So the Doves

HEIDI JAMES

DOVER PUBLICATIONS, INC.
MINEOLA, NEW YORK

Bibliographical Note

This Dover edition, first published in 2019, is an unabridged republication of the work previously published by Bluemoose Books Ltd, West Yorkshire, UK, in 2017.

Library of Congress Cataloging-in-Publication Data

Names: James, Heidi, 1973– author.
Title: So the doves / Heidi James.
Description: Mineola, New York : Dover Publications, Inc., 2019. | "This Dover edition, first published in 2019, is an unabridged republication of the work previously published by Bluemoose Books Ltd, West Yorkshire, UK, in 2017."
Identifiers: LCCN 2018057271| ISBN 9780486829746 | ISBN 048682974X
Subjects: LCSH: Journalists—Fiction. | Banks and banking—Corrupt practices—Fiction. | Arms transfers—Fiction.
Classification: LCC PR6110.A456 S6 2019 | DDC 823/.92—dc23
LC record available at https://lccn.loc.gov/2018057271

Manufactured in the United States by LSC Communications
82974X01   2019
www.doverpublications.com

For my vanished girls, Michelle and Louise. Always love.
And for my Charlie, the best of all dads.

So the doves cooed softly to each other, whispering of their own events, over Janey's grave in the gray Saba Pacha cemetery in Luxor.
Soon many other Janeys were born and these Janeys covered the earth.

Kathy Acker, *Blood and Guts in High School*

You could say that Newton's third law had been my guiding principle. That for every action there's an opposite and equal reaction. You might think it strange for a journalist to apply the laws of physics in their work, but to me it was clear: all I needed to do was follow a series of events and their consequences and everything would all add up like a formula, an equation. A neat sum of facts, arriving at the truth.

I'd succumbed to the seductive powers of determinism. You could say that I was wrong.

You could also say that I've come to understand that lies are facts yet to become reality, though that took me longer than it should have. It's all a con. Another physicist said: "What we take to be true is what we believe... What we believe determines what we take to be true." We live in an alternative-fact world. Honestly.

And yet, for a while, I was the purveyor of truth, a crusader for justice – all right, not quite that, but people read my work, they trusted me. I won an award or two. I was the good guy: I exposed the corrupt, the dirty, and the unfair. And I believed, completely and totally, in what I was doing. It mattered. You're probably thinking how could I be that naïve, how could I be a hack and still idealistic? That would be a fair point and perhaps I did lie to myself, but you have to believe in what you're doing. At least I did.

For the record, I was on to something with the St. Clair bank and their links to terrorist organizations: that was real. I say was, because it isn't now. Now it's a poorly researched article written in bad faith. And Melanie? I was seventeen when she disappeared, just a kid. It's as if she was a figment of my imagination, though she was flesh and blood – alive. What I mean is, she became a story, a myth, a series of actions and consequences folded into my own history. That was my fault.

Nothing ever really goes away; isn't that another law of physics? A material version of Nietzsche's eternal recurrence, atoms reorganized, reconfigured, but never totally destroyed? There's only so long before a new version of truth reveals itself, the skeletons in the wardrobe rattle and clack and the body is discovered.

And there's always a body, dead or alive. Every story needs a body.

Pride Comes

I t's the kind of assignment that signals one of two things: that you're on the slide, in decline, ready for the chop, or that you've just pulled off one of the biggest exposés in American journalism and you deserve to take things easy for a while. Or both. "Here he is, our man of the moment, scourge of the corrupt, crusader of the truth! I don't know how you do it, but I'm fucking glad you do." Edward, my editor, his face sun-raw from his latest jaunt to the Maldives, raised his arms in greeting like a rock star to his audience. "How're you doing?"

"Knackered, but pretty good."

"As you should! Circulation has shot up fifteen percent in the last week. I'm sure it's not all down to you, but you take some credit." He guffawed. "Sit."

I sat.

"There's a story just come in from the police, from Kent, Medway actually. Your neck of the woods, right?"

"Yeah, I grew up there."

"Thought so. A body's been found while they were clearing old farmland for the Cross Euro Speed Link."

"Really?"

"Yes, really, I'm sending you down there."

"Me? Why? Can't a junior cover it? Or pick up the story from one of the local rags?"

"I'm thinking that after your, our, latest triumph, my friend – which, by the way, has the bigwigs upstairs both nervous and delighted in equal measure – you deserve a little break."

"Why don't I just go on a long break somewhere hot and far away?"

"You will, just not right now. We'll probably need a follow-up on the St. Clair story and I can hardly trust anyone else now, can I?"

"Then I should stick around here."

"Marcus, why are you being so difficult? I thought you'd be pleased."

"I don't know, wouldn't someone else be better at this local crime kind of thing?"

"It's hardly just a 'local crime.' The delay in construction has got the Government hopping, especially with the EU wankers already pissed off. It could be a big story. Go down and get what you can. You can add a different perspective, the story behind the story. You could take a few days, see your family. Your mother's down there, yes? Now's your chance to spend time with her."

"Wonderful."

"Exactly. You'll be killing two birds with one stone. That's it then. Go now, today."

I rolled my shoulders and swallowed hard to quell the dread rising and expanding like gas in my gut. "Any other information?"

"Like?"

"Condition of the body? Who to contact?"

"Jesus, you need me to do your job for you?"

I stood up. "Alright. I'll do it."

"Stay in touch," he called as I left. I felt his sweaty gaze on the back of my head all the way out, like the red laser dot of a gun sight. Hyperbole: that's another thing they accused me of.

I got out of the city in under two hours. Grabbed my bag – habit of the job to have it packed and ready – locked the flat, got in the car. I called Mother on the way down, her surprise underscored by a long silence and the need for me to repeat my expected time of arrival.

"Here," she said. "You're coming here?"

I pulled off the motorway onto the slip road into town, crossing over the river where it's just narrow enough to allow the span of a cast iron bridge, all Victorian curlicues and fuss, with the cathedral spires competing with the ruined crenellations of the castle ahead of me. From that angle the town looks historic, the best England has to offer, but just out of sight around the river curve there's the decommissioned dockyard, a victim of Thatcher's government, all gussied up now as a museum. It's a shit hole, but a pretty one if you stick to the old High Street with its antique shops, tearooms and pubs, the half-timbered buildings leaning like old men.

I turned away from the river towards my mother's house, driving up a wide avenue of Victorian and Edwardian houses, now all past their best and divided into flats and bedsits. I crossed the junction to the White Horse Estate, where Melanie had lived, and passed a bus stop crowded with kids in the Danner Comprehensive uniform, chunky headphones like earmuffs clamped over their ears. The town seemed to fold in on itself like a fairground fun house, trapping me inside.

1989

H e first saw Melanie from the top deck of the number 84
bus, on his first day at Danner Comprehensive School.
Co-Ed. Locals called it the Danner bus, packed with rowdy
kids in the uniform of black blazer, green tie, gray trousers
or skirt. Long legs blocked the passage between seats, bodies
sprawling and shouting, all red spots and hair spray and newly-
bulged Adam's apples and shoving and smoking and spitting.
Only one or two old people on their way to work or the shops.

He hunched down in the middle row, breathing in
second-hand smoke, hoping that maybe he would get away
with being the new kid, unnoticed on the bus as it dieseled its
way through the wide roads of Forestdale and the mock-Tudor
semis. Then up through the estate and past the playing fields,
picking up more and more kids until there was only standing
room. He sat as low in the seat as he could, his collar around
his ears.

It was September, the beginning of the new term, and
it was pretty obvious that 1989 was a disaster, what with
Hillsborough, the Kegworth air crash and a train crash
somewhere in South London; having his heart broken and
being expelled was just icing on the crap cake. Rumor had
it that it was the second summer of love and everyone else
was out raving and taking drugs and having real sex, but he'd
spent the entire holiday inside reading, crying into his pillow
and waiting for Anthony to phone. It was no wonder he was
as pale and lumpy as rice pudding. But that morning of the
new term he got up early to do his hair in a Morrissey quiff,

and sprayed himself all over with the aftershave that Joyce, the housekeeper, had got him for Christmas. This time he would keep himself to himself. This time he would get it right.

That was when he saw her, not on the bus but walking along the street, going in the wrong direction, her long dark hair loose around her shoulders. Her school uniform accentuated her somehow, marking her out rather than blending her in, as if it was especially made for her and her alone. She wasn't tall or as obviously pretty as the other girls with their permed and blonde-streaked hair: she just had that something that drew people to her, what his mother called charisma.

"Oi, Gorgeous, where you going?" A thickset boy, about the same age as Marcus, had stood and pressed his full-lipped mouth to the small opening in the window, yelling down to her. All confidence and swagger with his Brylcreemed curtains of blonde hair flopping into his eyes and a pop star slouch. Darren Shine. His gang of look-a-likes laughed and banged on the windows.

She looked up at them, leering at her from the top window of the bus, waved, smiled and just kept going in the wrong direction.

"Slag," said one of the look-a-likes. Darren punched him on the arm.

"Shut your mouth, Mazzer, or I'll shut it for you. Got it?"

Mazzer tutted, rubbing his shoulder, "Just having a laugh, ain't I?"

"Well don't." Shine looked up and almost caught Marcus watching, just before he turned back to the window.

"He just isn't right for Coombe Hall, I'm afraid," the headmaster said when recommending that Marcus finish fifth form at a local comprehensive. "They have decent facilities there. He will fit in, I should imagine, or at least, better than here. After this last, uhm, event." He blinked and swallowed hard, lifting his chin to make enough space in his tight throat to accommodate his embarrassment. "I just don't think Marcus is truly able to

7

benefit from all we have to offer. It's not that his intelligence is in any doubt, just his, ah, character, his commitment to his education. We won't expel Marcus, if you withdraw him from the school with no fuss." Poking the words out of his mouth with the tip of his tongue.

Marcus stood in the corner, holding a plastic bag stuffed with all his school possessions. His mother didn't argue: a state school meant saving her a fortune – so Marcus heard her say on the phone later – and anyway, Anthony's parents had kicked up such a stink that arguing was futile. "Can't I go to King's? Or come to your school?" Marcus had asked, but she frowned, "King's won't take you, you know that, and I run a girls" school, Marcus, or hadn't you noticed? My God, what on earth will you do with this... this shadow hanging over you?"

Danner Comp was modern, built only a few years before, all straight lines and flat roofs, with large rectangular windows and low ceilings. The classrooms were flimsy, the partition walls rattling whenever a door was slammed by a moody teenager. Everything felt temporary, like a theater set, unlike Coombe Hall with its old stone walls and vaulted ceilings, solid oak paneling and book cases. The comprehensive was ugly but huge: it was easy to be swallowed up, anonymous, among a thousand or so other kids. For that he was grateful.

A short, thin woman dressed in a matching blue polyester skirt and blouse greeted Marcus at the office, signing him in, before handing him a timetable and walking him to a classroom. She didn't say a word, just plodded along the corridors and past the stinking toilet block and the computer lab that hummed with the few pcs and word processors necessary for the nerdy IT A-Level kids and the girls doing secretarial skills BTEC. Outside, the school fields were dusty and featureless. The white lines marking out the running track and football pitches had dried up in the sun and floated away like chalk rubbed off a blackboard; the goal posts had not yet been put back up. Marcus felt himself relax, his shoulders loosening under the polyester blazer, imagining he could fit in, or that at least no one would notice him.

The morning passed in a blur of lessons and introducing himself to the teachers, who in turn introduced him, blushing and blinking and sweating, to the other pupils. They looked through him or grimaced or – rarely – smiled, before he was instructed to find somewhere to sit and try to follow the class.

Lunch was a ham sandwich packed by Joyce, which he ate sitting on the wall by the staff room. Afterwards, he took his place in registration, a couple of rows behind Darren Shine, told to sit there by the English teacher, Mr. Laugham, whose six-and-a-half-foot rugby bulk was wrapped in a Fred Perry shirt and Sta-Prest trousers.

Halfway through the register (there were three Claires, two Sharons and four Darrens in the class), the door opened and she walked in. The other kids turned and watched her as she strode, head up, towards Marcus. Mr. Laugham paused and looked up from the register.

"So, Miss Melanie Shoreham, you've decided to join us, have you?"

"Yes sir, I have indeed." She brought her right hand up to her forehead and flicked a swift, oddly respectful salute his way. Marcus couldn't take his eyes off her, despite Anthony and his aching heart.

Mr. Laugham stared at her too, as if trying to figure out what to say next, his mouth pursed and twitching; she smiled at him and sat down in the seat next to Marcus. Relieved of having to say or do anything by her perfectly acceptable behavior, the teacher continued calling out the names of the rest of form and ticking them off the list; a little bald patch at the crown of his big head was just visible, shiny in the fluorescent lighting.

She was so close Marcus could smell her Lux soap, Impulse body spray and cigarettes. Her hair, draped black around her shoulders, looked greasy at the roots and her nails were unpolished and a little ragged. Her skin was smooth and soft and tanned. She glowed and Marcus blushed, his schoolboy ears pink at the tips.

"Right then, class." Mr. Laugham got up and wrote *Sons and Lovers* on the blackboard. "Take out your books." He turned back to the class. "Darren, why don't you get us started?"

The kids tittered.

Shine shouted, "Which Darren, sir?"

"You, Shine. Let's hear a gem of insight from you, shall we?"

"Didn't read it, sir."

"There's a surprise. Any particular reason? Or was the entire summer break not long enough for you?"

"That's about right." Darren laughed and his mate slapped his palm under the desk. Laugham, if he saw, ignored them.

"Has anyone completed their homework? Or can't any of you morons read?"

Melanie raised her hand. "I have."

Laugham turned to gaze at her.

"Have you now?"

"Yes sir, I have." She was matter-of-fact, not a trace of defiance or sarcasm.

"So, Melanie, if you have read it, tell us: what do you think is the theme of this novel?"

"The theme, sir?" she said, her hand resting on the battered book, almost touching Marcus.

"Yes, Melanie, you must have some idea of the theme. If you've read it, of course." Pleased with himself, Laugham puffed out his chest.

"I'd say the main theme is the Oedipus complex, except of course what's funny is that Paul actually kills his mother, rather than his father. So it's not that simple."

Laugham flicked his head to shift his fringe out of his eye. "Can you explain the Oedipus complex?" The class watched him deflate a little.

"Isn't that your job?" Melanie said. Everyone fell silent, stopped fidgeting and whispering, stopped scrawling on the desks; they sat up sensing trouble, hoping it was all going to kick off. Marcus held his breath and stared at his desk.

"I'm asking you." Laugham turned an odd shade of pink, like undercooked pork.

"It's a theory from Freud. Basically, boys fancy their mothers and want to kill their fathers. In girls it's called the Electra complex: girls desire their fathers and want to kill their mothers. Freud said it's how we develop our sexuality, sir."

The class laughed, and one of the Darrens said, "You'd know all about that, Melanie!"

She turned and blew a kiss in his direction. Marcus felt it breeze past his face.

"All right, settle down you lot. Thanks Melanie, you've been very insightful." Laugham turned towards the blackboard.

"Hang on, sir. I haven't finished."

Laugham stopped and turned back. "Is that so, Miss Shoreham? Do carry on."

"Well," she said, standing up and leaning forward a little so her hip pressed against the biroed desk. "Perhaps Paul is gay, and so it isn't quite so ironic. He kills his mother because she stands in the way of his relationship with men."

Embarrassed laughter rippled through the class. Darren Shine yawned theatrically.

"But Lawrence makes it clear Paul is attracted to women, as well as his mother. Paul has relationships with other women, which you'd know if you read the book all the way through."

Melanie smiled to herself. Marcus looked up at her from his seat. Her face was lit by the fluorescent strip lights that hummed in the background; her expression was almost pitiful, like one of those mournful statuettes of the Virgin Mary that old ladies used to have on the bedside table. "But people are more complicated than that, sir. Maybe he's suppressing his feelings. Maybe. Perhaps Mrs. Morel feeling like she's being buried by marriage and all the class and women's lib stuff is actually Lawrence telling us that everyone is trapped by society, by rules and expectations."

"Well, that's certainly a way of looking at it, Melanie. I'm sure many English scholars would argue differently, as would Mr. Lawrence himself if we could ask him."

"If you say so, sir. Personally, I think Lawrence is a woman-hating dickhead, but I doubt you or your scholars would agree with me."

"Oh my God," said Darren Shine. "This is disgusting. Stop talking about queers and sickos or I'll puke." Darren's little gang made puking sounds and heaved into their desks. Marcus's heart buffeted like a loose balloon under his shirt.

"Enough, all of you! Melanie – OUT! Go to Mrs. Murphy's office and wait there." Laugham was shaking so much he dislodged the covering of hair from his bald patch. It was much bigger than it first seemed.

Melanie looked down at Marcus and winked, then she picked up her bag and walked slowly out of the classroom, carefully closing the door behind her, leaving her copy of the book on the desk; a smudged black stamp saying PROPERTY OF DANNER COMPREHENSIVE half-obscured the title. Marcus laid his hand over the cover, absorbing what she'd left behind.

No More, No Less

The indicator ticking like a cartoon bomb, I pulled into our lane, behind the old village green that marked the original center of the town before it spread like bacteria in a post-war Petri dish. It was quiet, no other cars on the road and no one about. It's a wide lane and most of the detached houses are Victorian, like Mother's, surrounded by tall yew hedges, the odd magnolia spilling vanilla petals in the spring. Pseudo-Gothic turrets and dormer windows punctuate the red brick. A couple of the newer neighbors have installed UPVC windows and tall electric gates, to the horror of the stalwarts. The saga of the newcomers' home improvements dominated my mother's calls to me for months. The houses, once the residences of doctors, clergy, local officials and the like, now belong to financiers, builders and wealthy businessmen not wealthy enough for London. The same old story everywhere: the movement and flux of money and fortune, the upwardly mobile and the ignoble descent, a rotation like the gulf stream of heat and pressure and the cold salty rush of loss.

I parked on the drive, behind Joyce's little yellow Fiat; she'd had the same car for years, like Mother and her Volvo. The cars have become part of their identity, a distinguishing feature. Not for them the three-year cycle of discard and replace, the lease/purchase finance deal, a steady consumption of automotive technology and perpetual debt. Not for them any change at all, if they can help it, only the diminution of age. The wisteria trailed purple around the front of the house, trained around the windows and front door, its lower branches as thick as my arms. I used to think it kept the house upright, whimsical scaffolding – now I'm certain it does. Someday it will bring the house down under its lilac weight.

"Hello stranger, long time no see." Mother stood with her arms open at the door, her short gray hair as practical as a schoolboy's. She wore her uniform of linen slacks, long sleeved linen tunic and, because it was summer, robust sandals with buckles fastening them to her wide feet.

"New car?" We hugged, her head on my chest, as I wrapped one arm around her, the other holding my bag, and squeezed her for a second before stepping back.

"Sharp as ever, Mother dear. I can't get anything past you, can I?"

"No need for sarcasm, Marcus." She pressed her hand between my shoulder blades and pushed me inside the cool, dark hall.

"How was the drive down?" She looked me up and down, appraising my general condition: sleep habits, diet and cleanliness. Astute as a farmer assessing his livestock before market, no detail escaped her maternal eye. A small nod indicated she was more or less satisfied.

"Not too bad actually, no traffic this time of day."

"Good, good. Is your hair different? It looks longer."

"Is it? Probably, I just let my barber do what he wants." That wasn't entirely true, but I'm embarrassed by my own vanity.

"Well it's very nice, you look like a pilot from World War Two. Very stylish. Would you like a coffee? Joyce has just put some on for us."

"Coffee would be great, thanks. I'll just take my bag up if that's OK."

"Of course, darling, your room's all ready. You remember the way I suppose?"

I rolled my eyes. "It's not been that long, Mother."

"Just a few years, Marcus. I'll get your coffee."

I dumped my bag on the narrow bed, pulling out my laptop and plugging it in to charge, and grabbed my voice recorder and phone. Nothing had changed. Mother didn't do redecoration or home improvements unless it was absolutely necessary. I could've been a kid again, listening to the ancient heating system that farted and belched through the night; same furniture – my wardrobe, desk and book shelves; the wall paper, sun-faded and patchy. Except now I'm forty-ish with a small paunch and a few gray hairs.

I considered unpacking and opened the wardrobe. As sturdy as a boat and about as big, it's a relic as old as the house. It's doubtful that it has shifted an inch since the day it was first brought up the stairs by at least two strong men, muscling the solid oak and walnut around the turns and corners into this room. I imagine them grunting and swearing, stopping part of the way to rest and wipe the sweat off their brows, men in shirt sleeves and flat caps.

The heavy mirrored door opened wide and revealed my christening gown, yellowing in the crisp folds of tissue paper along with wedding dresses: my mother's, her mother's, an aunt's. My grandmother's full-length mink that Mother could face neither wearing nor throwing away, and a wooden box, mine, half-filled with photos, letters and my journal, the evidence that Melanie had existed. Behind the box, obscured by the dusty fur was a hiding place that no one has used for a long time.

History freighted the house like ballast, keeping us steady, on course and captive to its weight. Dragging us down.

I closed the wardrobe, left the bag on the bed and went down the stairs. Dust spun in glittering orbits in the Joyce-disturbed air; she flicked her yellow cloth at the banisters and side table.

"It's a dust trap this house, never ending," she said as I rounded the last steps into the hall beside her.

"I know, I don't know how you manage." I kissed her cheek, leathery and dry. She smelled of beeswax and lemon.

"I tell her to get rid of all this old junk, but she won't listen to me."

"She's stubborn, like someone else I know." I nudged her elbow and raised an eyebrow. "Who ignored their doctor's advice to retire and take it easy?"

"Easier said than done. Now, get out of it, go on. You can see I'm run off me feet here."

Mother sat at the kitchen table, her hands folded around her coffee mug. She smiled as I sat opposite her, in my old chair. My mug was already there, waiting for me, next to a plate of biscuits. I almost heard the click as everything slotted back into place.

"So, how are you? It's been so long since I've seen you."

"I know, but I was working on a huge story, and I couldn't get away."

"No, I suppose not."

"It's not a nine to five job, Mum, you know that."

"Yes, I do. It's very important, I know that. I would just like to see more of you."

"OK. I'm sorry."

She sighed. "So tell me more about the bank story. Did they really buy all those weapons?"

"It's not quite that simple, but basically yeah, it looks like it. How they got it past the Government Licensing Committee, God only knows. How about you?"

"As you see, all present and correct." She sipped her coffee and watched me over the rim. "So what brings you down here now?"

"Work. A body's been found at the rail link construction site, delaying the work, and Edward insists I cover it."

"Really? Why you?"

"He said that he thought I could bring a local perspective." I gulped the coffee, almost burning my throat. "Bloody hell, that's hot."

"Be careful, darling. Perhaps he thinks it needs your expertise?"

"Who knows what he's thinking?" I half-smiled.

She reached for a digestive and nibbled the edge. "So how's life otherwise? Are you seeing anyone special?"

"Are those new curtains?"

The kitchen cupboards and scrubbed surfaces were still clear of the usual kitchen clutter of jars of coffee and tea and biscuit tins and sugar bowls. No mess or frivolous home comforts. No postcards or fridge magnets or any of my childhood paintings on the fridge or cuttings of my work. No unpaid bills piling up on the kitchen table, no drawer full of flat batteries and elastic bands and dried-up pens. Everything necessary was neatly organized in cupboards and drawers.

"You know full well they aren't, stop avoiding my question. Is there anyone in your life?"

"No, still too busy, still no one."

"Don't sound so exasperated. I'm entitled to ask. I want you to be happy, to meet someone who'll support you. God knows I understand how lonely it can be. Aren't you lonely? Who do you talk to? Who do you share your worries and your accomplishments with?"

"My readers, Mother. I communicate with them and I've got you. How can I be lonely with you around?" I finished my coffee and rinsed the mug at the sink, heading off the guilt trip that would come my way. "Right, I'd better get over to the police station."

"Already? But we've barely spoken and Joyce has made lunch – we've got smoked salmon tart."

"Later? I promise." I pressed a kiss to her temple and squeezed her shoulder.

"You're always leaving as soon as you arrive," she said, but I was already at the door.

Blue and white police tape flicked and dodged in the breeze, tied to metal posts pushed into the newly turned soil. All the trees and hedgerows were gone, hacked down, roots torn up. A temporary access road cut across the clods and ruts for the plant vehicles that were parked across the far side of the site. There was nothing left of the orchard or the farm it had been part of. Flattened and cleared for progress, for connection, the new high-speed rail that would slice through, speeding all the way to the Channel Tunnel and into mainland Europe.

Uniformed officers (*Gavvers*, that's what Melanie had called them, I could hear her as clearly as if she were beside me, *so now you know*) blocked access to the site to the small crowd of hacks, photographers and a few ghouls who love being near a murder site; standing alone, a tall man with expensive jeans and haircut was tapping furiously at a Blackberry. We all stood watching the forensics team in white paper suits moving back and forth, crouching and bagging up, taking notes and photos. Two men and a woman in civilian clothes, obviously the SIO and his DIs stood watching the proceedings at the edge of the field.

I hadn't worked on a criminal case for a long time, not since the early days of my career, years ago, but I could still reel out the abbreviations: Senior Investigating Officer, Detective Inspectors, Detective Constables... Like riding a bike. Some things you just don't forget, like my first editor's repeated directive to "just find the story, that's all there is to it. The Facts. Details. Corroborating evidence. No more, no less." I used to repeat it to myself like a mantra when I was starting out. If only it were that easy. It had been, then.

They were huddled together; one of them, the older male, graying hair, not much taller than the woman, looked upset, as if he were being comforted, his head hanging. I watched closely, wondering if there was more to this story after all, waiting to see what would happen next. The female DI gripped his arm, but then they broke apart and the scene changed completely. They were professionals, working: there was no drama, nothing but the job. I stepped back to refocus, and look again. It was a crime scene, clear as day, not a soap opera; being back there was already clouding my judgment.

The three detectives turned and started moving towards us, towards the perimeter and the small crowd feeding off their work, and for a moment I thought I recognized the SIO. Before I could place him, the guy in the expensive jeans put away his phone and strode towards them, attempting to meet them at the gate.

"How much longer is this going to take?" he bellowed. His voice had the heft of someone used to giving orders, orders he expected to be followed. "We are losing millions every day this drags on. Why is no one giving me any answers?"

"Sir, step back, sir." The uniform stood in his way as the detectives signed themselves out of the area like travellers crossing a border.

"I need bloody answers. There's a lot at stake here."

"Sir, move away." The uniform moved closer but he stood firm.

"For fuck's sake!" He raised his hands, a gesture caught between tearing out his hair and smashing the uniform in the face. He did neither. Just dropped his arms by his side. His pulse flared in his neck like a coded warning for a heart attack.

One of the detectives turned back – the younger male, tall, broad-shouldered, blondish hair cut short around the temples. "Mr. Williamson, am I right?"

He nodded yes.

"I'm DI McMahon." He held out his hand and Williamson shook it, all the fight gone from him. "This is a serious crime scene and we need to be thorough, I'm sure you understand that. We also understand you have a job to do, so we'll be out of your way as soon as we can." He was good. Very good.

"When?"

McMahon flexed his fingers, exposing the palm of his hand, "When we can, and it'll be sooner if I can get on with my job." He stepped back, watching Williamson for a second, confirming his message had registered. He turned to go, and caught my eye. "Press?" I nodded. "There'll be a press conference tomorrow morning, eleven a.m. at the station. Our press liaison will give you more details." Then he was gone, into the waiting car and pulling down the track.

The tension ebbed. The uniform returned to his post, his hands crossed over his clipboard. The other hacks, young, locals – as you'd expect – climbed into their cars; there was nothing left to be gained there.

Williamson didn't move; he looked stuck, as if he'd run out of steam. I felt sorry for him: I don't think he'd experienced that kind of impotence before.

"Mr. Williamson?"

He looked up, blinking as if roused from a sleep. "Yes."

"I'm Marcus Murray, from the Sentinel. Could we talk?"

"The Sentinel?"

"Yes, you're big news. Major international contract, government involvement, delay costing millions, this is a big deal."

"You can say that again."

"Would you be willing to talk? Just on background first, if you like."

He pressed his lips together, and pushed his hands into his pockets – everything telling me I wouldn't get anything out of this guy, but then he said, "What can I tell you? I know nothing. The police have all the answers now."

"That must be very frustrating." I waited, turning myself to him, opening up, softening my shoulders, my expression. It worked. It always did.

"I'm fucking drowning here and the minister is doing nothing. It's the coroner apparently. Nothing they can do. The law must take its course. Yadda yadda yadda. I've got everyone breathing down my neck. There's men ready to work, being paid whether we're on the job or not. There's the equipment, the regulations, the bureaucracy. The French are going mad: we're holding them up – like it's my fault. We've only just got rid of the green lot..."

"The green lot?"

"Yeah, the protestors. You must've heard about that."

"Right, don't want the link damaging the wildlife."

"Yeah, this fucking site in particular: there are fucking skylarks nesting on the ground here, according to them. The police were no fucking help then either." He looked over at the uniform, but his comment fell on deaf ears.

An image of a skylark broke my train of thought: a skylark hovering high in the air singing the lines of his territory, and Melanie, sitting in the long grass telling me why they sing and how they nest.

"Murray?"

"Yeah, sorry, I'm listening."

"So what else can I tell you?"

"Ah yes, who do you report to?"

"I supervise this and a few other sites, but I'm part of the overall negotiations."

"Of course. You liaise with the Government?"

"I haven't got time for that: I'm the one who gets things done on the ground. The real work. When I fucking can, at least." He expanded his chest, pulling his shoulders back. He was a real display animal that one.

"I get it. So, what did your men discover?"

"A body. They were finally clearing the ground, getting somewhere, then there's a shout and one of the diggers has uncovered a body. Been there a while too, they reckon."

"Who does?"

"The police, my blokes. Nothing much left of it, which is why I don't see the hold up. How much evidence can there still be?"

I shrugged. "I'm no expert. Anything else you noticed?"

"No, I didn't see it, thank god. The men were a bit shook up, but that's fair enough."

"OK, well thanks for talking to me, I really do appreciate your time. You've been very helpful." I shook his hand. "Give me a call if you think of anything else or you want to talk." I gave him my card and walked back to the car.

I called Edward on the way back to Mother's. He didn't answer, so I left a message: There's not much here, no big

21

story, a disgruntled site manager. He texted back within a few seconds: YOU MIGHT AS WELL STAY AND SEE WHAT YOU CAN GET OUT OF IT. It didn't occur to me to be suspicious.

Joyce had gone and I found my mother sitting out in the garden, under the pergola, the twisting vines warping the shadows on her face.

"You're back! How'd it go?" She smiled and raised a glass of red wine. "Would you care for a glass?"

"Sure." I sat opposite her on one of the rickety cane chairs she left out in the garden regardless of the weather. I watched as she poured, her hand steady. Over seventy years old but she had more energy than me. She handed me the glass and we clinked cheers.

"So, your day, big story?"

"Nothing much to tell, honestly, I think it's nothing. Certainly not worth me coming down for." She winced. "Though it gives me a reason to be with you and spend some time together." She inclined her head and smiled, raising her glass again. Rescued. My mother has an unerring sensitivity for rejection, which seems to increase with age. It's part of the reason why I visit so seldom, which doesn't help the situation, of course.

"On the radio they said it's possible the victim was an undercover police officer."

"They said what?" My scalp contracted around my skull.

"That an anonymous source said it might be the body of a missing policeman."

"Which radio station?"

"The local BBC news bulletin. Why?"

"Because it's the first I've heard of it. There was no mention of the victim at all."

"Perhaps they only just found out."

"Maybe. Or I'm losing my touch."

"Surely not?"

"Perhaps I should go back up there and see."

I got up, trying to think where best to go first. Should I head down to the police station, or call the news desk at the radio station? If I spoke to the radio journalist, maybe I could salvage something and then leave, go home. Send Edward the article he wanted, so I could get out of there.

"You're not going out again are you?" Her face sagged with disappointment. Guilt and pride smothered my urge to get the story, to get in first. What difference would it make? I didn't have an exclusive; I was chasing around like a junior. It could wait, so I sat back down.

"No." I swallowed the wine and pushed the glass closer to Mother for a refill.

1989

"Do you always do that?"
"What?"

"Come and go as you feel like it?"

"You make it sound like it's a weird thing to do," she said, circling her left foot as it dangled from her crossed legs.

"Isn't it?" he asked. "I don't know anyone else who wanders in and out of school whenever they like."

"Why would you stay somewhere if you didn't like it?"

They were sitting on the grass bank round the back of the school canteen, out of sight of the staff room, catching the last warmth of the autumn sunshine. On the field in front of them, a group of fourth-year boys played football, turning their heads to stare at Melanie whenever they jogged past with the ball. They'd started talking on the rare occasions that she was in class – usually English, French and History, rarely Maths, sometimes Biology, but never PE – and then hanging out at lunchtime, if she stuck around long enough. He didn't know why she singled him out, perhaps because he was new and knew nothing about her or the rumors that had done the rounds about her and her mum, or maybe simply because she liked him, though he found that hard to believe. Why would someone like her want to hang out with him? But being her friend, standing in line at the lunch queue and having her call out his name and link arms with him, or catching her eye and igniting that slow smile that filled her eyes, made him feel untouchable, special. When he plucked up the courage to ask her why she hung around with him, she laughed, her eyes wide and dark-lashed.

"Don't you worry about your grades? Missing all the classes. Won't your parents go crazy when they find out? Mine would, my mother would have a total breakdown."

"My mum has other things to worry about. Besides, she knows I'll be alright. I'm a wanderer; you can't keep us cooped up for too long." She picked a long blade of grass, pressed it between her thumbs and then blew, producing a long, unwavering note. Marcus tried, managing only to cover his hands in spit. He wiped them on his trousers and waited for her to mock him. She didn't.

"What are you doing here, Marcus? Posh boy like you." She tipped her head back and leaned into the sun. She had dark skin, olive his mother would say, or swarthy, and he felt pasty next to her, self-conscious about the freckles and zits merging together on his face.

"I'm not posh, that was the problem," he said, sweating, damp spreading across the back of his shirt and across the soft stubble on his top lip.

"That's relative, mate. Here you're posh."

"It doesn't matter, I hated that school. I hated them all."

"Then you're mad. I'd kill to go to a school like that."

"Why? So you could bunk off the subjects you hate? Anyway it's awful there. Everyone is a stuck up prude and the lessons are ridiculous. They think everyone is going to join the army or be a dentist or politician. And they made us play cricket."

"So what? I bet it's challenging and brilliant. It makes a difference, going to a school like that. You have a chance. People take notice of you."

"Yeah, to kick your head in on the way home. Honestly, it was hell. It's full of rugger-buggers and snobs."

"If you say so." She stood up, brushing her skirt down and squinting her eyes against the sun. "You coming? Let's go down town and get some chips."

The town was divided into two distinct sections: the old, picturesque half that tourists visited, spending fortunes in the overpriced fudge shops and tea rooms and antique shops, and there was the newer part, by the dockyard and the crowd of protesters with their placards and banners about Thatcher and her gang, with the new red brick shopping center and High Street. According to Melanie it was ugly as fuck and rough as a badger's arse. Marcus had never been to the shopping center: he was too afraid he'd get his head kicked in by the gangs of boys that his mother had warned him about.

"Won't we get into trouble?" What an idiot thing to say. He waited for her to laugh at him and leave him behind.

"Nah, we'll be back before they miss us. But you can go now if you like. I won't mind."

"No, it's alright. But let's get the chips and head back, OK?"

"Sure," she nodded. They walked down the hill, the two of them, her dark head in line with his shoulder, her hands swinging by her sides, towards the ugly half of town, under the new concrete by-pass that carried traffic over the old streets and ferried them into the spanking new multi-story car park behind the shopping center.

Even though the council had laid new paving and put in benches and railings and flower beds, and pedestrianized the streets leading towards the center, they'd done nothing about the inhabitants, who were just as worn and scruffy as before. Old ladies with curlers in their hair shuffled along pulling their tartan shopping trolleys behind them. Middle-aged women stood outside the bingo hall, smoking fags and talking in quick, sharp sentences, their jaws and teeth clicking like the workings of a machine.

The chip shop was next to the Oxfam. "How much money have you got?" Mel asked as she dug into the pockets of her blazer. "I've got a quid."

Marcus pulled a fiver from his pocket, and handed it over.

"Bloody hell, how much can you spend for lunch?"

"What do you mean?"

"How much change do you need to give your mum?"

"Oh, I see. None."

"Seriously? Kushtie, we can have a feast. What you having then? You look like a cod and chips man to me. Am I right?" She walked in through the open door, straight up to the counter, unscrewed the lid of a large jar and plucked out an onion between her fingers; she crunched it between her teeth, the acid tang of vinegar dominating for a moment the smell of hot fat.

"Alright, Pete, he'll have a cod and chips and I'll have chips and curry sauce with a cheese and onion pie. Thanks."

"Not having your usual?"

"Nope, I've got money today." She held the five pound note up by the corners, flexing and snapping it flat it like a card sharp. "You'll have to find some other mug to feed your scraps to. We'll have a couple of cans of Coke too, please."

Pete, his black hair greased back in a tall quiff, wrapped up the order, shaking vinegar and salt on first; his fading tattoos were just visible as blue lines, like veins, under the black hairs on his arms.

Mel paid him, and he squeezed her hand as he handed over the change. "How's your mum?" he said, slamming the till shut and folding his arms over his thick body.

"Alright," she said, grabbing the hot paper parcels from the counter before turning towards the door. "Get the Cokes, Marcus, you dingalow. I'll tell Mum you asked for her, Pete. Cheers."

Marcus watched Pete watch Melanie, before picking up the cans and following her.

"How'd you know him?" They walked down the side street, past the mini-cab office towards the benches by the war memorial.

"He was almost one of our dads. Lived with us for a bit, but then me mum changed her mind. Let's sit here, I like reading the names on the plaque."

"Why'd she change her mind?"

"Who?"

"Your mum."

27

"Oh, he was lazy, expected us to wait on him hand and foot."

"He looks a bit scary. Was he violent?"

"Pete? He's as soft as a baby's arse. No, he's all mouth and no trousers."

"All mouth and no trousers... Joyce says that about her son."

"Oh yeah? Who's Joyce?"

"Our housekeeper."

"Your housekeeper?" She looked at him, a quick turn of her head to take him in, to scrutinize the alien, the rich kid, the queer. Or so he thought. He would take a long time to understand her and by then she would be long gone.

"Yes, she's lovely, but she says her son is a sod." Shame, a feeling he knew well, worked like fresh blisters under his skin.

"Right, well it takes all sorts, I suppose."

They sat eating, the grease oozing through the layers of paper onto their laps. Marcus watched her, gazing up at the monument, chewing her food delicately, taking small bites, as refined as if she were dining at the Ritz rather than eating chips from newspaper on a wrought iron bench. His mum would approve, not that that mattered, except it did. She wore no make-up, and didn't seem to care about making her uniform more sexy or cool by shortening the skirt or anything that the other girls did. She didn't seem to care about her appearance at all, and so of course she was all the more beautiful for it. His chest felt tight. He could feel his pulse in his fingers just like he had when he was with Anthony, except he didn't want to touch her, he didn't want to kiss her, but he knew it was love. Some kind of love.

"Do you want some?" He broke off a chunk of fish and offered it to her.

She shook her head. "I don't eat meat or fish, but thanks though."

"Oh." He sat there for a minute, not sure what to say. "I've never met someone who doesn't eat meat before. Don't you miss bacon? Or steak?"

"No, I'm a vegetarian like Morrissey, you know? Meat is murder."

"Yeah, of course. Right." He wondered how he'd tell his mother that he wanted to be a vegetarian. "Do you like the Smiths then?"

"God, yeah. He's a poet. What about you?"

"They're alright."

"Alright?" She laughed, "Just alright! What a cheek. Go on then, maestro, tell me what music you like."

"I like some American bands, you know and hip hop, that kind of thing." He hunched, almost curling around the words, defending them. He was so used to being teased, the butt of jokes and, if Mel had made fun of him, she would've been just like the others; diminished, smaller somehow and he didn't want that. He wanted her to like him, for her to be different. He wanted to be different.

"Oh yeah, like who? Which bands?" She turned and faced him, scrutinizing, testing his reaction.

"Sonic Youth. NWA. Beastie Boys. Dinosaur Jr." He put a chip in his mouth and she snapped her fingers, a sharp click in the air.

"That's so cool! What about Black Flag?"

"I've only heard a little bit of their stuff, but it's good."

"Good? I'll have to convert you," She smiled, tipping her head so that dark shadows collected under her eyes, "what about the Pixies? Nirvana?"

"Love the Pixies, of course. I don't know Nirvana, who are they?" She was an angel with a neon halo above her head. She even knew a band he'd never heard of.

"Come on, finish your chips and I'll take you up to Vinyl Exile, they've got a copy of Bleach in. I'm in LOVE with the singer. You look a bit like him, actually. If you bleached your hair and didn't wash for a few days."

"Oh thanks." He attempted a shrug, trying to hide how chuffed he felt.

"It's a compliment. Honestly. He's perfection."

"Shouldn't we go back? I mean, lunch time will be finished in a minute."

"Marcus," she said, her voice low and soft, "do you honestly think that what you learn in class today will be of more value to you than what you'll learn in Vinyl Exile? Come on." She stood up, raised her eyebrow and cocked her head in the direction of town. "Let's go, my rebellious friend."

She dumped the wrappers and cans in the bin and turned back towards the High Street, past the mini-cab office again and the drivers leaning against their Ford Sierras, eyeing up Mel's legs and boobs. Marcus stepped between her and their gaze, shielding her as they walked towards Woolworths and the Co-Op.

The record shop was down an alleyway between the pool hall and the launderette. Puffs of sour-smelling steam pumped out of the vent from the dryers, not quite masking the smell of piss. The lettering on the sign above the door was made from broken pieces of records.

"Have you been in here before?"

"No. It's a bit..."

"Out the way, I know."

"I was going to say, a bit of a dump."

"Well, yeah, that too. Cheap rent. He refuses to stock CDs. Don't ask him if he has any, or he'll kick you out and ban you from ever entering the premises again." She widened her eyes and smiled, then walked in, pushing through a beaded macramé curtain into a deep rumbling bass line and wheedling guitar feedback that seemed to expand in waves through the dingy space. The only windows were in front by the door, but with little light finding its way down the alley or between the buildings, the windows were redundant. There were lamps though: desk lamps, table lamps and one shaped like a Hawaiian maiden in a grass skirt, a pineapple shade over her head. The walls were papered over with band posters and flyers, layers and layers of them, with racks of bin shelving along the length of the walls and another load in the middle of the narrow room. At the end, perched on a stool was the owner. Tall and skinny, with long, mid-brown hair hanging over his shoulders, he was wearing jeans and an open shirt over a Frank Sinatra t-shirt. He looked old, at least twenty-seven.

He watched them as they walked in: Marcus, self-conscious; Mel, the same as always, light as if she skipped through the world unchanging, untouched by her environment. If anything, it seemed that her surroundings adapted to her. He nodded to Mel from his stool and didn't acknowledge Marcus. A couple of Goths stood huddled together in the corner, intently reading the back cover of The Cure's latest album.

The racks were full of alternative bands, rare imports and bootlegs. By the till there was a small display of fanzines and books. Marcus browsed next to Mel, watching as she flicked through the records, the tips of her fingers walking across the spines, rejecting, pausing, flipping and moving on until she found what she was looking for.

"See?" She held it up for him to see the black and white cover.

"It looks like an X-ray."

"I know. It's in negative, beautiful isn't it? Turning the light in on itself." She spun around and took the disc up to the guy by the till. "Can you put this on please?"

"Again? Why don't you bloody buy it?" He pressed pause on the tape machine behind him and then slipped the record from the sleeve and held it between both hands, his fingertips pressed at the sharp edge of the disc.

"I will. Soon." She tilted her head over to her left shoulder, and lifted the corners of her mouth. Other girls would look like they were flirting if they did that, but Mel, she looked as though she were bestowing a blessing. In spite of himself the man smiled back.

He put the record on the turntable and placed the needle down with the care of a surgeon. The opening bass line penetrated the room like strong fingers pressing deep below the surface of his flesh, digging at something only just hidden from view. Then the drums and guitar joined in before Cobain's voice, with its American whine and drawl and growl and roar. Marcus felt a percussion of blood thumping in his head, his fingertips tingling. Mel nodded at him, in time with the beat. Even the Goth kids swayed in time. Caught mid-sway, mid-nod, the owner lifted the arm of the record player with a jerk. "That's enough, are you buying it or not? Because in case you haven't noticed, this isn't a youth club, this is a shop. So buy something or sod off."

"Alright," she said, "thanks." She linked her arm with Marcus and led him out through the door and down the alley back to the main street. "Poor bugger, he's a very miserable man."

"I thought he was rude. How did he know we weren't going to buy anything? He didn't even give us a chance."

"Because I hardly ever buy anything from him, so he could be pretty certain. What did you think of the music?"

"Well, I didn't hear much..."

"I know that, but still, didn't it grab you?"

"It was amazing. Really."

"I know." She squeezed his arm against her body and he didn't pull away. "What next?"

"School? If we go now we can go to History."

"Can't go now, silly arse! We've missed registration. Better to take the whole afternoon and tell them you had to go home sick."

Swayed by her logic and previous experience, he ignored the grain of fear dissolving in his stomach and mingling with his bloodstream.

"Well then, let's go. You know you're really cool, Marcus, you're not like other boys."

"Really? Why's that?" His cheeks flushed hot.

"Because you don't pretend to know everything." She let go of his arm and walked off, light and merry. Her dark hair swung as she walked, her arms relaxed and loose at her sides. She moved as if propelled by laughter and yet, in the midst of all that energy, there was a stillness about her, something unreachable. He followed her down the pedestrianized main street, the shops on either side, past mothers and their pre-school children, old women and their men, their hands in their pockets, or carrying shopping bags, tagging along being helpful. Trailing behind her, caught in her wake, he wished he could be in love with her for real, in a way that was useful, or that could make him what he wanted to be.

"Melly!" A large girl grabbed hold of Mel, as sudden and engulfing as a wave, wrapping her arms around Mel's hips and lifting her in the air.

"Georgie!" Mel slipped down and stepped back into her own space. "Look at you!" She turned to him, "Marcus, this is Georgina, Georgina this is Marcus."

Georgina grinned, pulling her lips back over her large square teeth. "Alright, Marcus!"

He smiled back. Sturdy as an armchair, Georgina had thick arms and legs and a soft, dumpy body; her hair was honey-colored and fell around her face in thick, soft waves. Her Levi 501s, white t-shirt, Doc Marten shoes with Grolsch bottle tops wound in the laces, and blue eyeliner drawn thick around her eyes marked her out as a Bros fan, a Brossette. Of course, he didn't like her: she was loud and brash and in the way. He turned towards Melanie to find her looking at him, so he raised an eyebrow and smirked. But she ignored him, blinking him away and held out her hand to Georgina. "What've you been up to? I haven't seen you in ages."

"College, babe. I'm a career girl now. Got me own flat, up by the hospital. It's lovely it is. You should come over."

"Yeah, I'd love that. What you doing at college?"

"Secretarial skills. I've got my typing, shorthand, the lot. My social worker has got a job lined up for me at TSB. I'm so chuffed. You?"

"Same. School. Mum. You know. Marcus has just started at Danner."

"Oh yeah." Georgie nodded. "Poor fucker! Where you from then?"

He started to blush, pink rising over his collar. "I, er..."

"He got expelled from up the road, you know, Manor Park."

Mel didn't look at him, the lie smoothing over his embarrassment, easy as that. He wouldn't have to confess to being a phony, a rich boy, a failure. He didn't have to say anything. She kept his secret, and him, safe. He began to understand what it was to be seen clearly by someone with a level gaze, someone whose vision was as sharp and discerning as time itself. He would cherish that feeling. He would do anything to protect it, to keep it alive. Or so he thought then, when he was a boy.

"Oh, don't worry." Georgina slung her arm around his shoulders. "I got expelled loads of times. Unteachable they said, and look at me now."

"She's a character," he said later, on the way home.

"What do you mean?" Melanie asked, her hands in the pockets of her blazer.

"You know. She's a bit... She's larger than life, shall I say."

"Shall you? Maybe she has to be large to live the life she's had." She quickened her step and said nothing else until she reached her bus stop and said goodbye. He was afraid he'd upset her, but her mood had changed before the walk home.

He'd followed them into Woolworths, Georgie making jokes that only she laughed at, so loud that people turned to stare, although Mel chuckled along companionably, her nose wrinkling as she laughed.

"I love Woollies," Georgie said, "it's got everything you could ever need. Let's have a look at the clothes." They followed her up towards the back of the shop, past the pick'n'mix sweet barrels, the toy section, the household paraphernalia, garden hoses, colanders and saucepan sets towards the clothing aisles. Tall metal baskets held pairs of black plimsolls secured together by elastic bands. Georgie nudged Mel and reached in, picking up several pairs. She shared them out between the three of them, "Come on, let's switch 'em! It'll be a right crack when someone tries them on." She pulled off the bands and began re-pairing the shoes. "I've got a three here, you got a four? We don't want to make it too obvious. Come on, quick." And they began undoing and swapping the shoes, with Georgie laughing to herself, her belly shuddering with each guffaw, as a security guard sauntered over and watched them. Georgie turned and smiled at him, "Just trying on some plimmies for school, mate." He nodded, the pouch of flesh under his chin wobbling, and sauntered further up the aisle.

"Come on," Mel started throwing the shoes back in the wire basket. "That's enough now."

"Yeah, fucking pig is a right buzz kill." Georgie stood up, dumping the rest of the plimsolls back. "Let's have a look at the music."

Georgie was embarrassing but Marcus followed them anyway, wishing she'd leave him and Melanie alone together. Georgie meandered along, stopping if something caught her eye: running her fingers over a three-pack of tea towels, or a child's book, looking for all the world as if she were an interested customer rather than a kid out for a lark. At the music section, where the top ten was displayed – racks of cassettes, CDs and some seven-inch singles, nothing of any interest to him – she stopped in front of a stand devoted to Kylie Minogue and grabbed an album, held it up next to her face and pouted in a vague approximation of Kylie. "I look like her, don't I?" She turned her head, pushed her chin in the air, sucking in her cheeks, and cocked her hip out. "See?"

"Yeah, yeah, identical bloody twins, that's what you are." Mel said and pointed towards a poster of Sonia, all red curls and Liverpudlian charm. "More like Sonia, I'd say."

"Fuck off!" Georgina laughed, punching Mel's shoulder. "She's much fatter than me."

"How d'you know each other?" Marcus asked, wanting to pull himself back into the circle of their attention.

"I love his accent!" she said to Mel. She turned to him. "You sound like a newsreader off the telly. Say it again." He repeated the question. "Love it. He sounds lovely, don't he! I was at Danner, same year as youse. Till they kicked me out. But we known each other years, ain't we, Smells?"

"Sure have, George. Her old foster mum lives over the road from us." Melanie looked at her, standing there under the strip lights, her eyes soft. It was like an embrace rather than an appraisal; attention, not judgment. Marcus and Georgie stood there, not moving, unembarrassed. Then Melanie stepped back and said: "Time I was heading out, I think. You should too, Marcus, if you want to get home at the right time."

"Already?" Georgie's disappointment rolled through her like an increase of gravity, dragging her down.

"Yep, gotta be off."

"Can't you come back to mine? We could watch a video."

Mel had started out towards the door back to the street; Marcus followed, the security guard eyeing them all as they passed him at the exit, assessing every bulging pocket and pouchy jumper. Out in the street Mel started walking towards the bus stop. "I'm heading home. You coming this way?"

"Hang on a minute, come over here, I want to show you something." Georgie crossed over the other side of the walkway, to the path leading into the multi-story car park.

"Hurry up, then," Mel said, and so of course he followed. The crowd on the street had changed: other school kids had replaced the mothers and children, men and women having finished work were pushing through the bodies, heading home. It was getting cooler; the sky glimpsed above the buildings was cloudy, pale gray wads blocking out the sun. They both gathered around Georgie, as she gestured them to move even closer, looking over her shoulder at the street.

"Here, look what I've got." She stepped in closer still and pulled out handfuls of sweets from her pockets – chocolate éclairs, jelly snakes, caramel cups – pushing them into their hands. "And this!" Reaching behind her back she pulled a cassette from her jeans. "Ta-da!"

Marcus laughed, unwrapped an éclair and popped it in his mouth. "What's the tape?" He leaned in to look at the cover.

"Jive Bunnies Party Mix, great huh?" She beamed, her curls bouncing around her head. He laughed even harder, almost choking on the sweet, high on being around these girls, being part of their gang. Fuck Anthony and his beautiful lips, fuck his stupid parents and fuck that school. He didn't need any of them.

"Take it all back," Mel said.

"Shut up!" Georgie laughed.

"Seriously, take it back." Her voice was flat, low.

"What?" Georgie blinked, looking at Marcus, then back at Mel, her hands still full of sweets and the tape.

"Go on. Take it back." The three of them stood there, awkward, Georgie still not sure if Mel was having a laugh, Marcus chewing the sweet as surreptitiously as he could, the toffee getting stuck on the fillings in his back teeth.

"You can't chore stuff like that. You starving? No. You shouldn't chore, George. Take it back."

"I'll get caught, and if I get caught I lose my flat, my job, college. They'll send me up the hill." Georgie began to breathe heavily through her mouth, the air hissing and huffing past her teeth. "They'll call the gavvers."

"What are the gavvers?" Marcus asked. They ignored him.

"That's why you shouldn't have nicked it all, George. You have to be careful."

"I can't take it back, Mel."

"Then give the tape to the Oxfam."

37

"What about the sweets?"

"Chuck 'em or eat them, if you can stomach them," Mel said, handing back the sweets Georgina had given her. "Don't chore, girl. You're better than that." Mel hugged her and turned away, leaving Marcus and Georgie standing there with the stolen goods.

"I'll see you then," he said. Jogging to catch up with Mel, he turned back to see Georgie stuffing the tape and chocolate back into her pockets.

At Mel's bus stop she handed him a pile of coins. "Your change from the chips earlier."

"Oh, right, thanks." He took the money and slid it into his pocket. He stood there for bit, unsure what to do or say; he'd ruined everything again, just like always. Leaning out into the road to look for the bus, he asked Mel if she wanted him to wait with her.

"No, you're alright. See you tomorrow perhaps."

"OK," he said and started off in the opposite direction, towards home. He walked about twenty steps before looking back over his shoulder: she was still there, leaning against the bus shelter, reading a book. He raised his hand to wave, but she didn't look up.

Barking Up the Wrong Tree

I parked behind the police station, between a riot van and a squad car. The street was in shadow, almost dark, pressed between the rough concrete building rising several stories high, and the hill lifting sheer and chalk-faced to the war memorial a few hundred feet above. There was no access to the public on that side, so I walked around the building, picking up pace to outrun the creeping sense of being crushed.

The brightly-lit reception was crowded, but the two officers manning the desk appeared unflappable; fielding calls and ignoring most of the people hassling for their attention. I took a seat on a perforated metal bench that was bolted to the floor in the corner of the room, prepared to wait. There were a few other journalists there, recognizable by their self-important tone of voice and the flashing of their IDs. A middle-aged woman, thin and well-dressed, was crying at the other end of my bench. She muttered to herself, then gulped and sniffed. She clutched a dog collar and lead so tightly that her knuckles were white.

The doors opened and a bruiser of a man was carried in, kicking and swearing, by several officers. His hands cuffed behind him, he bucked and writhed like a bulky eel, red raw from booze, the smell rolling off him so strong it canceled out the stink of industrial strength pine disinfectant. It was a relief when they were finally buzzed through the security door.

"Missing, missing, missing," the woman said, huddled at the end of the bench. One of the reception staff leaned over the desk, resting on his elbows. "Misty gone walkabout again,

Mrs. B? Never mind, she'll be back, she always comes back. Have a tea and then get yourself home. OK?"

She stopped crying, nodding and wiping her face as if that's all she was waiting for: acknowledgment and reassurance.

"I'll get you a tea then, shall I?"

"No, that's alright." She stood, looked around to check that she hadn't forgotten anything, then shuffled out, still clutching the lead and collar.

The desk clerk watched her until she was gone: it was over. He answered the phone, tapped on a keyboard. Ready for the next scene, next drama. Next story. There's always another story.

I'm writing this as I remember it, without notes or recordings. It isn't as simple as I thought, when it's your story, your life. A neat sum of events and consequences: that's a joke. What comes back are trivialities, flimsy components that collapse under the telling. Anyway, I'll keep trying.

Finally, two women emerged from the dark interior of the building: a small woman with a clatter of bangles jangling up her wrist and the detective from the day before, tall and slim with her black hair pulled back in a bun.

"Right. Press, have you all got your visitor's passes and signed in?"

I hadn't and I crossed to the desk clerk, scrawling my name and showing him my press ID. He slid the laminated visitor pass over. Eyes rolled around me; I was the hold up, rookie, amateur. I probably felt the heat of embarrassment ooze up and over my collar. Probably.

"All done? Good, we're moving up to the press room. I'm Jennifer Brooks, the Media Liaison Officer, and this is DC Okonjo. I'll give you my card in a minute and I'll be your contact for now. Detective Chief Inspector Sutton is heading up the investigation: along with David Finborough from the Department of Transport, he will be answering your questions and give you all the details. Follow me please."

We followed them up a flight of stairs, carrying cameras and equipment cases, then along a corridor past the incident room. The door was open on the desks and computers and a blank white board ready for the mess of detail and witness statements, the rosters of objects brought in and photos of the scene, all still waiting to be amassed and collated, catalogued and numbered like museum exhibits – fragments of a story ready to be fitted together as a whole. I repeated the names she'd mentioned, Sutton, Finborough, Okonjo, Sutton, Finborough, Okonjo as if they would somehow rearrange themselves into the article that would magic me out of there. I just needed to focus, but I suddenly felt so tired.

The room was large and windowless. The Kent Police insignia was emblazoned on a blue background on the far wall; just in front was a large desk with four seats tucked behind it. A door, closed, was partially hidden behind a screen. We were ushered into the plastic chairs that fanned out through the rest of the room. I took a seat as close to the front as I could, pushing but not actually shoving my way through. Not that anyone cared, it's standard behavior: who has the time for manners when reality is being forged and documented? There were a few minutes of chaos and noise as microphones were placed on the desk and plugged into wires that were rapidly unraveled across the room and connected with cameras and recording devices, then we sat and waited.

I took out my voice recorder and note pad, writing down the names I'd been repeating: Finborough, Sutton, Okonjo. I underlined Sutton, then Finborough, then realized it didn't mean anything and sat back. I was lost, sitting there in that airless room, which was ironic considering I was in my hometown, doing the job I'd done for twenty years, but I felt foreign, out of my depth, vulnerable. Why did I imagine I was any different to anyone else?

"Busy isn't it?"

I turned to the voice on my left. "Sorry?" It was a woman in her twenties, thin lips, no make-up, nervous. Cheap blouse and trouser suit. Good hair, thick and shoulder length. The details presented themselves, directing my judgment of who she was and who she wasn't, what she might become. She smiled. Perhaps she thought I needed reassurance. What signs and signals, which details did she pick up from me? My lack of a wedding ring? My pressed shirt, courtesy of Joyce? Did I look lost? Straight?

"Government, potential embarrassment, the EU... Murder. Makes sense it's busy." She tilted her head to the rest of the room, indicating the crowd.

"Right. Sure, makes sense."

"I'm Annabelle Walker – Anna, from the Messenger. You?

"Marcus, Sentinel." I shook her hand.

"I thought I recognized you! Marcus Murray, right?" I nodded. "I really admire your work. You really get under the skin of your stories. Wow, I'm so pleased to meet you."

"Likewise."

"So this must be pretty big, for you to be here, right? What's going on? Corruption? Is the body just a diversion? I thought it was a bit convenient, just appearing like that." She stopped, filled up with breath and waited for me to answer. I didn't, and didn't have to because the door behind the screen opened and a team headed by DCI Sutton came into the room. I stared at Sutton, trying to place him. Where did I know him from? The girl leaned in, her head almost touching mine, trying to get a better view.

Sutton and Finborough sat down behind the desk, joined by the Superintendent. To the left, just out of view of the TV cameras, I spotted McMahon, from the site the day before. He was leaning against the wall as Okonjo joined him, while a couple of uniformed officers took their places around the room.

At the desk the Superintendent sipped from a glass of water and neatened the pages of the statement in front of him. He tugged at his uniform, straightening the line of silver buttons down his front. He almost sparkled under the bright lights. It struck me as odd that only the lowliest police officers and the highest rank are uniformed.

"Good afternoon everyone. Thank you for your interest in this case. We good to go?" He looked to the back of the room, the cameramen nodding. He cleared his throat. "Kent Police are investigating the discovery of a body found on the North Kent access site of the International Speed Rail Link. Formerly farmland, the site was at one point used as an orchard. The body was found on Tuesday the twentieth of June as the ground was being cleared." Annabelle scribbled on her notepad, her shorthand illegible. I looked back up and checked I'd switched my recorder on. "At the moment we are keeping an open mind..." Sutton was sitting back in his seat, watching the room from under heavy, almost drooping eyelids, his hands resting on the desk. Beside him the junior minister looked hot and uncomfortable. He swallowed from his glass then wiped the moisture and sweat from his top lip. "The investigation is at a very early stage and we are working with the forensic team..."

We are keeping an open mind. Early stage. The uniforms; theirs and ours, Annabelle and her cheap suit; the signs, the clichés; all so flimsy and constructed it was like a joke. I almost laughed. Corpsing, isn't that what actors call it? Breaking character, laughing out of place? Shattering the illusion of reality? Isn't that what the dead do? Shatter our illusions that we are exempt from mortality. I swallowed the impulse and shifted in my seat like a child. I was out of sorts, unsettled. I needed a holiday.

"We will of course update you as soon as we can and we ask if anyone has any information to please come forward. Thank you." He made to stand up, tucking the statement under his arm. No invitation for questions.

"Marcus Murray, the Sentinel. Is there any truth in the speculation that the victim is a missing police officer?" My voice rose above the camera shutters clattering around the room. I hate that sound: so final, got it, caught. That moment, that image, mine. Possessed. I caught McMahon's eye and he frowned.

The Superintendent sat back down and looked over at Sutton, who leaned forward and said slowly and deliberately: "As the Superintendent said, it's too early in our investigation to speculate. The post-mortem is taking place and our colleagues in forensics are at the site gathering evidence now."

A voice from behind chipped in, "Joanne Cline, Radio Kent. And what about allegations of corruption and the mishandling of EU funds? Does that have any bearing on this 'discovery'?"

Both police officers turned to Finborough, who now looked as if he would pass out.

"Which allegations?" He reached for his water again, but put it back down. The camera flashes flicked points of light against his damp skin.

"Allegations that funds have been misappropriated; concerns that were raised by MEPs at the Transport committee last month and then reported by the French press. The delay caused by the discovery of this body seems a little convenient, doesn't it?" She had him on the ropes. Cliché. Hyperbole. Once I thought I could write, or at least get a story straight.

"I would just like to say that we will work with the police to ensure that all the evidence is collected, and then work will continue as before and without too much delay. Thank you." He stood and walked from the room, a patch of sweat soaked right through his suit jacket. Brooks, Sutton and the Superintendent followed him out, trailed by a volley of questions from the other journalists.

"She hit him where it hurts."

"Yeah, so did you. Do you think there's anything in the rumor it's a police officer?"

"What?"

McMahon and Okonjo were standing close to each other, McMahon listening intently to whatever she was telling him, while keeping an eye on the room and the slowly dispersing press.

"The body? Your question, remember?"

"Right. Who knows, I just thought it was a place to start."

Disappointed. She was disappointed. I knew the signs, the tiny slump of the body, the open expression almost pitiful – hopeful that I'd say or do something to change her rapidly deteriorating impression of me. "What about the misappropriation of funds?"

"It's interesting but I doubt it, the bureaucratic checks are too tight. But if you think there's a story there then you should follow it, Annabelle."

"Just call me Anna. I will. It'd be great to get your handle on things though. I mean this is your area, right? Political scandals and dirty deals? It would be such an honor for me." There was no expression on her face as she spoke and I couldn't decide if she was being sarcastic or not. I didn't say anything.

She packed her things away and stood to leave. "Anyway it was good to meet you." She handed me her card. "Stay in touch?"

"I won't be around for much longer, but sure."

"Do you have a card?"

"Not on me, but you can get my email from the website, I'm easy to find." I looked past her and kept my eye on McMahon: if there was any juice in this, he'd be the one to squeeze.

"OK. Thanks. See you soon then." She dithered, taking a half step back then forward, and a part turn of the feet before moving between the chairs and out across the room. I half expected her to trip to complete the picture, but she didn't.

The room was almost empty. I got up, preparing to interrupt McMahon and Okonjo, but I didn't need to: she was moving away, behind the screen and through the door into the building off limits to me.

"Detective McMahon?"

"That's right. And you are?" He looked me up and down and smiled, a wide, snaggle-toothed, cowboy smile. Yeah, he was hot.

"Marcus Murray – from the Sentinel."

"Right. A bit out of your way isn't it? What brings someone like you down here?" He looked as if he might hook his thumbs in his belt loops and rock on his heels. He crossed his arms instead.

"This case, the story."

"We are honored."

"Why's that?"

"Didn't I see you on TV the other week? Talking about dirty politicians and financial scandals."

"Probably."

"What did you do to get sent here? Upset someone?"

"Maybe this is a bigger story than it seems?"

"It's not. Trust me."

"Convince me. What else can you tell me about this case?"

"You mean aside from the briefing you just heard?"

"Yeah. I'd appreciate having access to the information the local radio station has. An undercover police officer, any truth in that?"

"Whoever spoke to that journalist was out of order. At the moment there's nothing to tell, and when there is we'll let you know."

"Well, if there is anything – off the record even – let me know, I'd like to help if I can." I gave him my card and watched him tuck it into his inside pocket. "See you." I walked out through the now-empty reception and into the sunshine and tried to remember why DCI Sutton seemed so familiar to me.

1989

"Your mum won't like me."

"She will, she'll be thrilled I've brought a girl home. She thinks I'm a poof."

"Well, you are ain't you?"

He didn't say anything because he hadn't admitted it to himself, at least not in those words. He loved and fantasized and had feelings that worried him, but they could be denied, ignored, pretended away. Couldn't they? Didn't being queer mean AIDS and being alone and sick and rejected? He'd read the papers, seen the adverts on TV. So he unlocked the front door, stood aside and held it open for her.

"Well, I bloody hope you are," she said as she went in, "because the last thing I need is another dirty bastard trying to get in my knickers." She laughed and turned on her heel to look around.

"Do you have a lot of dirty bastards in your knickers then?" He shut the door and moved past her across the hall and into the kitchen, leaving her with the question. He'd dumped his bag and turned round to offer her a drink before he realized she wasn't there.

She was still in the hallway, her lower half anyway: the top was leaning through the doorway of the study, holding onto the doorframe for balance, her head and shoulders out of sight. He walked to stand next to her as she said, "Now I understand," so he pushed the door fully open and nodded to her to follow him inside.

"Understand what?"

"Why you don't know who the gavvers are. You're like *really* fancy. Bloody hell, look at this place, you've got a library! How many rooms have you got downstairs?" She ducked out into the hall again and counted the doors, "one, two... five!"

"No, that door there is to the pantry, a cupboard. So, four and it's just a study, not a library."

"Study, library call it what you want. Our entire house only has four rooms if you don't include the karzi. Jesus. This hallway is bigger than my living room. No wonder you've got a housekeeper." She walked back into the study, smiling. "Look at all these books. All yours?"

"No, these are mostly my dad's and some of my mum's too."

She walked over to the far side of the room, reaching out towards the bookcase. "A whole room lined with books. And a piano. You lucky fucker. Are you rich?"

"Oh God no. Not at all." He shook his head, embarrassed but proud to be impressive for once, even if it was for the wrong reason. She turned to look at him, her face hidden behind a blank expression. He leaned back against the doorjamb and crossed his arms, unsure what might happen next. Did she hate him already? He expected her to eventually, but not this soon.

"What does your dad do then?"

"He was a vicar."

"Oh." She moved away from the books and towards the French doors, pushing aside the curtain and breathing a patch of condensation onto a glass panel. They both stood still, watching it shrink as if it were pulling into itself from the outside edges in, to a place beyond the glass.

"If you're not rich, then you're posh. Old money. I knew it, you're like a character in an Evelyn Waugh novel." She dropped the curtain and walked over to the desk.

"Some of my family would like to think so. But my mother says we are 'jolly old Anglican middle class'. She hates all that stuff."

"What stuff?" She picked up a photograph in a silver frame from the desk, stroking a thin film of dust from the glass.

48

"Snobbery, but she's still a bit of a snob I think."

"Ain't we all. My mum's a right one, judges everyone, *look at the state of her net curtains, her sheets, kids...* She thinks everyone but her is filthy." She held up the photograph for him to see. "This your dad?" He nodded.

"He was handsome. You look like him. You've got his nice square chin. Do you miss him?"

"Sometimes. I was only six when he died." She placed the frame carefully on the desk. He didn't like to talk about his father, not even with his mother, but with her, he wanted to. He cleared his throat. "He wrote a book," he said.

"Really?"

"Yes." He walked over to the shelves, the orderly, perfectly alphabetical, shelves. There it was, a slim volume bound in maroon fabric-covered board. *Christianity and the Necessity of Sacrifice* by Dr Alexander Murray. He took the book from the shelf and flipped through the pages. There was no pressed flower or note in there of course, nor any dedication at the front: neither parent was sentimental. He placed it in Mel's outstretched hand. "He went to America to meet a famous French philosopher for his research."

"Wow," she breathed, tracing the lettering on the cover, her hair falling around her face. "It's impressive. You must be proud of him." She flipped the pages open and began reading, her voice clear and fluent, reading as if she had rehearsed and was performing for an audience:

Christ's sacrifice, of dying for our sins, paying for our sins with his life is of course the ultimate gesture of love. This is, I suggest, the exemplar for Christian participation in all relationships—one of sacrifice, of relinquishing self, body and soul for our fellow man. It is in always valuing the other above ourselves that we ourselves feel the full expression of love, both the love of God and of our fellow man.

My esteemed and valued peer, Girard, writes, "If left unappeased, violence will accumulate until it overflows its confines and floods the surrounding area. The role of sacrifice is to redirect violence into "proper" channels. The scapegoat, so called to bring to mind the lamb substituted by Abraham in place of his son, I suggest, is a willing participant in the event, demonstrating God's love in becoming the locus for societies' fears and hatred and dispelling them without causing greater harm, rather than a victim of a functional, carnivalesque release of social tension. It is a sacred act, a cultural ritual affording a transcendent proximity to Christ's passion, and yet ambivalent, for Christ died so that we might not.

She closed the book and he stood there for a beat, his father's words, her voice fading slowly like tobacco smoke. "Have you read it?" She turned the book over and stroked the back cover.

"No, not all of it."

"Why not? Your dad wrote it. You should read it."

"I don't know. It's not my kind of thing."

"How do you know if you haven't read it?" She shifted her weight onto one leg and drew the other foot in, like a dancer preparing for a step.

"It's complicated. All the God talk."

"What does your mum think?"

"About the book?"

"About the God stuff."

"We still go to church sometimes. She thought Dad's missionary work was arrogant and colonial, going off to Africa and India and imposing the Bible and the stories of Jesus and Mary on people with perfectly good stories of their own. Anyway, that's what she says."

She tilted her chin a fraction, encouraging him to keep talking but he didn't know what else to say. "Well, it's not for me. All that talk of sin and saving people from themselves, sitting in judgment and ain't *that* supposed to be a sin? Contradictions and lies." She handed him the book. "You should be proud of your dad though: at least he tried to do what he thought was right."

"Maybe." He slid the book back in its place.

"How did he die?"

"Malaria. Caught on his missions, or at least I think so. I just remember him getting sicker and sicker and then just not being there. It's not really talked about. My mum gets upset."

"Yeah, that's fair enough."

"What now?" he said, changing the subject or trying to, clumsy and gangly in all respects.

She smiled. "Time I educate you, I reckon. Despite all these books you've got some serious gaps in your knowledge. Right, let's start with the gavvers. The gavvers are the police, also known as the filth, pigs, rozzers. Best avoided at all costs. OK? Repeat after me. Gavvers. Come on, Gavvers..."

"Gavvers," he croaked.

"Filth, pigs, rozzers."

"Filth, pigs and rozzers."

"And they are?"

"Best avoided?"

"You catch on fast!" She took his hand, and pulled him towards the door before releasing him, dropping his unpracticed hand. "Come on, I'm parched. I need a drink before your next lesson."

In the kitchen she watched as he took the juice from the fridge and poured it into glasses, then wiped down the side with a cloth. With most people, being watched felt like an affront, as if they were trying to possess him, to catch him out, but when Melanie looked at Marcus like that, it didn't feel sinister, there was no agenda: she was just giving him her full attention. It was unnerving but comforting; like being watched by God or one of his agents. But if he'd said that to her, she'd have laughed so hard that she'd have exploded snot from her nose. She did that sometimes, despite being as graceful as a ballerina.

"Your mum never remarry then?"

"How'd you know that?"

"The photos on the desk: there's a few family ones, ones of you and your dad, your mother, but they're all from a while ago.

You're a little boy in the pictures. No updated ones, no one here to replace or be jealous of the past. Plus, in the hall there's no men's coats or nothing." She picked up her glass and gulped, wiping her mouth on the back of her hand. "That tastes good."

"You should be a detective."

"Nope, I just pay attention. Best way to avoid trouble." She raised her eyebrows and winked. "I don't like trouble."

They went upstairs, ducking their heads into each room to finish off her tour. She asked questions, pointed to photos and paintings, wanted to know who was who, when and what. He was her tour guide, giving her the abridged and exaggerated family history. He had never felt so fascinating.

In his bedroom, she kicked off her shoes and sat on the bed, leaning back against the wall, while he perched on the chair by the desk.

"Nice." She nodded at the posters of Sonic Youth and the Beastie Boys tacked up over the pale blue walls. She reached out and grabbed Cecil from the plumped pillow.

"You still have a teddy?" She sat him on her lap, facing Marcus and finished her juice, her face magnified by the curved glass.

"Well, I don't cuddle him at night, if that's what you're asking."

"That's alright. There's nothing wrong with needing a cuddle from your teddy." She laughed and put her glass on the bedside table, before sitting back and turning the toy towards her. "What's his name?"

"The bear?" The soles of her socks were worn thin, and there was a small hole by her big toe. She saw him looking and tucked her feet up under her bottom.

"Of course the bear."

"Cecil."

"Hello, Cecil. Nice to meet you." She pressed the paw of the bear with her fingers and pretended to shake his hand. "Anyone else you going to introduce me to?"

"Not right now," he said, unsure if she was teasing or not. He knelt down by the stereo stack and pressed play on the CD. Prince, intoning like a preacher over a wavering organ chord, oozed from the speakers.

"Good choice. Unexpected, but good. Love this album," She put Cecil back and lay on her side, her head propped on her hand. "It's a shame you've only got Cecil, 'cause I have a bunch of busted-up Barbie dolls for you to meet." She pulled her lower lip into her mouth, resting her top teeth there for a moment.

"Can I ask you a question?" He'd settled back, sitting on the floor by the fireplace.

"You can ask. It doesn't mean I'll answer."

"What's going on with Georgie?"

"What do you mean?"

"You know, you seemed a bit upset that day, after we saw her."

"Was I? I don't remember feeling upset."

"Well, quiet then."

"She has a lot to lose, that's all. And she wants to be liked so much that sometimes she tries too hard, she does stupid things."

"Oh, OK." He'd never heard anyone their age speak like that before. "I thought you were annoyed at me."

"Really? Why?"

"I don't know, you just went quiet and I thought I'd done something wrong."

"Nope. I'll tell you if you upset me. My turn to ask a question." She turned over onto her stomach, resting her chin on her hands. "Why did you leave Coombe Hall?"

"Because I hated it." He swallowed the flood of nervous spit in his mouth with a loud gulp.

"Really? Do you like Danner?" She raised her eyebrows.

"Eh, no, but it's better than Tomb Hall. Seriously, you have no idea how awful it was there."

"OK, if you say so." She turned over onto her back, closed her eyes and lay still except for her fingers that twitched and plucked at an air guitar. The music filled the space and he picked up the CD cover and pretended to read the back, blushing. He didn't plan to be honest about who he was. The thought didn't occur to him, not then; it wouldn't until much later. She would always be the one to uncover the truth, to see it clearly. She made it happen. She was the catalyst.

"I was kicked out of Coombe Hall." He put the cover back down. She didn't sit up, she just turned her head towards him a fraction to indicate she was listening.

"Someone found a love letter I'd written and gave it to the Headmaster."

"Kicked out because of a love letter," she said, almost under her breath; not so much a question or a statement, but an acknowledgment, letting him know she'd heard but not pressing him to continue. She watched as he pressed the heels of his hands into his eye sockets, plugging up the tears that stung his lids.

"It was to my best friend, Anthony. His parents found it and went mad."

She sat up on the edge of the bed and leaned forward, her elbows resting on her knees, her hair covering most of her face. He could hear her breathing, slowly, calmly. She looked up through her hair. "What did your mum say?"

"She thought they'd overreacted, that they'd misunderstood my letter, that they were the perverts, not me. She couldn't do anything about it though, and I didn't want her to. I wanted to leave."

"And Anthony?"

"I haven't heard from him since." Then he started crying, heaving as though he might be sick. Half-blinded by a mess of tears and spit and snot, he felt rather than saw Mel put her arms around him. She pulled him in close and starting rocking back and forth as if he were a baby, slowly keeping pace with the rhythm of her breathing. Her hipbone pressed against him and he could feel her soft breast against his arm. The contradiction of her body, hard bone and soft flesh, was pure comfort and he let her hold him, crying a little harder so she wouldn't let go.

Then, aware that his tears had become a lie, he shifted and sat up, rubbing his face.

"Sorry. What a cry-baby."

She got up and moved over to the shelves by the desk where his CDs and vinyl were stacked in neat rows.

"Let's have a DJ change, this song is sad." She peered at the spines of the covers, chewing on the inside of her cheek, and he wiped his face on his school jumper. "This will be perfect." She pulled a CD from the shelf, plucked it from the case and swapped it in the machine. "The Beastie Boys! You can't beat these bad boys to cure what fucks with you. Hang on a sec, I just need to find..." She pressed the forward button until she found what she wanted and then got up, bouncing around the room and rapping along to Fight for Your Right. "What do you think? Have I got the moves?" She started banging her head with the beat, flipping her hair around her shoulders and banging imaginary drums.

Looking in from the outside, it would be easy to assume a sweet and clumsy teenage romance was in the offing, but this was no such thing. Later, when he is a grown man, Marcus will pity those who confuse love with the ancient urges of the body. He will think love is something pure, untouchable.

"Come on, dance with me!" She pulled him up next to her and wrangled his arms to make him dance, pushing and pulling them to shift his body in time to the music. "Come on!" She let go of his hands and he stood there watching her as her dancing slowed to a halt. "What's up?"

"I can't dance."

"Everyone can dance."

"I can't." He folded his arms across his chest, still embarrassed and raw.

"Who says?"

"Everyone who has ever seen me try."

"And are you positive those people were equipped to judge your dancing? Was Wayne Sleep on the panel?"

"Pardon?" He was clueless, but no way was he admitting that he rarely watched the telly or, more accurately, that his mother rarely let him. That was a confession too far.

"Doesn't matter. Everyone can dance, trust me. You just have to let go. Who cares what other people think? Just have a good time."

"I care. I look like an idiot."

"Then we'll close our eyes. Come on, it's good for you." She closed her eyes and started dancing again, her shoulders and hips zigzagging. He joined in, not wanting to be a bad sport, his public school manners automatic and absolute. Closing his eyes, he shuffled on the spot. When the song ended, he opened his eyes to find her watching. "OK, so we gave it a good try." She rolled her eyes and sat down on the floor.

"I did warn you."

"You'll just have to practice, because the alternative is that you can never, ever go out clubbing and then you will be alone and a virgin forever."

"Right. I'll keep that in mind."

She smiled, looked down at her hands in her lap – long fingers curled in towards her palms, the nails short with ragged cuticles – and the mood changed. It was a slight shift in her attention, no big statement, but they'd gone from larking about to a certain stillness in a second, just with the change in the direction of her gaze. It was strange, and at first he felt anxious wondering what to say or do, but then he realized that he didn't have to do anything, that he could just be there, with no need to say anything. It was just peaceful. No one was being scrutinized. It was just *being*. There was no other way to describe it.

Then, "Tell me a joke?" She had turned back towards him, her cheeks plumped by her smile, revealing one slightly chipped tooth. Returned to real time, the room resettled back in the world, tangible and precarious.

"I don't know any."

"Well that's no good."

"I'll tell you something funny, if you like? It doesn't qualify as a joke, I don't think. Or at least not a good one."

"You're not selling this to me, you know."

"Well, I'm just not good at jokes."

"Come on then." She shifted as if she were settling down and getting comfortable for a long story. "I'm all ears."

"A Roman walks into a bar holds up two fingers and says, "Five beers, please."

He held his fingers up in a V and laughed. "Get it?"

"Yes, I get it." She stretched her arms above her head and yawned. "I'm not sure you're supposed to laugh at your own joke, though."

"Can I ask you a question?"

"Another one? Go on then."

"Have you had your heart broken?"

"Nope," she said and shook her head decisively from one shoulder to the other.

"Really? Have you ever been in love?"

"Yes, I'm madly in love with Kurt Cobain."

"No, I mean someone real."

"He is real."

"You know what I mean. Someone we know; someone local or at school."

She smiled her lazy, easy smile that lit up her eyes. "I'm saving myself for Kurt."

"Would you like to stay for supper, Melanie?" his mother asked, her voice metallic, shiny and resistant. She had come in from work, a pile of files balanced under her arm, her hair damp from the soft mizzle of rain.

"Thanks, Mrs. Murray, but I have to look after my brother for my mum."

"I didn't know you had a brother?" Marcus said.

"Well I do."

"Oh, how old is he?"

"He's two."

"Where does your mum work, it's a bit late isn't it?"

"In a pub."

"Marcus, stop asking Melanie so many questions. Another time, then." His mother walked over to the Aga and stirred something in a pot. "You're always welcome."

"Cheers," Mel nodded, her expression serious. "You have a lovely house and I love all your books."

"Thank you, dear. Feel free to borrow one, any time."

"I will, thanks a lot." She picked up her bag, tipped her head at him and left, pulling the door shut behind her.

"Are you not going to see your guest out?"

"She didn't give me a chance, Mum." They both looked at the closed door as if expecting her to come back in and say goodbye. She didn't.

What the Heart Can't See

I woke early, after a crappy sleep squashed into my old bed, and felt nervous as if I were about to embark on something dangerous. But as I stood in the kitchen drinking my coffee I realized that it wasn't the usual anxiety about work grating the lining of my gut, but something else, something half-recognized, a feeling with all the texture of a memory, something just out of reach.

I rinsed my coffee mug and checked the time – 6:03. Then I walked through to the study and sat at my father's desk, pulling the phone and a note pad and pen over. David picked up after the second ring. It was never too early to call the news desk.

"David?"

"Marcus?" His voice was still morning-slow and thick.

"How're you doing?"

"I'm fine. You?"

"Yeah, pretty good considering I'm in the wilds of Kent. What's going on there? Anything interesting breaking?"

"Well, you know, there's always something..." There was a pause, and I heard him swallow. "Pretty quiet without you around. What's up?"

"I just wondered if you'd heard anything about the supposed misappropriation of funds for the high-speed link?" I leaned back in the chair, ducking the sun as it cut through a gap in the heavy curtains, slicing through the room like a cheese wire.

"Why do you ask? You got something?"

"Not really, just following a potential lead. I'm trying to get a handle on this piece Edward has got me on."

"Right, yeah, the body that's turned up and scuppered work on the link."

"That's the one. What about rumors of a fall-out at the Department of Transport? Or anything on Finborough?"

"Not that I've heard, mate, nothing."

"Alright, if you do hear anything let me know, yeah?"

"Of course. By the way, has Edward called you?"

"Why?"

"It could be nothing, but Edward was holed up in his office with lawyers all day yesterday. Then Jennifer said he'd been called to an emergency board meeting. I'm surprised he hasn't spoken to you."

"Why would he talk to me?"

"The St. Clair story, Edward has asked to see all the files. There are... whispers. I hope your sources are reliable, Marcus."

"Of course they are, Edward gave me the go-ahead himself."

"Fair enough. Look, I'd better go, but don't let on that I mentioned it, especially not to Edward. OK? I'm sure it's nothing but, just in case, be careful." The phone went dead, and I put it on the desk, slowly.

St. Clair was a private bank, one of those banks that operates behind closed doors and moves a series of promises and digital IOUs around the world, creating ever more vast black holes in the global economy. When I was first approached by my source, a tentative phone call to my desk, I thought it would be the usual story about reckless City thugs risking the country's economy while they got ever richer, but I couldn't have been more wrong. My story exposed them, exposed the false companies set up to bounce funds back and forth around the world, funds constructed of pixels on a screen like the dot in a game of Pong, sent one way then another before arriving in an account in Libya where the strings of codes were translated into cash, then weapons: weapons manufactured by British companies, companies partly owned by the

St. Clair family. The story was huge and, most importantly, it was rock solid. My instinct for a story had never been wrong.

I sat there, thinking about my source: the risks she took; the documents she showed me; the emails; the twisting trail of numbers; the recorded phone calls and photographs; the meeting with her colleague in a deserted Starbucks on the Brompton Road. It was rock solid. I had nothing to worry about; David was prone to overreaction. It was a major story and I knew there would be blowback. I'd been through this before, the scrutiny and scramble to protect the paper, the due diligence, etc. etc. It was nothing. For a moment I considered calling Edward, but I couldn't do that to David, and anyway, I trusted Edward. Sort of.

I'd known him for years: we met on my first day at the Sentinel, hired because I'd just won the Student Journalist of the Year, which promised I'd have promise. Edward was the type that usually won all the awards. A rising star at the paper, he was the son of a milkman from Enfield and after attending the local grammar had been a star scholar at Cambridge and the editor of Varsity. Edward was the type who won no matter what, even now after all this. Anyway, together we'd made an all-right team, as long as I'd got the stories and kept my nose clean.

I padded back into the kitchen, flicking on the kettle just as Mum walked in, fully dressed and ready to go. She eyed my boxers and t-shirt. "Morning, darling."

"Morning, Mother." I kissed her cheek, and she stepped back, flaring her nostrils like an animal.

"What're you doing up so early?"

"Just doing a bit of work, actually. Coffee?" I dumped two spoons of instant coffee into the mugs and filled them to the brim.

"Please. You OK? You look pale."

"Fine, just getting on with work."

"Well that's wonderful." I handed her the coffee and she sat at the breakfast table. "What are you up to today?"

"Going back up to the site, see if I can turn anything up."

"Will you be out most of the day?"

"Looks like it." I wrapped my hands around the warm mug.

"So you'll get dressed, then? Soon? Joyce will be here at nine."

"Yes, I'll get dressed. Don't worry, I won't embarrass you any more."

"You don't embarrass me." She looked down at the table, her lips pinched. "I just don't want to shock poor Joyce." She looked back up at me, a smile relaxing her mouth. We'd always been at odds, irritating each other, but we were close, too, my mother and I.

My childhood had been a clammy mix of Calpol, heavy blankets and books. Boiled sweets and the radio, like a child of the fifties not the eighties. She was over-protective but, to give her her due, she had coped with a queer son and a dead husband with all the stoicism of the Queen. I didn't like to upset her.

"Fair enough, it's the least I can do. How does she clean this house all by herself? She's got to be seventy at least."

"We manage. I think if she could persuade Maurice to leave his precious allotment she'd move down to Australia with her son just like that. Poor Joyce. I hope you don't leave the country."

"Why would I want to do that? I don't need to emigrate, Mother. My life is here." I smiled at her. "Besides, I couldn't leave you."

She looked at me, her eyes searching my face to see if I was sincere, then reached for my hand. "Sit with me for a bit." I sat opposite her as I always have since I was a child. "I had the oddest experience yesterday."

"Really? What happened?"

"It will sound silly, crazy even. But I was in the garden, deadheading my dianthus, you know, the lovely white flowers in the front beds..." She paused and waited for me to nod

62

and indicate that I appreciated her fine garden. "And I saw this woman across the lane, and you know I think she was watching me."

"What do you mean? Like she was spying on you?"

"I don't know. I mean, possibly. You hear about these people who prey on the old and vulnerable, watching their movements and habits so they can rob them."

"You're not old or vulnerable."

"Hunh." She snorted, looking down at her hands. "I'm getting there."

"So what did you do?"

"Nothing. She saw me looking at her and she walked away. But you know what was really odd? I thought it was Melanie. It was like seeing Melanie as a grown woman. But that's impossible, isn't it?"

"Yes. It is."

"Unheimlich."

"What?" I asked.

"It's Freud. It means uncanny. Strange." I knew what it meant, but she always enjoyed the opportunity to educate me. It puffed her up a little: once a headmistress always a headmistress. "Poor Melanie. Such a shame, I suppose we'll never know what happened to her, will we?"

"No, I don't think so, not entirely," I said and drained my mug before standing.

"Have I upset you? I'm sorry. I should've been more thoughtful and not mentioned it."

"I'm fine, mum. Honestly. Will you be all right? Shall I stay?"

"No, Marcus, I'm just a silly old bat. Just a coincidence, that's all. I'm sorry I even mentioned it. I'm sure it was nothing and nobody."

I never wanted to believe that Melanie was dead. How could she be? She was so full of life, it's impossible to imagine that extinguished. For years I expected to run into her, standing on a street corner in New York, her hand raised for a cab, or pushing a baby carriage through the Tuilleries in Paris. Always romantic, soft-focused, ridiculous. Once, while in Madrid covering a summit on the Euro, I was drinking coffee in a pavement café when Kool Thing came on the radio, Kim Gordon's voice fuzzy in the warm air. Perhaps it was just the music, my mind suggestible and easily tricked, but I saw her. Dark hair coiled in a bun at the back of her head, her nose and chin in profile and a slither of gold chains coiled around her wrist. I stood to get a better look and the woman had gone, stepped across the street or transmogrified into a stranger. Melanie was dead, and if she had lived, none of these lives would've been hers. How preposterous our futile ambitions for the dead become, freed from the limitations of living.

There were more press at the gate this time, but no sign of the contractor Williamson and his stylish hair. I made my way towards the front. There was less activity around the burial site, but officers and forensics in their paper suits had spread out across the entire field and, bent at the waist, were searching the soil with their fingers. McMahon and his sidekick Okonjo stood watching and waiting. I looked around; there was no one I recognized, not even perky Anna.

David's warning to be careful had rattled me more than I wanted to admit. It was his surprise that Edward hadn't called me, the sensation of being in the dark, out of the loop, the object of discussion and gossip. Why? We weren't friends, but we'd worked well together over the years. I brought in stories, big ones, and he protected me, backed me up when needed. We had readers, we broke exclusives and won the odd award and that's all that matters in this game. *There are whispers,* he said. Paranoia boiled up like spit on a grate, but I ignored it. Do your job, make no assumptions, I thought, I've rattled some cages, that's all there is to it. It'll blow over. Focus on what's here, now. The facts.

"You're back again."

I turned to find McMahon standing behind me. "Looking for the story, just like you."

"I'm not looking for a story, Murray."

"No, I suppose you're not. You're looking for evidence, Detective."

"That's right, I am."

"Any closer to knowing who the victim is?"

"The post-mortem will be finished soon, if not already, and then a statement will be released to you lot."

"Fair enough. I don't suppose there's any chance of a sneak preview?"

He laughed. "No."

"What about a drink and a chat – just a chat? Any background information would be useful, and I'm buying of course."

He inhaled sharply, narrowing his eyes – assessing, considering – and nodded. "Sure. This evening? Six-thirty at the Queen's Head. You know it?"

"I'll find it. See you there."

"You will."

"McMahon?" Okonjo glared at me over his shoulder. He joined her and I watched as they left in an unmarked car.

"What did he want?" Annabelle appeared at my side.

"Jesus! Why is everyone creeping up on me?"

"Jumpy! You OK?"

"Yeah, fine. You?"

"I'm good, just got here. Been following up on those funding rumors."

"Anything?"

"Not really. They've closed ranks. What about here?"

"They're doing a search of the whole field."

"I see that. What did the handsome policeman want?"

"Nothing. Just said there'll be a statement released tomorrow, with findings from the post-mortem."

"Oh. Good. You had lunch?"

"Yes."

"Already? That was early. How about a coffee then?"

"Can't, have to do some work. Next time though?"

"We could work together on this, pool resources."

"The thing is, Annabelle..."

"Anna."

"Anna. The thing is, I don't think there's much here. Someone buried a body after killing them, and that's awful, dreadful, sad, etc., and it's delayed the building of a train track. That's it. No corruption, no conspiracy. Nothing juicy here, and if there is, I don't think it's worth the squeeze. Sorry."

"Right. Well it seems you've reached your conclusion. You know best. I'd still like to have a chat. You know, maybe learn from you. I'd love to know how you've got so many sources to trust you and reveal so much. It seems you're the master at coaxing secrets from people."

"I'm hardly that, Anna."

"Oh come on, everyone in the office is talking about it." She tilted her head to the side like a lapdog wanting choc drops.

"About what?"

She arched an eyebrow and smirked, shrugged a little. As if she'd got me cornered. "That you're the best, that's all."

I stepped back, putting my hands in my pockets. "Right, well, people talk."

"That's certainly true. See you tomorrow at the station then." She turned and trotted away, jaunty, before turning back and waving at me. I was embarrassed to be caught watching her go. Did she imply...? What did she imply? Nothing.

I got in the car and drove straight to the Queen's Head.

1989

He hadn't got away with being the new boy. What an idiot, to think that getting up twenty minutes early to do his hair and wearing Nike high tops like all the other boys would work. It should've been obvious that it was only a matter of time before they decided his accent and prissy ways needed a good kicking. It was only natural; it's the way of things. Everyone gets it, eventually. Everyone is cut down to size, by the mob or death: it's inevitable.

"Oi, Marcus, Marcus ain't it? Come over 'ere, you." One of the Darrens – the thick-set, muscly one with brown eyes and a thug's nose that spread across a face covered in acne – flicked his head back to beckon him, as if he'd not heard his command and needed a clue where to go. They stood there in the lower corridor outside the toilets, four of them with Darren Shine in the middle, their hair falling into their eyes. The air stank of piss, ripe socks, sweat and Kouros aftershave.

"Yeah?" He walked over, almost green with fear, taller than them but thin and long limbed.

"Where you from then?" This time the short one with braces wrapped like razor wire on his teeth piped up.

"What d'you mean?" Marcus almost squeaked.

"Where you from? Which school?"

"Oh, Coombe Hall." The sweat began to run down his back in thin streams. Other kids, passing through the corridor, slowed to watch.

"Fuck me," said Shine. "Too good for us here then, aintcha?"

"No, of course not." They closed in, sealing him off.

"Think your shit don't stink?" They were tight around him, their warm bodies close. He got an erection, of course. The short one noticed, of course.

"Oh my God, he's got a fucking stonk on!" The others laughed and looked down at his groin where his pleated trousers betrayed him.

"Fucking bender! You a queer boy, Marcus? You a homo?"

"They're all poofs up the private school."

Darren Shine said, "You better not be poking that dick in my direction, fucking bender," then grabbed his shoulders, yanked him down and kneed him in the balls. Marcus went down like a sack of potatoes, all the wind knocked out of him and wanting to be sick.

"I fucking HATE benders," one of them hissed in his ear. Down on the scuffed lino, he focused on the pattern as he tried to catch a breath before they started kicking.

"He ain't a queer, you fucking idiot!" And there she was, Mel, bent down next to him, appearing out of nowhere. Checking he was OK before pulling him to his feet. "You alright, babe?" She kissed him on the lips and stroked his face, before pushing the hair out of his eyes.

"What the fuck? You screwing this cunt, Mel?" Shine turned pink with incredulity. "You turn me down for this poof?" White foamy saliva gathered in the corners of his full mouth.

"Where did you come from?" Marcus gasped, barely able to stand.

"The loo, where d'you think?" She winked and turned back to Shine.

"Yes, I'm seeing him. Now give it a rest and fuck off with your little gang or I'll have a word with Charlie, shall I?"

They stared at each other for a few seconds until Darren shifted his gaze to Marcus, and after a pause Marcus held out his hand. "No hard feelings, OK?"

"Just stay out of my way, poof. Got it?" Marcus's hand hovered in the air, and as if they were of one mind the Darrens slouched off, barging into his shoulder as they passed.

"Oh my God! Thanks." Almost sick with relief and his groin feeling like it was on fire, he couldn't believe he'd made it without getting his face smashed in. He leaned over to catch his breath.

"You're alright. Come on, I'll walk you to your class."

"Who's Charlie?"

"Me dad. He knows Darren's old man."

"Oh."

She held his hand as he limped down the corridor, past the other kids who kept their eyes down.

"You know everyone will think we're going out with each other now?"

"So, they'd think that anyway. Dozy idiots think if a boy and girl are mates they have to be fucking."

"Don't you mind?"

"No. Do you?"

"No. I quite like it actually." He squeezed her hand.

"Give over, you old softie." She bumped her shoulder against him, gently. "Right. I'm off, I'll see you later."

"Where are you going?" he whined.

"Out. This place is doing my head in. Adios amigo!" And off she went, walking down the corridor in the opposite direction to all the other kids, her hair swaying around her shoulders, her hands in her pockets. It seemed to Marcus that she moved in slo-mo with an iconic song playing in the background, something cultish and hip, with the light softening around her. Like in a film. It was almost one of those moments where life imitates art, except that the room was badly lit, the backing track was scraping chairs, sniffing, coughing and laughter and everything moved in real time. But still, it was one of those moments.

"You really seeing her?" Shine, being brighter than the other Darrens was in the same maths set and had taken the seat behind Marcus.

"Erm, yes," he nodded, balls throbbing on the hard wooden chair.

"Bet she's a right goer. That's what I've heard. A bit of a slag."

"What?" He turned to look at Darren, at his smooth face, his full lips, the mineral blue eyes.

"She shags around. I heard she was doing a married man."

"No she doesn't."

"Yeah, where d'you think she goes when she's off on her jaunts?"

"It doesn't matter, she can do what she likes."

"Don't it? I wouldn't let my bird get about like that." He leaned back in his seat and ran his thick-fingered hands through his hair. A poster of a smiling Einstein was tacked on the wall behind him, and it looked like Einstein was laughing at the stupid boys beneath him.

"Have you slept with Mel?"

"Me? Nah, wouldn't touch it."

"What about the others?"

"No way, she's spoiled goods. Sloppy seconds and all that."

"Right. So if none of you have done it with her, how do you know that she's spoiled then?"

"Everyone knows, sorry, mate, don't want to upset you or nothing but you're new here and us blokes should look out for each other. Know what I mean?"

Marcus didn't have a clue, it made no sense to him, but what could he do? He played along, despising himself. "Sure, thanks."

"And I'm sorry about earlier, just a bit of a laugh, know what I mean?"

"Yeah, it's fine."

"I mean, you're not a bender, are you?"

He shook his head.

"No hard feelings then?"

"No, no hard feelings."

"You two going to do any work this afternoon or are you going to sit there gossiping like two old ladies?" Mr. Brooks walked towards their desks, blinking rapidly behind his gold-rimmed glasses. Marcus noticed the teacher's watch, gold colored with a second hand that whirred around the face in a smooth arc instead of jolting, second by second. He opened the textbook and squinted at the blackboard, feigning concentration, balls swollen and throbbing. Brooks stopped, nodded, pivoted on the ball of his foot like a dancer and walked back to his desk muttering: "That's more like it."

No Smoke

I found a table outside in the beer garden, a well-tended garden with hanging baskets and troughs of geraniums and rosemary bushes trimmed into shape. It was a quiet place, serving food. Not the kind of pub where kids come to get pissed, or score: a grown-up pub, for families and couples. The kind that has premium beers on tap, sea-salt and cider vinegar crisps and small jars of olives or hand-roasted cashews in earthenware pots.

I paced myself, drinking slowly, trying to enjoy the sun. I read a paper, not ours, left discarded on the bar. No mention of the St. Clair story, or of the body in the orchard, or the DfT; either because there was no story or because it hadn't broken yet.

I called Edward but he didn't pick up, so I left a message that I was meeting with a detective on the case and that I'd have something for him by tomorrow. Then I called my mother. It wasn't like her to be fanciful and she'd seemed unsettled that morning, imagining she'd seen Melanie. I thought maybe it was the beginning of dementia or she'd had a mild stroke, but then she picked up the phone and her voice, resolute and clear, with a hint of exasperation – I'd interrupted her in the middle of doing her accounts – reassured me otherwise. Perhaps it had been a trick of the light? The brain sees what it wants to see, looking for patterns and the familiar, what we know. Perhaps that was it? We're trapped in the wireframe of our memories, building our present from old images. But why Melanie? Why not her sister, or my father even?

The lunchtime crowd left, leaving just me and one other drinker – an older bloke, hunched over his pint inside close to the bar, his position unchanged each time I went in for a fresh one or a piss. By six it began to fill again: after work drinkers, pre-dinner drinkers, dates. I sent a text to Edward, who hadn't returned my call, repeating that I was meeting McMahon, and for him to call me. He replied fifteen minutes later, GREAT, IN A MEETING. WILL CALL TOMORROW. See, I thought, nothing to worry about.

I kept an eye on the crowd, half-expecting to recognize or be recognized by someone I went to school with or who knew Melanie; while there was no one I knew in the small groups talking and drinking and eating, it was strangely familiar. The flat lull of estuary English, the dropped Ts and Hs, the jeans and polo shirts and clean trainers on the men; the clumpy wedge heels and long strappy dresses on the women. The blonde highlights and shaved heads. The smell of beer and cigarettes, perfume and hot chips.

McMahon arrived at six thirty on the dot, showered and changed from his work suit into jeans and a short-sleeved shirt that showed his tanned, strong arms. Carrying two pints, he walked straight over as if he knew I'd be in that exact spot. Like he'd been watching me the whole time.

"Been here all day?" He sat opposite and placed the beer down on the table between us.

"How'd you know?"

"I've got my sources." He swallowed from his beer and smiled.

"Spying on me?"

"No need, your face is bright red from the sun... and the beer."

"You got me. It's a fair cop, Detective. Thanks for the drink."

He laughed and we both drank.

"So, any news?"

"That's it? Straight in there, no foreplay? No softening up with dinner and more drinks?" He looked me straight in the eye. I looked away.

"OK. Let's play it your way, Detective. So, first name?"

"Callum."

"Callum McMahon. Nice Irish boy."

"Yep. Dad was from County Clare. Lived here for most of his life though."

"So you grew up around here?"

"No, I grew up in Surrey with my mum." He leaned forward, his elbows on the table. He was wearing an expensive-looking watch, especially for a policeman. No wedding ring, though. "Moved here for the job a few years back. What about you?"

"London. Here for the story."

"So you're from London originally?"

I considered lying, for no reason other than simplicity, but didn't. He was a detective, lying would be stupid. Even with something to hide, and I had nothing to hide.

"Actually no, I grew up around here. Moved to London for University and that was that. I didn't come back."

"That so? Marcus Murray from Medway, you don't sound like a local."

"Why's that?"

"Your accent, you haven't got the estuary twang. You sound more like a member of the royal family."

I laughed, "Yes, I've been told that before."

"So, you still have connections around here? Family, friends?" He tipped his glass high and finished his drink.

"Mother. That's it. Lost touch with everyone else."

"And your mother? How's she doing?"

"Am I being interrogated?"

"Sorry, it's a bad habit. Just interested. I like to know who it is I'm talking to."

"Well in that case, officer, she's fine, thank you. She lives up on Highstead Lane."

"Very nice."

"So what made you become a policeman?"

"Ah, you know. I wanted to catch the baddies, be a hero. What about you? Why journalism?"

"Similar reasons, believe it or not. I wanted to be a hero, but I've never been much good in a fight and I can't stand the sight of blood. My secret weapon is the pen: revealing the establishment's dirty secrets, working for the public interest. All very noble and selfless."

"So you're one of the good guys?"

"Yep, I'm a good guy."

He grinned, his lips rising above his teeth in a thin crescent, crinkling the corners of his blue eyes.

"I'm a good guy," I repeated, as if I was trying to convince myself.

"I think that calls for another drink," he laughed, exposing dark metal fillings in his back teeth.

"Same again?" I said, picking up the glasses.

"Sure. Do you want to eat? Maybe get a menu?"

At the bar I positioned myself so that I could see him through the window. He was sitting back, relaxed, just watching the punters.

"You both look comfortable. Mind if I join you?" Okonjo was standing by our table, a glass of wine in her hand.

"Of course." Callum moved our dirty plates and glasses out of her way, pushing them to the end of the table to make room. Soft lights strung around the trees and fence glowed in the thickening dark. A young woman lit the patio heaters dotted through the garden and then gathered up the empties from our table. The crowd was getting rowdier; a glass shattered on the paving stones to a round of applause before being quickly swept up.

"Trouble brewing?" I asked.

"No more than usual," Okonjo said. She stared at me then drank from her glass. "How long you two been here then?" She directed this at Callum.

"Long enough." He laughed and then, without looking at me or seeming to move, he pressed his knee against mine under the table. I waited to see if he would move away, if it was a mistake. He didn't, so I pressed back. Then he turned to Okonjo and moved, leaving a point of heat on my leg. "You OK, Ada? You seem tense."

"That might be because I've been in the office and not the pub for the last three hours."

"Best catch up then."

"No, I don't think so. I'd best get home, early start tomorrow." She drained her glass and stood. "Nice to meet you...?"

"Marcus. Nice to meet you too."

"Tomorrow then, Callum. Don't do anything I wouldn't do." She bumped his shoulder and got up, giving me one last look as she left.

"She doesn't like me."

"I wouldn't take it personally: she's just not keen on the press."

"That's not uncommon."

"Neither is hating the police," he said and raised his glass. "To our maligned and misunderstood professions."

"I'll drink to that." We tapped our glasses at the rim.

"So, the body. Who is it?"

He sighed, "And I thought you were here for me, not just information."

"Maybe it's both."

He tipped his head back and looked at me down the length of his nose. "You charmer." He sat up straight and rubbed his head, ruffling his hair. "Off the record?"

I nodded and opened my hands, palms up.

"I'm serious, I don't want to see my name in the paper tomorrow. Alright?"

"Yes, off the record, no names."

"OK. We've a pretty good idea who the victim is; we're just waiting for DNA tests to confirm the identity."

"Cause of death?"

"Looks like a head trauma, but again, too early to tell conclusively."

"How long has the body been there?"

"A long time, twenty years or so, maybe more."

"Is there any truth that it's a missing policeman?"

"No comment."

"Is that a 'yes,' no comment?"

"It's a 'no comment,' no comment." He finished his drink.

"Another round?"

"I don't think so, work tomorrow," he reached over the table and stroked my arm, resting his hand on my wrist. "Can I see you again?"

I pulled my arm in. "I don't know how long I'll be around."

"Really, is that it? Or am I being rejected?"

"No, I really don't know how long I'll be around, that's all. So it seems sensible to not start anything."

"I'm not asking you to be my boyfriend, Marcus," he laughed.

"That's good."

"Why's that? You not into relationships?"

"You could say that," I shrugged. It was getting late, the pub emptying. Settling down for the night.

I tried to remember the last guy I'd been with – his face, his voice, his body – but I couldn't, only the overwhelming need that drove to me to the sauna and the release among bodies, breath and heat. The perfect hygiene and purity of anonymous sex that was just sensation, nothing else: no guilt, no shame, no responsibility and no risk of hurt.

"So no significant other, no husband or boyfriend for me to worry about?"

"No. You?"

"No, single. You could come to my place, tonight. No strings, I promise."

We stood, and I followed him through the pub out into the car park.

"We shouldn't drive," he said.

"I know," I said, grabbing his hand and pulling him back against the wall behind the cars before kissing him. He pulled me in, pushing his body against mine, his tongue in my mouth. A burst of laughter and the slamming of car doors intervened and we pulled apart for a moment, waiting for them to leave. I pulled him further into the shadows and dropped down, unbuckling his belt and tugging open his jeans. His hands were on the back of my head as I sucked him in, then he tried to pull me up to face him,

"Let's go back to mine." But I stayed where I was until he finished, only standing as he buttoned himself up. "You don't take any prisoners," he said, breathless.

I kissed him and let him taste himself, before pulling away.

"See you at the press conference tomorrow then?" I walked out into the road, too pissed to drive, and made my way back home, my tongue still thick with him.

1989

M el was waiting for him on the bench opposite the school gate, her tatty school bag at her feet.

"Hello, I'm your security!" The wind was up and her cheeks were flushed from the chill. Autumn was shifting into winter, and she'd pulled her woollen socks up over her knees instead of leaving them to wrinkle around her calves. Behind her, the grassy bank dropped steeply towards the river as it curved towards the dockyard and factories that lined the way towards the estuary and the sea. Hundreds of Danner kids filed out over the hill towards the bus stop and the High Street.

"You OK? Get any more grief off that div, Shine?" She stood and linked her arm through his.

"No. Though he tried to warn me off you. You know, man to man."

"Really? Well I never."

"Yes. Where did you go today then?" He shrugged his shoulder to pull the strap of his bag closer and she let her arm drop back by her side.

"Out and about. Why?"

"Just wondered."

"Did you now? You know what curiosity did?"

"Killed the cat?"

"So they say."

They idled down the hill, watching the crowd of pupils pushing onto a bus. Darren and his gang were nowhere to be seen. A couple of stragglers huddled together puffing on their fags.

"Do you know what they say about you, Mel?"

"Who?"

"Darren and everyone."

"Nope." She bent and tugged up her sock.

"It's just that, you saying we're going out with each other, I think it confirms their impression of you."

"Speak English, Marcus."

"I don't know how to say it. It's horrid."

"Just say it. Come on!"

"He called you a slag. He said that you're a right goer and that you're sleeping with a married man." He waited for her to get angry, with him and them, or defensive and upset, but she didn't. She laughed.

"No way! That's funny."

"Is it?"

"Yes. Very funny and ironic actually."

"Why is it?"

"Because it is, Marcus. It's ridiculous."

"Do you want me to tell them the truth about us?"

"Why would you do that?"

"To set them straight. To stop them spreading rumors about you."

"No. That's sweet, but you're alright. I might as well be hung for a sheep as a lamb."

"What does that mean?"

"It doesn't matter, just something my Nan says. Look, you can't change no one's mind for them, so leave it. Why care what they think?"

"Because it's awful, and they're wrong. They're bloody arseholes. Wankers actually."

"It's not their fault really. They can't figure me out, so they take the piss to feel better. You can't let that bother you, mate. You'll be upset all the time. I know who I am and the people that matter know me and that's what counts. People lie and talk shit all the time to make themselves feel better, might as well shrug it off."

"Well, if you're sure."

"Yes, unless this is your way of fake dumping your fake girlfriend?"

"No!" The bus stop was almost empty now as they drew closer. "You want to come to mine for supper?"

"Can't, sorry. Got to babysit for me mum. Another time?"

"Sure, see you tomorrow?"

"Maybe," she winked at him and swung onto the bus as it pulled up. He watched her disappear up the stairs and then reappear at a window on the top deck. She blew a big, silly kiss and, laughing, he blew one back as the bus shut its doors and pulled away, hydraulic brakes hissing. Waiting for his bus, hands in pockets, still reeling from being beaten up for being gay to now dating the coolest and most talked about girl in school, he wondered if he could live like this forever, be straight and have a girlfriend like Mel. He could marry her. That would work. It might. They could be happy.

Without a Fire

"Look what I've dug out."

Mother handed me a photo: Mel and me in the back garden sitting on the bench under the pergola, both in our school uniform. Mel is squinting at the camera, the autumn sun in her eyes, her legs tucked up under her; my arms are stretched out across the backrest, my left ankle resting on my right knee. I look shy, she looks bold – we look like a couple in love.

"Look at you both, my handsome boy. So skinny then, my goodness!"

I put my half-eaten croissant back on the plate.

"So young, the two of you."

"What made you look for that?"

"I don't know. Silly I suppose, I wanted to look at her, at her face, rather than rely on my memory. I wanted to prove to myself that I didn't see her the other day."

"That really rattled you, didn't it?"

"I'm almost embarrassed to admit it, but yes. It did," she blinked and looked away, suddenly fragile. For a moment I didn't recognize her: my strong, independent mother had been replaced by a vulnerable old woman and I felt ashamed that I was failing her somehow, as always.

"It's understandable, Mum. So did the photo reassure you?"

"Yes, yes it did. It wasn't her, of course not," and with that the woman opposite returned my mother to me.

She sipped her coffee, watching me over the rim of her cup for a second before carefully placing it on the saucer. "You mustn't worry about me, it's my job to worry about you. Come on, eat up. You must be exhausted, I've no idea what time you got in last night and you were up early this morning. I could hear you tapping away on your computer."

I stuffed the rest of the croissant in my mouth, buttery flakes of pastry falling into my lap as I chewed and tried to swallow, the photo of Mel and me on the table by my plate. "Sorry, I was interviewing a source last night and wanted to get started on the article."

"Your car isn't on the drive."

"I left it at the pub."

"Now what will you do? I can't drive you, I've got all sorts on." She pulled her cardigan around her body, tucking her elbows in under her breasts, her chin lifting, ready to fight. She couldn't hide her indignation at my fecklessness, all trace of fragility gone.

"I'll get a cab and pick it up."

"Oh, right. That's sensible. And I forgot to tell you, Edward phoned for you when you were in the shower. He asked you to call him back on a new number, I wrote it down for you."

"Did he? He called the house phone? Here?"

"Yes, why? Didn't you give him the number?"

"Yes, probably, it's just strange. What else did he say?"

"That he needs to talk to you and that it's very important that you call him back as soon as you could. He's quite forthright, isn't he?"

"You could say that."

"Perhaps he wants you to go back to London? Another story?" She stood and started clearing the table of breakfast things, piling them in the sink for Joyce.

"Maybe. Where did you leave his number? In the study?" I pushed myself away from the table, scattering pastry crumbs all over the floor, and pocketed the picture.

"Marcus! Joyce has just done all the floors."

"I'll sort it in a minute. I'll just go and call the boss first. Where's the number?"

"In the sitting room, I think. I was reading the paper when he called." She lifted her mouth into a smile, "Work comes first, off you go."

I went through to the sitting room, guilt rolling like a marble behind my eyes, hard and clear, though I'm not sure why I felt so bad, only that something was horribly wrong, I couldn't see clearly and being in that house, being back wasn't helping. I stood rubbing my temples as my eyes adjusted to the light; it was a dim, thick-curtained room. A glass cabinet with my father's trophies in the far corner was the only point in the room that seemed capable of bearing the pressure of light. The furniture was dark and heavy, with Victorian wooden chests and thick-ankled settees, sagging slightly in the middle. An armchair, leather and buttoned, dominated the space by the fire, next to the poker and the brush. The small pad my mother kept for messages and to-do lists was on the side table close to where she always sat. Edward's new number was neatly printed in black ink.

He picked up immediately. "Marc?"

"Edward, lost your phone?"

"No, I just needed to talk to you privately."

"What? Are you on a burner? That's a bit dramatic isn't it?" I laughed. David's warning took shape again: *there are whispers, be careful.*

"Maybe. Look, how are things going there?"

"Fine, I don't think there's any dodgy stuff going on, nothing untoward with the DfT, but I've got a detective talking to me on the quiet, so I'll get something to you later today."

"That's good. Take your time," his voice low.

"What's going on, Edward?"

"Nothing to worry about, not really, just push-back from the St. Clair camp, not much more than what you'd expect. You're a pro, Marcus, you know the drill. Stay there, cover this piece and keep your head down. Right?"

"Shouldn't I come back?"

"No. It's best that you don't for now, we will deal with this: the legal team are ready, I've spoken to the board and we're all behind you. Alright?"

"If you say so."

"I do, it's better this way. Just reassure me, for my sake, we're a hundred percent on this, aren't we?"

"Of course we are, you gave me the go ahead yourself."

"I know, but... Good. Fine. I'll call you later."

"OK."

Ridiculous as it seems now, I decided he was right, it was part of the job, nothing to worry about. If you rattle a cage, they go for you. I could ride it out, I thought, it'll be fine. The sense of foreboding I had was just paranoia, irrational. Stupid. So I tore the page from the pad and crushed it into a ball; walking outside to the bins by the garage, I tossed it with the soggy leftovers, empty bottles and tea bags, irretrievable and unnoticed. I'd call him on his usual number: I had nothing to hide, nothing to fear. Then my phone buzzed, a text from Callum. "PRESS CONF PUSHED BACK TILL TOMO. COFFEE?"

"WHERE?" I replied.

As I turned to go back inside I caught sight of a bloke, thick-set and bald, wearing a black jacket. He was standing at the edge of our drive looking towards the house; as I moved closer, he turned and strode off behind the yew hedge that separates our property from the neighbors and the road. I waited to see if he came back. He didn't. I told myself it was probably nothing, that I was losing perspective.

1989

L eysdown. The North Sea slapped and folded on the mud
flats that slid from under the shingle where Marcus and
Melanie sat. It was cold, but the sky was clear and that hard
blue that promises no rain. They had caught the train three
towns down to Sittingbourne, and then a bus that juddered
through the flat farmland to the village. Melanie wanted a day
out and Marcus wanted to be with Melanie.

It was a tiny place: one street lined with amusement arcades,
some fish and chip shops, a café and a holiday park whose
guests stayed in caravans and prefab chalets resting on brick
foundations. The highlight of the holiday park was a small
outdoor pool with a slide and a double set of swings for the
kids. Small bungalows and narrow houses were plotted in neat
cul-de-sacs that led from the main road.

Winnings from the slot machine jangled in Marcus's pocket
like a cowbell. Melanie seemed to have a knack for it, for
knowing when to play on until the jackpot paid out and spilled
fifty-pence coins into the trough. A fat bloke with no front
teeth and a long wiry beard watched them from his cubicle,
piles of change arranged in neat rows on the ledge in front of
him, protected by Perspex and a locked door.

"That's enough," she said, breathless with laughter, her
hands scooping up the money and dropping it in his trouser
pockets. "Ice cream?"

Though it was off-season, it stayed open for the locals,
although he and Melanie were the only people around apart
from the bloke in the amusement arcade and a few older women

in the cafes. A strange halfway place, it wasn't quite a seaside resort, not quite a normal town. Even the shingle, the broken shells and pebbles were almost ground to sand, but not quite. Everything seemed half-finished, or half-broken, depending on how you looked at it. The lights flashed around the entryway of the arcades as if inviting in the ghosts of the apocalypse. It felt unreal, like a sham set-up for a con or a film set without actors or crew. Melanie loved it, she said it was honest; Marcus wasn't so sure.

He sat licking his ice cream, conventional and ordinary, while she bit through the bottom of the cone and sucked the pink sludge down. She threw the empty wafer to the gulls who waddled just beyond reach, gray and bulky like the tankers out at sea that were just visible as gunmetal slivers on the horizon.

"My hands are sticky," she said, walking to the shore where she bent down to rinse them. Then, instead of straightening up, she flipped upside down and walked through the fizzing surf on her hands, her skirt flopping over her head, showing her pants. Marcus leapt to his feet, clapping and whooping as she took a couple more steps before she dropped upright, curtsied and ran back laughing. The tips of her hair were wet like a paintbrush, her hands red and damp. He took them in his and wrapped them in his coat to dry.

Feeling the cold, they turned to leave and catch the bus. They trudged up the beach, the shingle moving underfoot, watched by a man who sat on the bench at the top of the sea wall. He had the hood of his dark coat pulled up, concealing his face, his hands folded under his arms. Melanie didn't seem to notice him but Marcus did. He felt him staring at them both as they climbed up to the street.

"Hello Melanie, up to your old tricks I see," he said as they passed, his voice gritty, the texture felt as much as heard. The color drained from her face. Marcus looked from her to him, and the man winked before tapping his index finger to his nose and pointing back at Marcus as if they were in on some secret together. Beside him Melanie had picked up the pace and was pulling him away, her head down, tucked into the collar of her coat.

"Tell your mum and brother I'll be over soon," he leered, his lips flexing up into his cheeks, flashing a gold molar before he turned back to the sea.

"Who's that?"

"No one," she said.

He had never seen her so afraid, and he wouldn't again until the last time he saw her, the last time before she left for good.

"You look scared."

"No shit? That's because I am."

"So who is he?"

"Is he following?" He could feel her trembling; her lips were white and pressed thin against her teeth. Marcus looked back but the man was still on the bench, his back to them. They were almost at the bus stop and the bus was due in five minutes.

"No, he's not following. Is he dangerous? Should we call the police?"

"Jesus, no! He *is* the fucking police."

"What do you mean?"

She didn't answer and it seemed best not to question her further, but she kept watch, staring at the man until the bus arrived. They sat together in silence until they reached the station. She finally relaxed on the train; as they got closer to home she was her old self again, at least on the surface. He promised himself that he would do anything to protect her, even though he didn't know what that might entail. But he promised anyway.

The Devil and the Deep Blue Sea

I used to trust the details: I collected them like rare objects or signs of revelation. It was a habit I picked up as a kid, noting everything around me, listing the particulars of surroundings, people, sounds and smells... recounting them to myself. It stopped me from paying attention to how lonely I felt. That was how I worked, how I wrote: focussing on the small, seemingly incidental details and let them reveal the facts, let the details build the story, report everything you see and hear, inoculate yourself from bias. I believed I was doing good, something vital; something to make it right, to atone. I still collect details, but I don't trust them. Actually, better to say that I don't trust myself to interpret them, so they just collect like a film of dust and obscure what should be clear.

"So how long since your last partner?"

Callum lay next to me, his head propped on his hand. He had a beautiful body, cut and ridged and unshaven. Fair hair spread over his chest then spun a trail down his stomach before fanning and darkening around his cock and balls. Retro. A tribal tattoo, patchy and faded in places, twisted on his bicep. I felt flaccid and pale beside him, and I sucked in my gut.

"What do you mean?"

"You know. Last serious relationship. When?"

"Why do you ask?"

"Just interested."

I sat up, pulling the sheet around my waist. "A long time ago. Work makes long-term relationships hard." I wasn't going to admit that I'd not had a long-term boyfriend for over twenty years: it would be a confession of my freakishness, my fear, that I didn't trust myself. How do you explain that?

"I can relate to that."

"Married to the job."

"That's the one." He ran his fingers down my back. His place was neat and stylishly bland, like a flat in those estate agent brochures. Everything matching, and revealing nothing about the owner except that they have no taste of their own. My place is similarly characterless, but that's because it's practically empty.

"This place is like a show home."

He smiled as if I'd paid him a compliment; perhaps I had, if you like that kind of thing.

"Actually, this was the show home. It did the job and there was no fuss involved so I bought it from the developers lock, stock and barrel."

"Wow."

"Yeah. I just needed to bring my clothes and personal things. Fill the fridge and get a TV. Simple."

"Saves time I guess." How light he must have felt, no history to drag him back.

"Yeah. Brett, my ex, kept our place and I didn't want to get into a war over possessions, so I just walked away. Left the lot, started again." He got up, pulling boxers up over his smooth rump. "Coffee? Beer?"

"Sure. Beer, if you're having one."

I lay back on the bed, pushing the pillows up under my neck. The sun dropped in a thick wedge through the window. A fan whirred and turned on the bedside cabinet. Details. No books on the side, no photos. His phone, face down. Everything clean. I considered looking in his wardrobe, one of those fitted types that open up revealing drawers and mirrors and tie racks, but he walked back in with the beers frothing from the popped caps.

"Brett's not going to be an issue though, in case you're wondering."

I shrugged, tipping my head in a non-committal nod.

"But you're not wondering, so it doesn't matter. Wow." He sucked from his beer.

"What's the matter?" I watched as he wiped his mouth with the back of his hand, his bottle almost empty.

"Nothing. You're just impressively casual." He finished his beer and flopped down on the bed beside me. "Mysterious. It's a bit of a turn-on." He pulled down the sheet and reached for me. I put down my beer.

The light had softened and retracted, we were showered and dressed. I admit I liked his company: he was funny and charming. It felt good to be around someone, even if it was pretense. We both checked our phones; mine registered six missed calls from Edward and a text – WE NEED TO TALK. Callum listened to a voicemail, his back to me, nodding to himself, then put the phone in his pocket.

"Right then, dinner?"

"I should get back, my mother will be waiting."

He laughed.

"I know it sounds pathetic, but I rarely see her. And I'd better work on this story, my editor has left a load of messages."

"Fair enough. So when can I see you?"

"At the press conference?"

"No, I mean SEE you?"

"I don't know. When I've filed this piece? Before I head back to London?"

He folded his arms over his chest. "So if I give you some details – anonymously, obviously – you finish up and I get to see you?"

"Something like that."

"So anonymous, right?"

"Yes. Strictly."

"And I get dinner?"

"And maybe dessert..." I didn't know why he wanted to be with me, beyond the obvious physical stuff, but I was flattered,

I felt myself letting go. What harm would it do? I was leaving in a day or so, there was no real risk.

"You're on. It's nothing we aren't saying in the press conference tomorrow anyway, you'll just get the jump on it. No reference to me though, right?"

"None."

"OK, so we've identified the victim, he was a police officer. He'd gone missing while working undercover."

"Undercover?"

"Yeah, at the time we had a problem with these local gangs bringing drugs in on the Isle of Sheppey. There are loads of small marinas on the estuary, so it was easy to bring the gear in – ecstasy, acid and speed mainly, some marijuana. He was working those. The team suspected the dealers he was investigating at the time, but they couldn't bring them in without blowing his cover and all the work he'd done. Besides which, with no body and no evidence they had nothing to go on, just that he had vanished."

"And now?"

"Well, now we have a body. Forensics are doing their thing, so with a bit of luck we'll be able to solve it. There are suggestions he wasn't squeaky clean as a police officer, but nothing solid. What we do know is he was killed by a blow to the head and then the body was moved to the burial site."

"So that'll make it harder? Less evidence?"

"Yeah, but you'd be surprised what we can work with now. The body was wrapped in a large rug which did a pretty good job of preserving it."

"That's useful."

"Actually it is in more ways than one. It's unusual, and we might be able to trace where it was made, then where it was sold and then who knows? Some of the blokes in the station knew him, so it's important to them to get the murderer. You know, a fellow copper, it hits us all pretty hard."

"I can imagine. The rug was unusual how?" Details, facts, build a story.

"Just unusual, I can't say more than that. But for your purposes, there's no evidence of a conspiracy or government involvement; the body has been there undisturbed all this time. So that puts paid to that theory." He watched my reaction.

"I thought as much, I suspected this was just a local interest story from the start."

"Not for the victim and his family it isn't."

"Right. Sorry. Has the victim got a name?"

"I can't give you that, even with a promise of dinner. We have to speak to his next of kin first and that's proving difficult."

"Why?"

"You know how it is. People move on, leave town, disappear. It was a long time ago. It seems a shame in some ways to disturb them now and tell them what happened."

"Perhaps it will bring them peace, to finally know."

"Perhaps."

"And the building work on the link? Can that restart?"

"Looks like it."

"Well, at least the DfT will be pleased."

I called Edward from the car. "I'll have this piece finished and ready tonight. Just a copper killed by a gang of drug dealers years ago, no evidence of anything else."

"Forget about that for now. Listen, this isn't easy," he said, "I'm sorry, Marcus, I really am, but I'm going to have to suspend you from work for the time being and I'm going to need your laptop and all your notes and files on the St. Clair piece."

"What are you talking about?" I pulled the car over to the side of the road. My body felt heavy, alien. I felt sick.

"Marcus, don't make this harder than it already is."

"Make what harder? What's going on? You said there was nothing to worry about."

"And that's what I believed at the time. But things have changed and you're being investigated, along with all your evidence."

"Investigated? Why? By whom?"

"By the paper for now, but the police aren't far behind."

"Why?"

"How did you get those emails? Who was your source? The security for St. Clair is tighter than a nun's proverbial."

"What are you talking about? How? You know how."

"I need to know who spoke to you."

"Hang on a minute, what is going on?"

"Who is your source? We need them to come forward and back you, back us, up."

"I'm not going tell you that, and I don't have to, you know the law."

"Yes, I do, and being a threat to national security overrides Article 10 of the European convention, as well you know."

"A threat to national security?"

"That's what they're saying."

"Who's they?"

"That doesn't matter."

"Of course it does. Who is it? Some thug lawyer hired by the bank? A smug civil servant?"

"Unfortunately not, it's a bit more serious than that. I'm under a lot of pressure here to protect you and the paper."

"This is ridiculous. They're trying to intimidate us."

"They've had to step up police protection for Lord Sunbury and his family. There's been a riot outside the Embassy building in Libya."

"You know that's absurd. The Embassy is closed, has been for months. They're using that to scare us off, to shut us up. It's the oldest trick in the book, come on Edward. Which of Sunbury's cronies has got to you?"

"I'm serious. This is serious. Speak to your solicitor, and if you haven't got one, get one. I need all your notes, transcripts and the identity of your source, otherwise they will take us to court for a disclosure order and if you don't comply they can jail you. You know that. Just give me what you've got. Let me help you."

"I can't. I can't do that."

"Don't be a hero, Marcus. You'll bring us all down with you."

"I haven't done anything wrong, Ed, and any investigation will bear that out."

"I hope so, I really do, because I've just had a meeting where it was made pretty clear that not only do St. Clair have evidence to prove your accusations wrong, they can prove that you illegally obtained access to their servers and possibly blackmailed one of their employees, so either you're a liar or they are."

"I'm not caving in to this, what do you take me for?"

"I don't know what to think now."

"You know me, you know my work and you know I wouldn't do that."

"I thought I did. You've been slipping lately, Marcus, last month you got the date of a meeting between the Prime Minister and her Brexit advisors wrong. You were lucky Laura caught it."

"Oh come on! One mistake doesn't make me incompetent."

"Doesn't it? When was the last time you had a big story?"

"What does that prove? I get a story when there's a story. I can hardly make one up, can I?"

"The situation is, if you don't comply the entire paper will be investigated, the whole operation, and after the way we took down International Media and their scummy lot, we will look like the biggest fucking, shit-eating hypocrites out there. I can't and won't let you take us all down."

"I thought I had your support."

"You did, and you will continue to have it if you work with me, if you work with us. Look Marcus, this is really fucking serious."

"Fucking hell, Edward. You cleared this piece, you and the lawyers said it checked out and now what? Now it doesn't?"

"Let me do my job and get to the bottom of this."

"You sent me down here to get me out of the way. I'm such a fucking idiot. David warned me, you know, and I ignored him. I trusted you."

"Trust is a fickle thing. I'll send someone to your mother's place to collect our property tonight, and if I were you I'd stay there for now."

The line went dead. Was I, am I, a liar? More than anyone else? I sat there in the car trying to think. Had I cut corners on this story, had I bolstered the facts? I hadn't. I had played everything by the book with the St. Clair piece. I followed my gut and it had never been wrong before. What was I forgetting? What was I hiding? So much. Everything. But nothing to do with my work. I was good, the best, at my job. But that was the shaky ground I'd built my life on.

1989

The woman was all in white. White make-up pressed into the lines and pits of her skin, crusted around her nose and the high ridges of her cheekbones. She wore a long white dress; her hair was gray, fading to white where it was held back in a long ponytail that trailed over her shoulder. Her ponytail and narrow waist were those of a young girl. As she strode past where they sat huddled on the grass under the cathedral, she shouted – at them, at phantoms – her hands lifting and then dropping to her sides as if she were considering taking flight. They looked at her, Marcus afraid and laughing to cover his fear. Melanie saw her but didn't watch – which is to say, she took nothing and imposed nothing by settling her gaze on the woman. She wasn't afraid. Why would she be?

"The story goes her fiancé was killed in the war. Her father was a deacon at the Cathedral and she was a genius who graduated from Cambridge with a double first in physics. When her fiancé was killed, she lost her mind. I bet he was handsome. She still lives in the house she was born in, all cobwebs and falling down now."

"Like Miss Havisham?"

"Exactly. My mother said the vicar and her doctor try to help her but she refuses. Apparently she's completely sane when she wants to be."

"Well, they sure have her all worked out." She picked at a loose thread on her skirt. "It's weird: it's like all romance and glitter and rags, as if it isn't enough to just be a person who doesn't fit, because that isn't worthy of respect. But then at the same time, the story demystifies her. Makes her a bunch of facts, an explanation. That's sad."

"No it isn't, if people understand they can help her."

"What makes you think she needs help? Maybe she's just fine, and wants to be left alone in her world." She shifted her weight back and crossed her feet.

"Alright, but if they have sympathy then they'll be kind."

"Why can't they be kind anyway? No matter what the facts are?"

It began to rain, tentative blots on the back of their hands, their faces. He waited to see if it would pass. While he tried to think of something to say, she said, "You're all telling yourself a story because you need the illusion of meaning – we all want our lives to have meaning. But it's just patterns, sequences that we think we recognize and then name."

"What's wrong with that?"

"It's our tragedy, as humans."

He blinked and sighed and let the rain fall on him. Even though he wasn't sure he knew exactly what she meant, he disagreed: there was nothing more important than finding a reason for his existence, even if that meant he was boring and shallow.

" 'We are condemned to meaning.' "

"Who said that?"

"Merleau-Ponty."

"I don't know who that is. Anyway I think it's sad, why not make her special, why not tell a story that works? I think we all do it and I think we all need stories; it helps us to understand and make sense of each other. I think your way is cruel. Life has to have meaning or why bother?"

She chewed her lip and then nodded, as if she'd made a decision. The rain came harder, heavier. Angry now, with her, at himself, he stood up. "I'm cold and I'm going to head off home. See you."

She smiled and raised her hand in her salute. "Bye."

When he looked back she was still sitting there, her face turned up to meet the rain. Then he understood, but only for a moment and then he forgot.

Truth Will Out

After that it all happened fast. I got home and checked through my notes, reread the transcripts of meetings and conversations with my source. Her emails. The spreadsheets, the lists of payments, lists of dates, contacts, lunch meetings. It was all there, plain. Hard evidence. Maybe. Yes. No comment. She was very clear and precise. Dates, facts, figures. Proof. Evidence? Or just a series of lies? Evidence. I copied everything onto a memory stick and hid it in my mother's desk.

I called the last number I'd used for her but the line was dead, which didn't necessarily mean anything; she might have changed her number which would be sensible, considering the controversy. I deleted her name and contact details, though I knew it was futile, and left the rest as it was. I called my solicitor and she told me to comply, to hand it all over and trust that I would be cleared. Sit tight, she said. We'll fight this. Don't worry. Don't worry. The paper will protect you. I'll protect you. Have I ever let you down before?

The phone bleated and buzzed: colleagues, rivals, strangers wanting a comment or to confirm the story. Was I a rogue journalist? Had I hacked into the servers? Was that how I broke my stories? Had I faked sources? Fabricated statements? Was I part of a leftist conspiracy? I didn't respond, just watched the screen flash with Twitter and Facebook notifications. The take-home message was that I was a queer, traitor, scum, cunt, hero, cock-sucking liar. I turned it off, knowing the story would billow then sag like a plastic bag caught in the wind.

One of the paper's drivers arrived at seven o'clock and stood at the door, strangely formal in his black suit and grim expression. I handed over my computer without protest, and he shook my hand. Though I can't say exactly why, I was moved by the gesture. I got a brief mention on the News at Ten. My mother just took it all in, calm and righteous. "The truth will out," she said. "You have nothing to worry about. You can stay here until it all blows over."

Edward called around five in the morning, using his own phone.

"You're awake."

"Of course."

"What happened, Marcus? Why risk your career, the paper?"

"What do you mean?"

"The emails are fake, the spread sheets, the documents, all forged. How did you let this happen? Didn't you check?"

"Of course I did. What do you mean fake?"

"I mean fake, those emails were never sent from the St. Clair server."

"That's completely insane. Why would anyone forge emails and documents if it was so easy to prove the contrary?"

"I don't know, you tell me. Why would you?"

"Listen, Edward. I don't know what's going on but those emails are real. Trust me."

"Marcus, stop it. You sound pathetic. I've got it all here, we've spent all night going over your notes and none of it, not a bit of it stacks up. I've seen their SMTP records, the lawyers and IT boys can't find a thing to back you up. So I'll ask you again, will you give me the name of your source?"

"No, I won't."

"Then I can only assume the fault lies with you. I know how determined you are to bring the high and mighty to task. Perhaps there is no source. Maybe you lied. Is that how you want it? Because that is how it looks right now."

"I checked my facts, I followed through, I did my job; regardless of what they say, this is the truth. I'm not turning in someone who came to me in good faith. You backed me, you gave me the go-ahead."

"Christ, you're naive."

"What's really happening here, Ed? What are they threatening you with? One minute I've hacked into their server, and the next I'm a liar and a forger. Which is it? Did I blackmail my source or are they imaginary?"

"What does it matter?"

"It matters! Of course it fucking matters."

"Tell me your source, or the only publication you'll be writing for will be a fake news site because right now that's exactly what this story is: fake news."

"For fucks sake, no. You don't intimidate me."

"You've giving us no choice. I'm sorry."

"What do you mean, no choice? I'm going to fight this, I'm not just going to roll over."

"Then you're a bigger fool than I thought."

He was interviewed on Radio 4 later that morning. "It's a blow, a serious blow. I feel very let down, devastated actually. Marcus Murray was the epitome of all that is great about our press. We all trusted him." His voice sounded hollow, somehow corroded and brittle, without substance.

"How do you answer the charge that the atmosphere at the paper is corrupt? As the editor it seems far-fetched to imply this level of impropriety was isolated to one journalist?"

"Look, investigations are ongoing, and we are cooperating fully with the authorities. All I can say is that I'm appalled that the actions of one member of staff have brought us all into disrepute and I'm positive the paper as a whole will be vindicated. I'd also like to apologize to the St. Clair organization and all their associates for the considerable distress caused."

"And will you be resigning?"

"No, I won't."

"Even though a number of Murray's other articles have been called into question? Including his expose of the NHS budget crisis?"

"No."

"Hasn't Miriam Conway come forward to say she was seriously misrepresented by Murray in a recent interview?"

"I can't comment on that. As I say, we're investigating."

I had been hung out to dry. Destroyed. All I had was my work – that was it. Nothing else. Sometimes, often, I would imagine Melanie still being alive and seeing what I did, reading my articles. I imagined impressing her. I imagined I could make amends for being a coward. But I was glad she wasn't around to see me like that. I shouldn't have been surprised: my mistake was imagining I was safe, innocent. Exempt. No one is safe, Melanie had said to me once.

Some things I remember so clearly, clearer than how I actually felt, like outside the bin men came and went, dragging the bins over the gravel and back again. Joyce arrived and pushed the vacuum around the house, grim-faced and heavy on her feet. A plane scored a white trail across the empty sky. But what I was feeling, I'm just taking an educated guess.

1989

They were on the bus, heading into town. It was a Saturday and Melanie was going to the library.

"What book do you want?" Marcus asked.

"I don't know, I just needed to get out of there."

"You OK?"

"I'm fine. My mum is on the rampage today, that's all. You know how it is: no one can do anything right, no matter what. Everyone is an arsehole, blah blah blah." She smiled.

"Yeah." Marcus had no idea. His mother took pride in maintaining a calm home and made a habit of declaring "Equanimity IS wisdom" whenever anyone threatened the peace.

"She's actually pretty scary when she gets going," she laughed. "Run for cover, Charlie used to say."

"I can't imagine you being scared."

"You haven't seen my mother on the warpath. She's terrifying."

The bus stopped and an old man heaved himself up the step to the driver, handing over change for his ticket. Melanie turned in her seat and, seeing that the rest of the bus was full, she stood and pulled Marcus up with her.

"Here you go, mate, sit here." She nodded to the old man, who glowered at her as he lowered himself down.

"Was that your good deed for the day?" Marcus said as they shuffled further down the aisle, holding onto the rail above.

"Shut up," she said. "Go on then, what are you afraid of?"

"Your mum, now!"

"You should be. But seriously, what scares you?"

"I'm afraid of dying."

"Are you? Why? You won't even know about it."

"Because I'll be sent to hell."

"What are you talking about?"

"You know, because," he leaned in and whispered, "God hates gays."

"You don't believe that, do you?" She looked up at him, as if trying to decide if he was joking or not.

"I don't know. I don't want to take the risk."

She sighed and reached both hands up to grasp the rail, hanging for a moment, letting her body sway with the movement of the bus. "Don't you think if there is a god, he or she will have bigger things to worry about than who we love? All that is a load of nasty stories people tell to control us. You won't go to hell and if you do, you'll be in great company."

"Shush."

"Nobody's listening or knows what we're talking about," she said, but quieter, moving her body to block the other passengers.

"You don't even believe in hell."

"Precisely."

"What if you're wrong?"

"Then God is a bastard and I want nothing to do with him or her." She shrugged. "See, shouldn't I have been struck down for blasphemy? You'll be alright. It's other humans you have to watch out for, they're the source of all the trouble."

At the library she took out three books: Kathy Acker's *Blood and Guts in High School*, a collection of short stories by Katherine Mansfield and Milton's *Paradise Lost*. Marcus insisted on carrying them for her, feeling safe by her side.

A Companion of Fools

I t was a question of credibility. That's all I had. As a journalist
nothing else matters, it's your currency, your means of
exchange, and they were taking it from me. I was letting them
take it from me.

I left the house before ten o'clock, leaving a note on the
breakfast table for my mother, and got in the car. It was
cloudy and humid, the air storm-heavy. As I pulled out onto
the street I dialed David's mobile number, paranoid maybe
but I didn't want to call on the Sentinel's line. There was a
car parked opposite Dr Addison's house, a black Audi. The
driver was just visible and as I passed he caught my eye:
the same bloke I saw earlier that week, loitering outside
our drive.

David finally picked up. "Hi."

"You OK?"

"Yeah, how about you?"

"Not great."

"I can imagine."

"What the hell is going on? One minute it's the scoop of
the year, the next I'm a rogue journalist."

"I know, it's crazy, but I can't talk here."

"Can you meet me at my place?"

"At your flat?"

"Yeah, you know the address, right?"

"By Battersea Bridge?"

"That's it. I'll be there in an hour or so."

"OK, I'll meet you there."

The drive was easy: rush hour had eased off and I was on the motorway in a few minutes. I turned the radio on and listened for the news headlines: if they mentioned me then I knew I was in real trouble. They didn't. It was a good sign. I switched to my iPod and The Stooges clattered out of the speakers. I turned the volume up.

It was only as I came off the motorway and drove through Blackheath that I noticed a black Audi, one car behind me. I drove up through Lewisham and into Peckham, past empty new apartment blocks, the convenience shops that offered everything from khat and tins of beans to wiring cash to family overseas. Past a couple of pubs and takeaway restaurants selling fried chicken, kebabs, Chinese food and Indian. The Audi was behind me all the way, but then so was the blue Corsa and a silver Range Rover that had traveled with me since I'd come off the motorway. I lost sight of it as I crossed over the junction at Camberwell but then it was in my rear-view mirror again as I went left around Vauxhall and turned onto Nine Elms. It was still there as I passed the power station and its teetering chimneys, right behind me. I could see the light ricochet off the driver's bald scalp.

He followed me to the roundabout by the park, but when I turned left onto Prince of Wales Drive he carried on over the bridge, towards the river and Chelsea. I softened into my seat, not realizing until then how tense I'd been. The wind had picked up, swirling fallen petals and dropped litter around mothers pushing their children in expensive, high-tech buggies and men jogging with devices strapped to their biceps.

I turned into my street and found a space a hundred feet or so from my building. It was quiet, no sign of David and, mercifully, no journalists from our competitors. As I reached for my door key I saw the Audi, parked a few cars down and in sight of the entryway to my flat. I started running towards the car, but as I got within a few feet it pulled away, casually: not screeching away like in a TV show, but as if the driver didn't care whether I saw them or not. This time the driver was a woman, her blonde hair cut in a bob like a gold helmet. I watched as she turned towards Clapham at the end of the street. It was a different car.

I let myself into the entryway and took a breath; I needed to calm down, to stop reacting as if I was in a TV show, my body and imagination carried away by the habits and stories of others. I needed to stop and uncouple myself from the postures and assumptions I used without thinking. I leaned against the wall waiting for the lift as it juddered down from the upper floors, the pine scent of disinfectant prickling my nose. David tapped against the glass siding of the front door, looking nervous and checking back over his shoulder at the street as I let him in.

"You found it OK?"

"Yeah, no problem. How're you holding up?"

"You didn't see a dark Audi out there did you?"

"I don't think so. Why?"

"Nothing, it doesn't matter. My mind is playing tricks on me."

"Oh yeah, you sure?"

"Yeah, it's fine."

"So you had the loons and crackpots hassling you?"

"Yeah, usual internet nutters, I've just stayed away from the internet. Turned it off at the source."

"Sensible. It'll blow over."

"Yeah. It's our lot turning on me that's worse. Edward of all people. I thought he knew me better than this."

David shrugged. "I think he's just trying to protect the paper."

"Himself more likely."

David said nothing.

The lift arrived and he followed me in, standing awkwardly by my side. He was around my age, but shorter with broad shoulders, his dark hair starting to gray around the temples. He wore expensive jeans, a precisely faded Sex Pistols t-shirt and pristine Converse, tightly laced. He'd invited me to a BBQ at his place last year and I'd actually gone along. He'd played guitar and sung Oasis covers while his wife swayed her Pilates-taut body at his side and their kids – dressed like mini versions of their parents – bounced like demented acrobats on a trampoline. Despite that, I thought he was a good bloke, honest and dependable.

He broke the silence as we walked down the hall towards my flat.

"It's quiet here, not like at my house."

"Yeah, well it's mostly professional couples and a few older tenants who've lived here for years and years. No kids." I stood aside to let him pass and pushed the door shut. Behind us, the lift began its descent to the ground floor, the gears and pulleys churning and humming.

"Nice flat. I've always liked these old mansion blocks." David stood in the middle of the sitting room. "I sometimes miss my bachelor days, without all the cushions and cashmere blankets my wife throws around the place to hide the mountains of Lego." He laughed to himself, then twisted his wedding ring in penance.

Everything was exactly as I'd left it. The weekend papers and magazines were still on the coffee table. My mug, ringed with dried coffee, on the counter. The remote control on the arm of the chair. A film of dust dulling the TV screen.

"Thanks. Drink?"

"Sure, what you having?"

"I'm going to have a beer."

"That sounds good. You're a vinyl man I see."

"What's that?"

He pointed to the stack of old records leaning against the amp and turntable.

"Oh yeah, I was. Mostly use the docking station now, though."

"Me too. Sad eh?"

I skirted past the breakfast counter to the fridge. A head of lettuce wilted above the rack of beers. I levered the tops off and, as I moved to throw them in the bin, something in the sink caught my eye. Hanging from the tap on a tarnished chain was a faded image in a half-locket. I lifted it up, hand shaking, to look closer: it was a photo of Kurt Cobain, its scant weight heavy with recognition. I put it on the counter by my beer and handed a bottle to David.

"Cheers," he said, sitting on the sofa.

"Yeah, cheers. Give me a minute will you? I just need to check something."

"Sure. You OK? You look like you've seen a ghost."

"Yeah, I've just remembered something. I won't be a minute."

My bed was untidy, the sheet pulled half way towards the pillows just as I'd left it. I opened the drawer in my nightstand. Condoms, porn, a watch my mother had given me, a pen, my National Insurance card, a stack of letters and greeting cards bound by an elastic band. I opened the wardrobe and the drawers in the chest under the window, then the small filing cabinet where I kept bills and bank statements, receipts. Nothing was missing, nothing had been moved. Except the locket, which had been in my nightstand, had been for years, undisturbed, half-forgotten. A gift from Melanie.

"Everything OK?" David was still on the sofa, his beer in his fist.

"I think someone's been here."

He blinked but didn't look shocked. "What makes you think that?"

"Something's been moved."

"Are you sure? Has anything been taken?"

"No. Nothing like that."

"You probably just moved it and forgot."

"I don't think so, it's not the kind of thing you would move and leave. It's sentimental, not a thing you get out and leave lying around."

"What was it?"

"This." I moved to the counter to pick up the locket: it wasn't there. "It's gone. Have you taken it?"

"Taken what?"

"The locket, a necklace with a photo on it."

"No mate, I haven't moved from here."

"I swear I left it on the counter."

"Perhaps you took it with you to the bedroom."

"No, I definitely left it here."

"Well I didn't move it and I promise you no one else has been in the room. Why don't you check and see?"

It was in the drawer of the nightstand next to my old watch. I put it in my pocket and went back into the living room.

"Find it?"

"Yeah, I'm losing my marbles." Outside the storm broke with a volley of rain and thunder, the room suddenly dark.

"Well, you've got a lot going on, it makes sense that you're distracted."

"Yeah, yeah, doesn't explain why it was moved in the first place though."

"Why would someone move a necklace? Wouldn't they have stolen it?"

"What if they came here to intimidate me, send me a message?"

"What message?"

"About the article? There's nothing here for them to take that will help them. It was all on my laptop and the paper has that. What if they wanted to scare me off? Show me they could come in here? Perhaps I should call the police."

"And say what? You've misplaced something? Nothing's been taken, the door wasn't forced. I think it's more likely that you're upset, stressed. Understandably so, you're under a lot of pressure. You probably moved it and forgot." He sipped his beer. "Have a drink, and let's think this through."

I picked up my bottle and sat, taking a swig. The beer tasted like swill from a trough. A swell of thunder rolled through the room.

"You're right, I've not slept since all this started. I'm a mess."

"Look, I get it, but it will blow over. You know it will."

"What's been said at work? They don't believe all this shit do they?"

"Of course not, we all know you. If you say the story is solid then it's solid. But I can't lie to you, it's not looking good."

"I know."

"Let me help. I can speak to your source, get her to come forward, go on the record."

"Her?"

"Or him, just a figure of speech. I can help you."

"You think I haven't tried?"

"I'm not suggesting you haven't, just maybe if I speak to them, reassure them that we will protect them, it might make a difference. Give me their contact details, it won't hurt to try."

"No, I can't do that. It won't help anyway. They've disappeared and can you blame them? You could try and speak to John Cullan, see if he can step in?"

"OK, but I don't know if the likes of me will have any luck getting through to the Chairman." He sat forward and looked me in the eye. "I really think the best way to clear your name is to prove you had reliable documentation and that St. Clair are manipulating the evidence. You need your source to come forward and corroborate your story."

"So you agree there's a conspiracy here?"

"I didn't say that, I mean let's not get paranoid, but something is off."

Before I could respond the entry phone buzzed like a trapped hornet. "Hello?"

"Marcus? It's Neil Mason from the Telegraph. How you doing? Can you comment on the allegations that you fabricated evidence against the St. Clair group?"

"No, Neil, I can't." As I replaced the receiver it started up again. "Look fuck off Neil, I've got nothing to say." The buzzing continued as soon as I put it down, filling the space and my head.

"Marc, you better come see this." David was at the window, peering out into the street. I pressed the do not disturb button and turned my back on the blocked questions to follow his gaze.

"Oh shit." Twenty or so journalists with photographers and cameramen were huddled in the rain outside the building. A BBC van was parked across the street.

"What the fuck?"

"You've got to get out of here, Marcus. Let this thing settle."

"I can't, I have to sort this."

"How? You can't find your source and you say you've got no other proof. Look, I'm not being funny but I'm worried about you, mate. Why don't you get out of here for a bit? I'll come down with you now and deal with that lot. You've just got to sit tight and wait. Maybe we'll find something or someone to back you up."

I nodded and followed him out, double locking the door. We went down the stairs and out through the service exit at the side of the building. We couldn't completely avoid the crowd, but it gave us a head start. They caught sight of us as we jogged towards the car, calling my name and shouting, their voices overlapping and merging like the cries of gulls, but I could make out some of their questions: "Did you forge the St. Clair documents?" "Were you paid?" "Who's behind all this?" "Have you fabricated other stories?" And one that I half-heard and made me falter: "Where's Melanie, Marcus?" But David pushed me into the car and the shouts merged again and I still can't be sure if the voice and question I heard was my own.

"I'll call you, now go," he said, slamming the door. The rain stopped as suddenly as it had started. Before sliding the car into gear I pulled the locket from my jeans and tucked it into the glove compartment, safe. David was already walking away, his back to me; as I drove past I saw him talking to the crowd, laughing, like he was telling the joke of the year.

The story was all over the news. It was reaching peak transmission, it would blow over and soon, I knew that and of course I wanted it to, I was totally humiliated, but when it was forgotten, old news, a tangle in the hyperlinked web, then I would be too, with no chance to prove myself, because who'd want to hear it then? It would be worthless, along with me. I switched off the radio and tried calling Edward, though it didn't get me anywhere: I either got his voicemail or his secretary fobbed me off, her usual warmth gone. Caught in the metal press of rush hour I was creeping forward towards the A2, checking my mirrors every few minutes for the Audi even though the cyclists, swerving the puddles, were the only ones moving. My hands shook.

I was fiddling with my iPod and the Bluetooth when my solicitor called.

"How are you doing?" Her voice echoed like a cartoon voice bubble bouncing around in a tin can.

"Not good."

"No. Where are you?"

"In the car, on my way back to Kent."

"Kent?"

"My mother's. My flat is surrounded by hacks."

"Already? Listen, I hear you've been harassing Edward."

"Harassing? What the hell does that mean?"

"Apparently you've called his phone repeatedly this afternoon and abused his secretary."

"Is this a joke? This is my life, my career. I want answers and they aren't even talking to me. What am I supposed to do? Roll up in a little ball?"

"I know that, but do yourself a favor and don't call Edward again. Stay away, at least for a while."

"Or what?"

"Just stop calling."

"I'm being set up, you know."

"We shouldn't get ahead of ourselves, right? Like I said before, stay calm, I'll do my best to protect you."

"Can you?"

"Of course, nothing has changed. Get to your mother's and stay there, and speak to no one about the article, the bank or the Sentinel. Relax, let me handle them and then we'll meet and talk."

"It's bigger than that now."

"What do you mean?"

"Someone's been inside my flat." Even as I said it I could hear how deluded I sounded.

"What do you mean?"

"Someone has broken into my flat."

"What have they taken?"

"Nothing... They moved something."

"Have you called the police?"

"What good would that do?" The cars in front rolled forward about ten feet, while the driver behind me, objecting to my three-second delay in moving, pressed the horn of his car until I shifted into first and closed the gap.

"Well if you think someone has broken in, then they—"

"Forget it. I'm talking nonsense, I haven't slept and I'm not myself." I checked my mirrors again, catching the guy behind shouting expletives, his lower lip between his teeth as he mouthed "Fu—" I looked away.

"Are you alright, Marcus?"

"No, I am totally fucked."

"I don't think it's that bad yet, not if you cooperate. There are rumbles from the St. Clair team that they will pursue legal action over the article, but so far there's been no formal complaint to the police. I suspect it's just saber rattling; talk is that the Sentinel has agreed to print a retraction and an apology and that a rather large compensation package will soothe the delicate souls at the bank. Not to mention that certain ministers would rather this all went away quickly."

"But what about the story?"

"That's over. You have to forget about that: in return for not prosecuting you, they'll want you to sign a gagging order. You might have to admit to a number of fabrications or errors too."

"I don't want to do that." I began to sweat, my hands slipping on the steering wheel.

"I'm sure you don't. But be sensible, you'll bounce back, find another job; a better one, everyone loves a media bad boy. Look at Piers!" She guffawed. "You know how this goes. All hot air. You'll have your own TV show before you know it, or a star column in a tabloid."

"Are you joking?" My jaw began to ache, a solid throb that traveled up and around my skull before meeting over my eyes.

"No, I'm not." Her voice tightened, its pitch narrowing over the phone. She sighed.

"Can't we fight this? What if I can find my source and get them to go on record?"

"Haven't you already tried? We can fight if you've got the stomach for it, but I wouldn't if I were you. I don't think it would end well. Chalk this one up to them. Play ball."

"Are you working for me or not?"

"Yes, believe me, I am and it's in our best interests to let this go. Do you understand?"

"Maybe you're right."

"I am right. Consider yourself lucky and let it go."

"Lucky?"

"Yes, lucky. I'll call you when I've spoken to their legal team again. Right?"

"Right."

She hesitated and I was about to disconnect the call when she said, "Marcus, is there anything else I should know?"

"No," I said. "No there isn't." I was a liar now. Untrustworthy.

"OK then," she said. I hung up.

When I got off the phone I had three messages on voice mail. One from Mother. "Where are you? I'm worried sick, they're talking about you on the radio"; one from Callum, "I've just heard the news. Are you OK? Call me when you can." And Annabelle, as if we were firm friends, though obviously sniffing out a scoop: "Are you alright? What the fuck? Listen I've just finished at the press conference, if you want a drink or a coffee? And by the way, they've released the name of the dead guy if you're interested, a Detective Steve Burrell, he was an undercover officer apparently. Anyway I'm so sorry this is happening to you. Give me a ring. Perhaps I can help, tell your side?"

Steve Burrell. I knew that name. I knew that name and I began to understand, finally.

1989

There's no way she'd have come along if he'd told her where he was going, but it didn't matter because she hadn't been in school anyway. It didn't stop him imagining her calling him an idiot and telling him to turn around and go home, but he carried on regardless.

He trudged up the hill towards the edge of town, the strap of his school bag cutting into his shoulder; half-tempted to dump it, he shifted it to the other shoulder instead. He'd taken a change of clothes with him and switched out of his uniform in the bogs at home time, but he regretted it now, loaded down and trying too hard. As he got closer to Coombe Hall's rugby pitches the houses got further and further apart, the hedges and gates higher, the drives longer. All newly built, they looked like American mansions he'd seen on the telly, with double garages and disconnected fountains standing dry. Only half of them were occupied; the rest had signs warning about guard dogs and electric fences posted on the gates.

The boys were still practicing their drills, running in rows and tossing a ball from one to the other as the coach yelled instructions from the side. Marcus walked over to the picnic benches set out for spectators and sat down. He was so nervous it felt as if his stomach was in his chest, swallowing his heart. He dropped his bag between his feet and jammed his hands in his pockets, then took them out and crossed his arms, and then put them back in his pockets, then he crossed them again. It was a mistake to come. Of course it was.

The team finished and he watched as they gathered around the coach and tipped water into their mouths and scratched their arses and shoved each other. Anthony was standing at the front, listening intently, his purple and gray jersey tight across his chest. They turned towards him and started back, a couple of stragglers left to pick up the cones and pellet shaped balls. The changing rooms were directly behind him: Anthony had to pass him, had to see him, had to speak to him.

Steaming like a herd of cattle, the heat and sweat rising from them, the team passed him. The coach eyed him up and down and, from his expression, didn't like what he saw, but he didn't recognize Marcus as he'd never been selected for any of the teams. Finally Anthony, beautiful Anthony walked past, catching his eye for a second then ducking his head and jogging off into the changing room.

He waited until the whole team had gone inside and then sat on the bench, his body suddenly all fluid and loose. His hands wobbled rather than shook and a ripple of sweat soaked his shirt and the seat of his jeans. But even though Anthony had just walked past, had seen him and said nothing, his look, that split second look said everything. He loved Marcus, he did, he was afraid, that was all. So he decided to wait. Excited now, he felt bigger and stronger, like a man.

So he waited, watching as the rest of the team left one by one, hair shower-damp, their bags slung over their shoulders, some unlocking their bikes and cycling off, others sliding into parents' cars. But no Anthony, still no Anthony, then the coach came out, looked around and spotted Marcus, still sitting on the bench.

"You Marcus?" he called, walking over, his eyes narrowed against the glare of the sun, lower in the sky now.

"Yeah." It was getting chilly and goose bumps rose on Marcus's arms.

"You have to leave."

"Why? I'm just waiting for my friend. I'm not doing anything."

"Your friend? Do you mean Anthony? Because he is pretty adamant that you are not friends, and this is private property, so you need to go."

"Can I just speak to him for a minute, just a minute, please?"

The older man looked at Marcus, assessing him, then half turned to look in the direction of the changing block. He turned back and slowly shook his head. "Listen, Marcus. I don't want to embarrass you or hurt your feelings, but Anthony asked me to make you leave. His parents are on their way and they don't want you here either. So, I suggest you go, OK? Don't make this any harder on yourself. Anthony doesn't want to talk to you. He really doesn't."

"Please, I just want to... I waited all this time."

The coach shook his head and bent down to pick up Marcus' bag. "You need to head home now." He handed over the bag.

Marcus stood for a second, his head too heavy for his neck, his body too heavy to move. Then, blinking back tears, he nodded, shouldered his bag and started walking, knowing he was being watched until he turned out of the gates and had left the school grounds.

The walk back to town seemed quicker, over gray gobs of gum flattened on the pavement; dog shit dried white in the gutters while plastic carrier bags half swollen by the wind rolled and turned like tumbleweed. He watched his feet taking steps beneath him, moving him forwards; he side-stepped other bodies, other people and waited at the side of roads until he could cross, stepping out without really seeing where he was going. Like a puppet, pretending to be human. It would be good to feel real. To know what he was really feeling and act on it rather than pulling his face and body into the shapes he thought were expected. He didn't trust his own reactions or feelings. Not really. He didn't belong in the world, not like Melanie. She belonged. His mother would say it was teen angst and he would grow out of it, but he didn't think so.

The traffic was building up now, people on their way home from work, driving back to family and dinner and the TV. He wasn't far from home either. He glanced right and then left and then right again; he walked out in to the road, his feet repeating – heel toe heel toe. Knees and hips flexing. There was no squealing of brakes or the drag of tires on tarmac, and he reached the curb seconds before he could've been hit, but a passing car blew its horn at him anyway and pulled up sharp beside him.

"Marcus!" Melanie climbed out and slammed the door shut as it drove away, giving him only a second to see the driver. "What are you doing? You look like a zombie."

"I'm going home."

"You could've been killed!"

"But I wasn't. Whose car was that?"

"No one special. Anyway, I'm worried about you. What's happened?"

"It doesn't matter. What about you? Who was that? It looked like that guy from Leysdown." The bloke was dressed differently, smarter maybe, but he was pretty sure he recognized the man who'd scared Mel into silence, except she didn't seem so scared now, only tired. Dark rings shadowed her eyes.

"Did it? Well it wasn't." She blinked. "Where have you been? You look sick." She reached for his hand and turned it over, tracing the lines like a palm reader. He felt her hot breath on the thin skin of his wrist, meeting his pulse.

"I went to my old school to see Anthony."

"Why?"

"Because I wanted to see him, I wanted to talk to him."

"That sounds like a bad idea."

"You haven't been around so I couldn't talk to you. You were gone, I was lonely." A shiver interrupted the expression on her face, but only for a second and he didn't take much notice, too caught up in Anthony.

"So what happened?" She moved her hand from his and tucked it into the crook of his arm, guiding him along the path away from the road, glancing once over her shoulder.

"The coach told me to leave, he said Anthony doesn't want to talk to me but I don't believe that. I think his parents and the headmaster made him say that."

"How do you know? Has Anthony phoned you or written to you."

"No, but that doesn't mean he doesn't want to."

"You can't change reality by wishing, and you can't make someone love you when they don't."

"I'm not trying to do that. I saw the way he looked at me, you weren't there and you don't know him, but I do. I know him."

"That's true," she said, "I don't. But I know you. Come on, I'll walk you home."

It was only after she'd gone that he realized she was wearing her school uniform, even though she hadn't been in for days.

Once Sown

"Do you remember how you used to help Daddy in the garden?" Mum stood in the study looking out onto the lawn creeping out from the terrace towards the stand of silver birch trees. I had taken refuge there, at home. No one followed me.

"Did I?" I replied.

"Yes, you used to potter around with him, helping him weed and dead head. You even helped him set those birches. You had your own little plastic watering can. Do you remember that?"

"I do, it was red with a yellow spout." I leaned back against the large armchair, trying to focus on her and what she was saying. Trying to maintain the illusion of being myself.

" 'The love of gardening is a seed once sown that never dies.' Your father used to say that all the time. I miss him. You know, I don't like to mope, but I do miss him."

"Yes, you must."

"He's been gone thirty-five years."

"I know, mum."

"I wonder what he'd make of us now?" She turned to face me, resting her hand on the window latch, graying and stout, suddenly smaller, it seemed.

"Oh God. I dread to think." I grimaced, and crossed my arms in front of my chest, my fist pressed into my shoulder.

"He'd be very proud of you. An eminent journalist, whose work has brought him awards, that's what he'd see in you. And this other stuff, he'd stand by you as I do, as I always will.

Anyone who knows you knows you're incapable of anything less than courage and integrity. Even Joyce says so."

"Well, if Joyce says so..."

She turned back to the garden, full and ripe with flowers just turning to seed. The grass needed cutting, waiting for the young kid she paid to run the mower around. Puffy balls of hydrangeas bounced in the warm air: it was hot, one of those rare English summers of dry relentless heat where the grass curls in dry, yellow wisps. It occurred to me that I'd never spent a summer with Mel; she'd already gone by then.

"Why don't we go into town and get some flowers for Daddy's plot? Shall we? That would be good for us both, I think. Don't you? Let's spend some time together and get out of here."

"I don't know, I've got things I need to do, calls to make."

"Come on, darling. You can't mope around in here all day. Please."

"Alright," I nodded. "You win, let's go."

I opened the car door and helped her in before climbing in to the driver's seat and turning the engine over. "Right then," I said, for no reason except to break the silence.

Mother patted my hand where it rested on the gear stick, then grasped the handbag in her lap. "Right then," she echoed.

I shifted into first and pulled out of the drive. The black Audi was down the street, parked under a rowan tree. A bird had shat on the bonnet, a thick white splash studded with cherry pits. I said nothing and drove on, watching the car in the rear view mirror. It didn't move.

1989

"Bloody hell, it's freezing in here."

"No shit, Sherlock," said Melanie's mother. "We don't want the flowers to wilt do we?"

"They're pretty." Mel said, watching her twist pink roses and a white frothy flower together, the tips of her fingers blue with cold.

"You think so?" Her mother turned, reached behind her for a large pair of scissors and snipped at a length of ribbon, still holding the flowers. She flipped and twisted and tied and cut in a dextrous blur and placed the finished flowers with their huge ribbon bow on the glass counter.

"This is Marcus, my friend from school."

The woman turned and ran her eyes over his face and down to his shoes before she nodded. "Hello Marcus."

"Pleased to meet you," he burbled, half-shivering, half-burning up from the look she gave him. He never could hide his shame, though what he was ashamed of then is hard to understand.

Melanie's mother was thin and hollow-cheeked, with blonde hair tucked up in a dark wool hat, her skin still freckled and sun-blotched, apart from her nose which was as blue as her fingers. She looked much younger than his own mother, but unsmiling, hard at the edges.

"Can I have some lunch money?" Mel jiggled on the spot, her hands in her blazer pockets.

"For God's sake, it's always something with you! Want want want." Her mother opened the till and took a pound coin. "Don't go to the chippy with it. Get a proper sandwich from the baker. And hurry up out of it, if Kathleen sees you I'll get gyp." She handed Mel the money.

"Ta, mum." Mel turned on her heel, her skirt fanning out around her like a dancer's. "It's as cold as a butcher's heart in here," she said as she dodged the buckets of lilies and tulips on her way out to the street.

Cold Hands, Warm Heart

"What was that, Marcus?"

"Huh?" I looked up from flipping through the stack of small cards the florist used for messages – condolence cards, new baby, birthday, anniversary, good luck – platitudes crammed onto a printed slip the size of a business card. The nauseating smell of the lilies with their indelible orange pollen hung in the chill. Mother tucked her purse into her handbag and picked up a bouquet of chrysanthemums.

"Thank you," she smiled to the woman behind the counter, who'd turned her back and was already working on another arrangement, singing along to the radio playing in the back room.

"I said it's as cold as a butcher's heart in here. It's what Melanie said about this place. Her mum worked in here, you know."

"Did she? I didn't know that. Mind you, I don't know that I ever even met her mother or father, did I?"

"No, I doubt it. They weren't the sociable type." She folded her arm in mine and pulled me close, the familiar smell of her perfume clouding my head.

"Would you mind driving up to the cemetery?" She sniffed at the broad mouth of the bouquet, inhaling the scent. "They don't really smell nice, but that doesn't matter. Does it?"

"No, it doesn't." We walked back to the car, avoiding mothers pushing buggies, old ladies tugging shopping trolleys and lunching office workers blinkered by their phones. We passed a newsstand with the local paper's headline, UNDERCOVER COP MURDERED, splashed over a photo of Steve Burrell, where even in black and white his gold tooth flashed dark and memorable.

1989

So together they took the pound and went to the kiosk at the end of the High Street, near the tattoo parlor and the dodgy pub that the skinheads and the National Front drank in. The kiosk was a trailer, like a horsebox only smaller and with a front hatch that opened onto the street. Racks of chocolate and sweets were in the front and magazines dangled from taut lines of string like laundry. A shelf stacked with cigarette packets was placed on the left wall, just beyond grabbing reach from the street.

"Can I get a couple of Silk Cut singles, please, Mahmoud?" Mel leaned on the newspapers laid out on the front ledge of the kiosk, peering at the boxes of crisp packets stacked up in the back. "And a box of matches and a packet of pickled onion Monster Munch."

Mahmoud bent under the counter and pulled two cigarettes from a packet, grabbed a box of matches and then the crisps. "You're sixteen?"

"Yes, I am." Mel pushed the pound coin towards him.

"OK." He gave her fifty pence change as she pocketed the fags and matches and chucked the crisp packet to Marcus.

They shared the crisps as the two of them walked over to the river, with Marcus glancing around every now and then to check they hadn't been seen.

"This'll do," Mel said and they sat on the low wall that lined the mud banks. The bile-colored river pulled and coiled in twisting currents heading for the estuary and then on out to sea. Mel lit both fags, shielding the match by pulling on her blazer lapel and tucking her head and the fags down towards her chest and passed one to him. He sat for a bit, smoking, not coughing and feeling sick any more.

"You don't look like your mum."

"Everyone says I'm like my dad."

"What's he like?"

"Like me, I suppose! Ha!" She laughed, which sounded more like a cynical cough really, then said, "I don't know, I never met him."

"Why?"

"Not sure. Mum says Granddad made him leave us, Nan says he did a bunk. Either way it amounts to the same thing. What does it matter now?"

"That's terrible."

"Why is it? You can't miss what you don't know, and I wouldn't want a dad who stuck around because of duty, hating us."

"Yeah, I suppose so." He thought about his own father, and the shirts and jackets still hanging in the wardrobe in his mother's room. At least his dad was dead; it would be stupid to take that personally.

"We're doing alright as we are. Mum's pretty solid most of the time." She held her cigarette up and examined the tip for a moment.

"I didn't know she was a florist. I thought she worked in a pub." He was embarrassed by how curious he was about Mel and her family, knowing it revealed something about himself. Why was he so curious? Perhaps it was partly because of her mystique, her hold over him, and partly because her world was not his. Were they really so different? Maybe they were and maybe he believed that if he could only figure her out, emulate her – her gestures, her attitude – then maybe he could be invincible, extraordinary, like her.

"She does."

"What?"

"She works in the florist and she does a couple of shifts in the pub."

"That sounds exhausting."

"That's work, I suppose. Got to pay the bills. What you gonna do when you leave here?" She jutted her jaw and jerked it forward as she exhaled, blowing a perfect smoke ring.

"Uni, then journalism, I think. I hope. What about you?"

"Anything, as long as I'm not here. Maybe I'll go to America and marry Kurt Cobain, and write songs with Kim Gordon, or maybe I'll just travel the world and dip my toes in every ocean." She tapped her ash over the wall into the mud. A bird's footprints zigzagged across the oily surface like crude stick figures drawn by a child.

"You could come to Uni with me," he said, taking a last puff before guiltily stubbing it out and flicking the butt out into the river.

Mel laughed. "As if. Girls like me are hairdressers or work in a shop if we're lucky. Or we end up pregnant, or if we've really fucked up, we end up on the game."

"That's not true. You're clever, you could do anything you want."

"Right? It's that easy is it? Just head off to Uni." She took a final drag on her cigarette, right down to the filter, and blew out a cloud of smoke.

"Yes, it is."

"For you maybe."

"For you too, seriously. You'll easily get good A-Levels and there's grants and things. You can get a loan."

"That's the point, I ain't doing A-Levels: my mum can't afford to put me through another two years of school. I have to get a job. I have to earn my keep, and I want to anyway. I want some money. I've had enough of it round here."

"But that's so short-sighted, you could have an amazing career."

"Doing what?"

"I don't know, anything. You could be an English teacher, or a nurse."

"Wow... That's some enticing career path you're sketching out for me there. Teaching little shits or cleaning up someone's shit."

"Well, something else then. I don't know. You'd figure that out at Uni."

"Well, mate, I don't have the luxury of five years to figure out what I want to do." She'd hunched her shoulders, pulling her chin down to her chest like a bird sheltering from the rain, her hands in her pockets.

"I suppose we should get back to school." He looked at her, to catch her gaze and smile, to apologize for whatever he'd said that'd made her sink down inside herself, but she looked past him and pushed herself off the wall.

"Come on then."

"You're going to come to class?"

"Yep. I suppose I'd better if I want a 'career.'"

She stayed for the rest of that afternoon, French and History, both teachers looking up from the register in surprise when she answered to her name. She answered most of the questions the teachers threw out to the class, too.

After she told Miss Graveney that Magna Carta meant Great Charter in Latin, he nudged her, hissing "See! You're clever. No one else knew that." She sat next to the wall of windows, which some architect no doubt intended to allow for lots of uplifting and inspiring light; instead, the expanse of glass made the room boiling in summer and freezing in winter. The sun picked out a halo of red highlights in her dark hair.

"It's not clever, I read and remember things. That don't make me brain of Britain. Anyway, you knew what it meant, and when it was signed I bet. Why didn't you answer?"

"I don't want to show off, give them more ammunition," he whispered, hair falling into his eyes – he was growing it out.

"Right." She gave him that long look, sucking him into her gaze, exposing him. "You should get a haircut, you're beginning to look like those twats." She turned back to the Darrens, sprawling at the back of the class. Darren Shine looked asleep. The short Darren saw them both looking; pressing his tongue into his cheek, he inserted his left index finger into his closed right fist and began a crude semaphore of fucking, all the while staring at them both.

"Wow..." she said and shook her head. "Jealous, Darren?"

"As if!" He sprayed little flecks of spit as he spoke.

She didn't go back in for the rest of the week.

A Long Silence

After the cemetery I dropped Mum home. It was strange, standing there in the bright sun, gazing down at my father's grave as if waiting for something – an answer or realization, a sensation of grief – while Mum tugged out the dandelions growing by his headstone (simple, just his name and the dates that plot his span like coordinates on a map) before she filled up the vase from the tap by the chapel and arranged the flowers in silence.

"I'm just going to run a couple of errands, Mum, alright?" I said as she climbed out of the car. My head was throbbing. This time the road was empty: no one in the street and the only other cars were standing on the neighbors' drives.

"Oh, OK then." She looked disappointed, and a familiar feeling crawled cold up my spine.

"I won't be long."

"Shall I wait for you to have lunch?"

"No, you carry on. Don't mind me." There it was, kindness and my failure to be worthy of it, same as always.

"Where are you going?"

"I won't be long."

"Where? Tell me or I'll worry."

"I've got to get a laptop, I can't keep using yours." My source hadn't called and her number was still dead, my emails bouncing back undelivered, but I still believed I'd need to work, that I'd write again. More than that, I needed to get out of the house.

"That's a good idea. Drive carefully then."

"Will do." I watched her as she fumbled for her key, then stepped inside without waving goodbye. I opened the glove compartment and checked that the locket was still there, tucked under the log book.

I drove slowly, up past the estate, flicking through the stations on the radio, avoiding the news programs until I found a classical music station. I let myself enjoy the sun and the music, just for a moment: no work, no Mother, no scandals, no lies, no guilt. No dead policeman. Not being followed.

At the edge of town I pulled into a new retail park. Six stores spread low and vast over the concrete, built from prefabricated cement and metal blocks, as if they were designed to withstand a hurricane in Mid-West America, not the mild English climate. There used to be orchards here, acres of cherry and apple trees planted in neat rows, but now our fruit is imported from South America and Africa, where the farmers are easier to exploit.

I parked right in front of Tech Whizzards and took less than twenty minutes to purchase a new computer, despite the salesgirl trying her best to deliver her pitch. My credit card was accepted, which of course it would be, except that I'd begun to imagine persecutions and calamities that weren't real, or not yet real. Nothing would surprise me.

I drove over to Melanie's old house. I couldn't get the image of Burrell out of my mind, or the idea that the locket being moved was a warning. I couldn't sit around the house, waiting. Waiting for what I wasn't sure, but I knew that at some point the police would come. I needed to get back on top, resurrect my old instinct for truth, for unraveling secrets. That was who I thought I was.

The estate hadn't changed that much, though there were more cars parked outside the houses and most of the houses were privately owned now. The old uniformity was gone, ushered out with Social Security, jobs for life and community, to make way for neighborhood one-upmanship and bad taste. I parked and sat in the car across the road from her place, memories flaring then guttering out, like a match flame held at arm's length. Images – of faces, a smile, a crate full of bottles of fizzy pop on the doorstep, the butter dish, two-pronged forks with plastic pineapples on the end – all those things that meant everything and nothing. I felt sick. A smell of stale cigarettes and vinegar hung in my memory like forgotten laundry.

All that time had passed since she'd gone and for so long I'd tried not to think about Melanie, or at least, not to think about her being here, being a scared desperate kid. I tried not to think about what I'd done or not done. I never confronted my part in what had happened to her, because she'd disappeared and I told myself it wasn't my fault. I was just a kid myself. It takes the lens of distance to see the elements of story in your own life, to become an outsider to your own circumstances. There I was. The coward returned, still trying to save his own skin.

I wondered if Charlie's pigeon loft was still standing, tucked behind the house, just visible from the back bedroom window. The house was pretty much the same, a squat two up, two down 1930s terrace, the kind that had the bathroom tacked on to the kitchen as an afterthought. Brown pebbledash was starting to fall off in small chunks, exposing the brickwork underneath. The front door was brand new though, the white plastic shiny and clean, the brass-colored handles and locks gleaming hot in the sunshine. The net curtains fell in pure white, evenly spaced pleats. I got out of the car and crossed the road.

A woman opened the door, small with dark hair, too young to be Chrissie, but still I asked anyway. She squinted up at me, examining my face as if she recognized me. But she didn't say anything other than to tell me she didn't know Chrissie, never heard of her, and that she'd bought the house four years before from a couple named Nicholson.

The door to the living room had been pulled closed but the stairs behind her were newly carpeted, the paintwork pristine. I smiled, thanking her and turned to leave, noticing a smell that I've always associated with that house and as I walked away I saw why – the curry plants Mel's mother loved were still growing in the small flower bed by the fence. I bent and crushed one of the leaves between my fingers.

"Why are you looking for her? Not the police, are you?" the woman called after me. She was still standing on her front step, watching me, her arms folded over her pale blue t-shirt. She was wearing jeans and a pair of those ugly boots that look like someone has gutted a stuffed toy and shoved them on their feet.

"We were friends," I said, the scent of curry leaves clotted on my fingertips.

"Try next door, later, after six. They won't be in now but they might know." She shut the door.

1989

H e felt shy when she opened the door in her mottled jeans and gray t-shirt, because he'd only ever seen Mel in her school uniform before and she looked like a stranger. She gestured him into a tiny hall, which was basically a square just deep enough to allow the front door to open. She had to stand on one of the stairs leading up to the bedrooms to give him enough space to come in. "Go in," she said, nodding to the door by his left shoulder. He did as he was told and walked into the sitting room, Mel close behind.

An enormous velvet rug printed with a brightly colored Elvis in his prime hung on the chimney breast over the gas fire; below it, on the orange brick mantelpiece, figurines of horses with cowboys on their backs bucked and reared. A brown velvet three-piece suite was pushed back against the remaining three walls, the armchair under the window. Dangling from the back of the chair in its white leather holster was a silver gun with an ivory handle.

"Is that real?" he asked.

"Nah, it fires blanks. My mum is really into Country, you know, the music, cowboys and all that. She dresses up for the barn dances: boots, hat, gun, the whole cowgirl Dolly Parton works," she smiled, watching his reaction.

"I've never seen one before. Can I hold it?"

"Sure." She handed it to him, holding the barrel in her fist.

"It won't go off will it?"

"Not now, maybe later."

"I think that is… fantastic. I'm jealous."

Melanie tipped her head, slowed time with her long indrawn breath and then blinked him back into the room. "I suppose you would say that." She took it back and polished it on her t-shirt before sliding it back into the holster.

Marcus looked around at the shiny horse brasses and the Royal Wedding commemorative plate hanging on the wall, the embroidered lacy cushions on the sofas, the thick pile carpet underfoot and the black ash coffee table right in the middle, topped by a clean ashtray. The room smelled of lemons, furniture polish and bleach. He hadn't expected it to be so sparkling clean, and was surprised that there wasn't an atom of dust anywhere, not even on the framed school photos, and there were lots of them, from primary class onwards – of Mel mostly, and a few of a little boy – on the wall above the TV in the corner.

She moved past him, cutting off his curiosity, and opened the door at the far end. "Want a drink?"

He followed her into the kitchen, the thick carpet giving way to patterned lino. Her mother was sitting at a table pushed up under the window, a rubber cap on her head. A skinny woman with bad skin and jet-black wiry hair cut short like a boy's was yanking tufts of Melanie's mum's hair through small holes in the cap with the tail end of a comb.

"Mum, you remember Marcus?"

"Oh yeah, hello love." She winked at him and took a drag on her cigarette. "Excuse the state of me, I'm just having me streaks done." She blew the smoke out through her nose and pulled a towel tighter around her shoulders. "Don't get bleach on me top, Dot."

"And this is my Aunty Dot." Mel gave the woman a quick squeeze on her arm and kissed her cheek as she moved to the fridge and grabbed two cans of Coke.

"Hello," he said, hearing himself stiff and prissy, blushing. Dot smiled and revealed a dark gap where her top front teeth should've been, before ducking her head and concentrating on hooking a twist of hair and teasing it through the hole.

"What youse two up to then?"

"Going to listen to some music in my room."

"What you listen to ain't music. Do you like that shouty stuff an' all, Marcus?"

"Erm, yes."

"Motown, that's music. Elvis Presley, the King of Rock and Roll." She took a drag on her cigarette. "Alright, but don't wake Jamie up, I've only just got him down. And put your ironing away, took me hours to do your washing, I don't want to come up there and find it on the floor. You hear me?"

"I hear you," Melanie said, and grabbed a pile of clothes from the plastic basket on the counter.

"And keep the door open, I don't want any funny business."

Mel's room was cramped, with just enough room for a single bed and a chest of drawers. What his mother would call "the box room." She put the pile of clothes on the floor. Two shelves were crammed with books, most of them with the pale green spines of Penguin Classics.

He picked up one the size of a brick. "Have you read this?"

"No, I just look at the pictures." She popped the ring pull on a Coke and handed it to him. "Yes, I've read it." He took the can and put the Proust back on the shelf next to the slim volumes of poetry by Anne Sexton and Sylvia Plath.

"Sorry, I didn't mean to be patronizing." He sat on her bed, ruffling the immaculate pink counterpane.

"You're alright. You can't help it," she said and sat next to him. The mattress sagged and tilted them towards each other. "Cheers." She bumped her can against his and drank.

"I don't think I've ever met anyone who actively chooses to read all these books. They're all so serious. Are they school books?"

"Do they look like school books?" She shook her head. "I borrowed some from the library, others I chored from W H Smiths."

"I thought you didn't approve of stealing." Stiff and prissy again, he swigged the Coke to shut himself up and almost choked on the sharp fizz as it hit his throat.

"Only things you don't need. I need these." She got up and pulled a CD out from a pile on top of the chest of drawers and slid it into a small portable stereo. "Goo, alright?"

"What do you think?"

She pressed play and lowered the volume. "Have to keep it low or Chrissie will have a fit, she's already pissed off with me."

"Are you in trouble? Do you want me to go?"

"Nah, she'll get over it."

"How come you have so many of the green ones?"

"Are you still going on about the books?"

"Sorry, I'm just curious. Have I offended you?"

"Not really, you're just a nosy bugger. I read those because they're classics and how else will I know what's good? Besides what Laugham and the Tory twats think we have to read, how else am I gonna know what is worthwhile or not?"

"I guess. That makes perfect sense." He thought of his mother and the pile of books she kept pressing him to read and the study, filled with his father's collection of books, faint pencil marks in his handwriting in the margins of the ones he cherished, and felt the feathery brush of guilt in his gut.

So they sat there together, Melanie leaning back on her elbows, eyes closed, her bare feet pointing up to the ceiling that looked like a wedding cake covered in swirls and peaks of stiff white icing. She was right he was nosy, he wanted to get up and poke around her things, to open the drawers and look under the bed. Instead he read the CD covers and the titles on the spines of all the books. He'd not even heard of most of them. On the window ledge there was a small animal skull with sharp little teeth, and a field guide to the wild flowers of Britain. Above them, a flock of paper doves hanging from a wire fluttered in the draft.

Over the music he could hear the low hum of the women's voices downstairs. The house was so small he couldn't imagine much privacy: even upstairs, in a separate room, there was a sense of being observed. But then on the other hand he imagined that he wouldn't be lonely either. Wherever you might be the family would be close by. He wasn't sure if he liked it or not. Exposed but together. He turned to Mel and she was watching him back, looking closely at his face. "Are you looking at my spots?" He reached up to cover his chin. "My mother says I should see a doctor."

She laughed, her head tipped so far back that he could see the metallic gray fillings in her back teeth. "You're nuts."

"If I'm nuts, what does that make you?"

"I'm entirely sane, thank you." She kicked his foot with hers, and rested her head on her left shoulder. "Do you like my rabbit skull then?"

"Your what?"

"The skull. I saw you looking at it."

"It's a bit gothic, I suppose. Where did you get it from?"

"I found it out near the orchards. I think it's beautiful, a reminder that there's more to the world than what we see. You know, under the surface."

The thing about Melanie was that she was brilliant at everything, but she didn't care. She didn't want it, this shininess she had. Even in sport: she was the fastest sprinter in the school, setting a district record when she was fourteen, but she turned down all invitations to join the athletics team and run for the county. She was brilliant, and she didn't give a shit. None of it, not the skull, not the books, her grace or insight, none of it was self-conscious or pretentious: she just *was*. And he worshipped her. And resented her, just a little.

"Has she fucked up my hair?" Mel's mum said, looking at herself in a small mirror over the kitchen sink, turning her head one way then the other to check the lines of bleached blonde that intersected the rest of her fair hair.

"Turn around so I can see properly," Mel said, her little brother on her lap, sucking his thumb, his blonde hair and blue eyes in direct contrast with her own.

"I think it looks fine, Mrs. Shoreham," he said, feeling bold and adult smoking the cigarette Mel's mum had offered him when they'd sat down with her.

"Mrs. Shoreham! You make me sound old. Just call me Chrissie. Mel?"

"Yeah?" She squeezed the little boy close and blew a raspberry on his neck, making him giggle and wriggle on her knee.

"My hair?"

"It's fine."

"You sure? Bless Dot, she's a darling, but she ain't much of a hairdresser."

"Why'd you let her do it then?" Mel put her brother down. "Off you go, Jamie. Go and play." The boy toddled off, his tiny flat feet leaving moist prints on the floor.

"Because she needs the money and it keeps her busy, poor thing."

"Is she your sister, Mrs.... Chrissie?" He crossed his legs and leaned back on the chair.

"God, no. Her mum and mine worked together in the kitchens up at the Army barracks, they were thick as thieves them two. Feels like I've known her forever. She used to come to my mum for her dinner after her mum got cancer. She was a pretty girl, you wouldn't know it now though." She sat down at the table with them and lit a fag. "That's what sorrow and heartbreak do to a face." She pushed the packet of cigarettes towards him and Mel.

"Looks more like fags and booze to me," Mel said, leaning back on her chair and balancing on the two hind legs.

"Amounts to the same thing don't it? And be careful of them chairs, I'm still paying for them on tick."

"Right." Mel dropped down and stood, walking over to the back door. "Come on, Marcus. Let's go for a walk."

"OK." He stood, almost knocking the chair over, puzzled by the sudden change in mood. Chrissie sat impassive, smoking, stroking the pad of her ring finger against the weave of the checked tablecloth. "Bye," he said as he followed Mel out. "Thanks for having me."

"Don't thank me, my love, thank your mum."

"Pardon?"

"For having you!" she said and laughed to herself as he pulled the back door shut behind him.

The Allotment

I turned down the alleyway, two doors down from Mel's old place, stinking of piss and with nettles over five feet tall that almost blocked the way, but I shouldered through towards the back of the houses and turned left. The path opened out, the nettles and bindweed cut back to allow access. I jogged to the end, past the gardens and houses: the washing hanging limp in the heat, the ponds and water features, plastic garden furniture and rusting BBQs, swing sets, the mattresses and building rubble, neat square lawns and barking dogs.

I felt tired, old suddenly, overwhelmed. I carried on to the end of the path that seemed much longer than I remembered. I wondered if I'd got it wrong, if I was in the wrong place. But then the path split at an angle and squared around the allotments just as I'd thought it would. I followed the tall wire fence to the right, the neat parcels of land full of late flowers, runner beans climbing willow frames, fruit bushes covered in netting and tomatoes swooning against their bamboo supports behind their glass frames. It was more abundant than I remembered, no doubt because of the new craze for organic and growing your own.

I reached the gate and rattled the heavy padlock; it was locked of course. So I carried on, skirting the perimeter, checking to see if anyone was around. Bantams were chittering and scratching in a wood-framed run on a newly-turned patch of soil. It was peaceful back there, the noise from the streets muffled by the vegetation. I could see the appeal of escaping there every day, digging and pruning and minding my own business. At the next turn I should've been by Charlie's plot, but it had gone. Or rather, all trace of him had gone. His shed and loft had been replaced by a summerhouse painted in pink and cream stripes, and raspberry bushes protected by netting. Of course he wouldn't be there. I was losing my grip, looking in the wrong places. Expecting the world I left to stay the same; that time would stop. I turned to leave, to get back to the car, to Steve Burrell, to Edward and the Sentinel, Mother.

"Who you looking for?" A woman, short and fat, leaned on the back gate of her garden. Behind her I could see a folding picnic chair and her discarded newspaper. She was breathless from the short walk down the path. I would've put her at around sixty but it was hard to tell; her hair was dyed the blue-black of magpie feathers.

"What makes you think I'm looking for someone?"

She laughed, a low huffing sound that teetered towards a cough. "You don't look like the type to be nicking potatoes off the allotment, now do you?"

I smiled back. "Probably not."

"So what you doing there? Admiring the view?"

I looked up at the skyline, where the pale blue met the brown roof tiles and gray satellite dishes, weighing up the question. I had nothing to lose; at the very least it would be another false lead among many. "Actually I'm looking for Charlie, he used to have an allotment right here. He had some—"

"I know Charlie, big fella, handsome. He don't come here no more. Had a stroke, he did. Here in fact. They had a right job getting him out and into the ambulance."

"He's alive though?"

"Yeah, take more than that to finish off old Charlie. He's in the sheltered housing down on Gladstone Road. You know it?"

"I'll find it."

"He'd like a visitor, I expect. You an old friend of his?" She cocked her head to one side, the flesh under her chin wobbling and adjusting to the new angle of her head.

"Yeah, something like that."

"Been away, have you? Easy to lose touch, I suppose. I've lived here all my life, born in this house I was, be taken out of it in a box I expect."

"Oh right." I wanted to get away, get out of the heat and find Charlie, but I stood there torn between the need to hide and the need for some answers, for some clarity.

"Make sure you ring first. The warden there is a right old cow. My aunt Ginny lived there after her Eric passed away, miserable she was. Terrible arthritis, so she couldn't get about much, you know. I used to pop over, take her some shopping, a bit of tea or what have you, that's how I know the warden. Nasty piece of work, never a kind word or a smile for anyone. They said cancer got poor old Ginny, but I reckon she was lonely."

"They say loneliness is a killer." I wiped the sweat collecting in the stubble on my top lip and rubbed my damp hand on my trouser leg.

"Do they? Well, there you go. Make sure you ring first, that's my advice."

"I will, thanks. That's really helpful."

"And tell Charlie Rita says hello, will you?"

I nodded and walked away, knowing that if I turned back she'll still be there, watching me go. Waiting for me to fall.

1989

"Come on, I'll take you to meet Charlie." She crossed the narrow garden, stepping over a plastic trike and a half-deflated paddling pool, and swung her legs over the low fence into the alleyway running between the gardens.

"Charlie, your dad?"

"My old stepdad, he was married to my mum when I was a kid."

"Oh, so is he your brother's dad?" He followed her through the passage, dodging the clumps of nettles and brambles still rich and tall from summer.

"No, he was born after Charlie left."

"Right. Have you had many dads?"

She turned and looked over her shoulder, her eyebrow raised. "What?"

"Well, you said the man in the chip shop was almost your dad, and there's Charlie and..."

She turned right into another alleyway, this one bordered by gardens on the right and a tall chicken wire fence on the left, beyond which a large field was sectioned up into different groups of plants and flowers with sheds dotted here and there, small plastic fencing dividing one section of ground from another.

"Sometimes things don't work out, and my mum doesn't like being on her own. She prefers a man around. It's complicated."

"Right."

"Can you stop saying that?" She'd stopped at a gate in the wire fence and was pulling at the catch.

"What?"

"'Right,' as if you were a social worker or something. It's doing my head in."

"OK, sorry. I'm just curious." She'd managed to open the gate and together they walked into the allotments; rows of houses, including Mel's, bordered the fence all the way around. "My mother hasn't had a boyfriend or anything since my dad died. I wish she would though."

"Why?"

"I don't know, it might be nice for her."

"For her, maybe. Be careful what you wish for."

Charlie's allotment was in the far right corner and, unlike all the others with their fruit bushes and ruler-straight rows of vegetables, his was a small patch of bare earth with a tool shed one side and a large aviary on the other which he was sweeping out as they arrived.

"Hello there, my treasure." He straightened up, smiling when he saw Mel, tucking the broom into a corner and stepping carefully out of the enclosure, leaving the door open behind him. "How are you?"

"I'm alright. You?"

"Mustn't grumble, you know. Who's this then?" He stretched out his large hand towards Marcus.

"Marcus meet Charlie, Charlie meet Marcus." His hand wrapped around Marcus's and squeezed, but not too hard; there was no macho crushing of the bones in his fingers.

"Hello Marcus."

"Hello." He let go and stepped back close to Mel.

"You come to see my birdies then?"

"Yeah, and you of course," she smiled up at him. His face was lined, dry as split wood, and his nose was broad and crooked at the bridge. Thickset and stocky, the bulky muscles of his youth were now covered by a soft layer of fat. He looked like a retired boxer, with just a hint of menace still lingering.

"You going to school?"

"Sometimes."

"You sure?" He turned to Marcus. "Is she?" He shrugged and Charlie shook his head.

"How's your mother?"

"Same."

"That Steve been back?" Melanie shook her head. "She alright then, is she?"

"Ask me no questions, and I'll tell you no lies." Mel smiled and pressed her face up against the fine wire of the aviary. "How's Lucinda?"

"She's alright. She's doing well actually."

"Can I show her to Marcus?"

"In a minute," he said. He opened the door of the little shed, pulled out a couple of folding chairs and wrenched them open. "Come on then, sit yourselves down."

They sat, side by side, as Charlie rummaged in his shed again, lifting out a large black bucket and upending it to make another seat. Bending his knees to sit, he tucked his right arm under his backside and scooped his trousers flat against his body as he sat down. Then he pinched the knee of his trousers and pulled them up his big thigh a little, to prevent bagging. It seemed strangely fussy for such a big, bulky man, especially one who looked like he could swing a punch as quick as he would shake your hand.

"Well then, this is nice," he said, his hands clasped between his knees. "Do you want a cup of tea? I've got me Thermos in the shed if you fancy it."

"Go on then," Mel said. "I'll get it shall I?" As she stood, a small flock of birds turned a tight loop over their heads, wings cracking the air. They dropped as one into the aviary and settled on the perches that stretched across the wire in front of nesting boxes.

"There they are, my babies!" Charlie stood and walked with Melanie into the enclosure, shutting the door behind them. Charlie held out his hand and stroked the plump breast of a large white bird with his finger. "Here's my Lucinda, here's my special one."

"Oh, is that a dove?" Marcus said, coming closer.

"No, she's a pigeon, but a beautiful one."

"She's not just a pretty face either is she?" said Mel, scooping up a fistful of grain from the feed tray and offering her cupped hand to the birds.

"No she isn't, she's a champion this one. Ain't you?" The bird cocked her head to one side as if listening, her eyes clicking open and shut. She puffed out her feathers and shook herself, the red metal ring around her ankle flicking like a bracelet before she settled down to sleep.

"What's the difference?"

"What's that?" Charlie said.

"Between a dove and a pigeon?" Marcus asked.

"There ain't one really, one is smaller than the other, that's all."

"Then I think Lucinda is a dove. It sounds better than pigeon don't you think?"

Charlie laughed, his eyes screwing shut. "He's a right one you've got there, Melly-Moo." A cough erupted from deep in his chest, a dark rattle that shook his whole body.

She nodded. "He's special all right. You should see a doctor about that cough." She rubbed his wide back.

"I'm not seeing no quack. Can't stand 'em," he said, wiping his mouth on the back of his hand

"Why? That's silly, you should get checked out."

"Because no one should know more about my body and its doings than me. Too much bloody power them doctors have. Keeping secrets from me, telling me what to do like I'm a kid." He started to cough again, his face red.

"OK. Whatever you say. You know best."

"Yes I do. Right, I'll better get on with clearing up this lot. Help yourself to that cuppa if you want one." His large body looked suddenly hollowed out, as if it was made of blown glass filled with bad air, rather than solid and strong as before. He seemed angry at his own weakness.

"Nah, it's alright, we won't deprive you of your tea. Right, let's go, Marcus Aurelius." She hugged Charlie, pressing her face against his chest and letting him hold her close for a moment.

"Alright then, bye, babe," he said. "Tell your mum I was asking after her."

"I will," she said as she came out of the coop and took Marcus's hand.

"He's nice," he said.

"Yeah, he's a prince, he really is." She smiled up at him, still holding his hand, and swung their arms to and fro, like kids.

"Isn't he worried his birds will fly away and not come back?"

"You what? They're homing pigeons, you silly berk. They always come back. That's how you race them."

"Right, I get it," he said, not getting it. He looked back to see Charlie sitting on his chair watching them go. He raised his hand to wave, which Charlie returned with the flat of his palm, fingers spread wide. Melanie didn't seem to notice.

At the end of the alley she kissed him on the cheek and said good-bye.

"Where are you going? I thought we were hanging out together."

She'd started to walk in the opposite direction to her house. "We have, and now I've got to go somewhere!" She laughed and walked away.

He went home. He never would find out where she went on her jaunts, though his mother once saw her sitting on the river wall behind the council offices, gazing out over the estuary. Other times she was spotted walking up the hill towards her estate, shoes in her hand, or getting off the train from London, still in her school uniform.

"She ought to be in school," his mother remarked. "Besides, it's not safe for a girl to gallivant around." He thought that everywhere was safe for Mel, so why be afraid of anywhere? But he didn't say so, because it would be disloyal, and anyway, deep down he suspected that he was wrong, that she was in danger, but he didn't want to believe that and it was easy not to.

Whenever he asked where she went, she would say, "somewhere, everywhere." And though he was tempted to follow her, to find out precisely where she disappeared to, in the end he couldn't do it. Perhaps he didn't really want to know. Perhaps he understood, even then, as stupid and ignorant as he was, that she deserved her vanishing.

Thick as Thieves

When the doorbell rang we were sitting on opposite sides of the sitting room; my mother was reading a book and I was trying to, but couldn't focus. We'd barely spoken all day and, even though nothing had been said, I suspected that even she thought I was guilty. The radio played the splintered chords of Scarlatti, which only heightened the feeling that my nerves were being slowly pulled through the pores of my skin, like the extraction of a tropical parasite, twisted from the flesh on a matchstick.

"Are you expecting anyone?"

"No, I don't think so." She stood, rubbing her fingertips on her skirt, as if the pages of her book had dirtied her.

"Sit, Mum. I'll go."

She sat back down and watched me as I left the room. I felt a sharp twist of trepidation in my gut. I wasn't ready to deal with the police or talk to fellow hacks, not with the image of Steve Burrell, gold tooth glinting, on my mind. I'd begun to question myself: maybe I was losing my grip, sliding, missing details, not thinking things through. What if I had missed something with the St. Clair research? Misinterpreted the facts. I could've. I had before, hadn't I? Even if I had been just a kid.

I took a breath, squaring my shoulders before pulling open the door. Callum stood in the dim light of the porch, his face clean-shaven and smooth, his eyes in shadow.

"What are you doing here?" I swallowed and rubbed at my unshaven face, the gray patch on my chin.

"You're not answering my calls. I had to come."

"How did you know where to find me?" I left my hand on the door latch, casual. Blocking the way.

He shrugged, holding up a plastic bag oozing a gingery chicken smell. "You told me the address. I thought you could do with cheering up. I have dinner." He raised his other hand. "And wine."

"I'm not alone, my mother's home."

"I know, that's why I've got enough for three. I figured you could do with some company. I've been a bit worried about you, to be honest. Your mob are baying for your blood."

"Yeah. So I've heard." I stepped back, letting him in. Mother was at the sitting room door.

"Hello?"

"Mum, meet Detective Inspector McMahon..."

"Hello, call me Callum, Mrs. Murray." He walked in and shifted the wine bottle into the crook of his elbow to clasp her hand in his. "Don't worry, this is not an official visit, I'm a friend of Marc's."

"Pleased to meet you, Callum."

"I've brought dinner, and wine. Hope that's not too presumptuous, but when I saw the news and I couldn't get hold of you, I thought I'd better come and see that you're both doing OK." He smiled. "Plates?" He looked over his shoulder at me. Behind him Mum tightened her brow quizzically. I shrugged.

"Through here."

I stood by the coat rack watching as she led him into the kitchen. His hair was short and sharp around his ears and neck, the cut of his shirt pulled taut by his broad shoulders.

"You won't mind eating in the kitchen, will you? It's quite cosy," she was saying, looking up into his face, intrigued and charmed. I couldn't hear Callum's reply, but he was nodding and sitting at the table, while she pulled out plates and cutlery. "Come on then, Marcus. Don't just stand there in the hall. Get the glasses and corkscrew, darling." I pushed the front door shut, checking that the latch was on, and joined them.

"I'm not surprised you met through work: he rarely makes time for anything else. Mind you, you were never one for large groups of friends, were you, darling?"

"No, I suppose not." I pinched the stem of my wine glass between my thumb and index finger and stared into the purple liquid as if it might reveal my future.

"No, he was always a loner really, just one or two close friends. Not very sociable. I suppose that's why nobody else has been to visit. None of his work or London friends has even called, except to get a comment about this nonsense." She spooned sweet and sour chicken over some rice on our plates.

"Well..." Callum began.

"There was Melanie, of course. She was lovely; she and Marcus were as thick as thieves for a while."

"Mum... please."

She pressed her mouth shut and picked up her fork.

"More wine?" Callum took the bottle and poured.

"I will, thank you. This is so thoughtful of you, to bring supper and everything."

"It's my pleasure."

"So how about you, Callum? It must be very hard at work at the moment, investigating a murder after so many years."

"It is, Mrs. Murray."

"Call me Philippa, please. Where do you even start?"

"We gather all the evidence we can. We see what forensics tell us: any details, DNA left behind, the weapon used, cause of death, then build from there. Talking to family, associates, and in this case going over the initial investigation when DC Burrell first went missing. It's not easy twenty years on, but not impossible. What about you, Philippa? What was your line of work?"

"I was headmistress at the girls' school, after Marcus's father died anyway. Before that I was the vicar's wife and all that entailed." She twisted her mouth in a wry moue. Girlish. I shifted in my seat, wanting to get out and up to bed. The syrupy remains of the food hardened and curled in their metal trays, the paper lids stacked in a neat pile on the counter.

I decided that I was going to see Charlie, and I needed to think about what I was going to ask him. I wanted to think about Steve and Melanie and the past and put it all in order. What I was forgetting or never knew in the first place. Then I was going to email Neil Mason at the Telegraph, see if he still wanted my story, see what he would make of the documents. They wanted to shut me up but I wasn't going to go down without a fight. I would prove I was right. Then maybe sell the flat, move on, start again somewhere new. Write a book.

"Marcus. You're miles away," she said. "It must be hard to hear all this talk about work, darling." She patted my hand, releasing the scent of her lavender hand cream. "Tell us about when you interviewed Philip Devereaux. That was such a coup! What was he like? Was he brilliant? He seemed brilliant, from your article."

"No, Mother. I'm sure Callum doesn't want to hear about that."

"Of course he does, don't you?" She tilted her head, as if emptying her ear.

"Absolutely," he said, watching me. He'd undone the top buttons of his shirt, looking entirely comfortable, as if he were enjoying himself.

"You see? We want to hear. Tell us about how amazing he was."

Well, honestly, he wasn't, he was ordinary. Disappointing. Like the rest of us, only he was guarded by a team of polished publicists and hotshot assistants. Of course I didn't tell her that.

What I said was: "Well, he was charming and extremely clever, as you'd imagine. And gracious. Well-dressed. That's about all I can remember. Sorry."

"That's alright. It was a marvelous article, they said you'd managed to really get him to open up, that you showed a different side to him. Did you read it, Callum?"

He'd been watching me speak and only turned away to answer her. I thought about the shape of him against his bed sheets. "Yes, I think I might have. I read his article on racism in the police force, obviously." He cleared his throat. "He's more handsome in the flesh than on TV though." He winked at me.

"Well, I think so, but then I'm his mother," she blushed. "He's written so much. Achieved so much. I can't honestly see how Marcus could be considered unprofessional after all he's achieved. It's beyond me. In light of these recent scandals, I mean honestly, how can they lump Marcus in with these phone-hackers and liars? He was instrumental in uncovering what they were doing. It's unjust." Her eyes were suddenly magnified by the brief lens of tears.

"Mum, really, it's alright. Don't get upset."

"I'm not upset. I'm angry, bloody angry. I can't understand how people you've known and worked with for so long can write such lies when lives are at stake, reputations – your reputation. You've done nothing wrong, worked so hard and for this? What's your opinion, Callum, as a policeman?"

"I'm sure Marcus will be fine. They'll investigate the claims and find him innocent, eventually. It's the waiting that isn't easy, for you both, for us, but they'll get to the bottom of it I'm sure."

"I hope so."

I watched them moving and talking easily. They thought they knew the situation, knew all the answers – getting to know each other, cosy. The boyfriend and the mother, at ease, comfortable. *For us,* he'd said. I got up and cleared away the plates, the foil containers and sticky cutlery. *There is no us,* I wanted to say, *and the investigation is over, I'm over,* but there was no point, it wouldn't change anything. They were convinced of their world, it was up to me to either confirm their view or stay quiet, both of which amount to the same thing.

"So tell me more about Marcus when he was younger. Who was this Melanie? Should I be jealous?"

"Well, at the time I'd have thought so, I was very naïve!" They laughed as I rinsed the plates under the tap, feeling the water warm over my fingers, reassuringly ordinary, banal. What danger could there be when the tap spills clean water over your hands?

"They were very close, the best of friends. Then she just vanished, ran away and then, a couple of years later they found her belongings – her bag and passport, some clothes – and signs of a struggle, in a bedsit in France. Presumed dead. Murdered. Just awful. That's about it, isn't it Marcus?" I turned to face them, to answer, but she continued, "Marcus was at the LSE by then, you got a letter didn't you? From her stepfather? There was no funeral, no saying goodbye. Tragic really..." I listened to them talk, discussing Melanie and me, watched them gesture, her hands lift and drop, not expansive, not dramatic, but practical, efficiently articulating her point, his frown and eyebrows indicating his concentration. "Oh he mourned," she said. "Didn't you?" I nodded and she pressed her lips together in that sad sympathy smile while he inclined his head, and I thought about all that I couldn't say, all that I'd worked to forget.

"All that promise," she continued, "Melanie was bright, very bright, at least that was the impression she gave." She fell silent, her face half shadowed in the low light. I pictured Charlie's broad cursive filling a white page with her name and commiserations and felt again the dull, insistent pressure of sorrow and guilt and the unknown. I turned off the tap.

"What a morose evening this is turning out to be! Let's lighten the mood." She stood, almost flouncing despite her usual stout, solid manner and as she left the room she turned. "I'll just be a moment." Her hand was raised, palm pressed against the air as if stilling our impatience. Theatrical.

"Sorry."

"What for? I'm enjoying myself, your mother's great."

"Yes, I suppose she is."

"I'm glad I came, I wanted to see you and your phone is dead."

"I've turned it off. My lawyer said to keep my head down until things are settled. Then I can make some decisions about the future."

"That makes sense."

"What does?"

"Keeping a low profile, avoiding the press."

"Yes, I suppose it does. Makes me look guilty, I think, like I've got something to hide. You haven't asked me if it's true, if I'm guilty."

"Are you?"

"No."

"That's that then." He laid his hands on the table.

"Are you always so easy to convince, Detective?"

"Only if the culprit is as sexy as you." He smiled.

"A charmer and worryingly unprofessional, that's not very reassuring." Why did this man find me attractive? Why would anyone want more than a quick fuck? I was used to a brief intimacy, a connection that dissolved loneliness momentarily, just long enough. How could he like me?

"Don't worry, I'm ruthlessly professional when I have to be."

"So how's the case going? I heard you've released the name of the victim."

"Yes, we're working on a few leads." He steepled his fingertips. *Look inside, there's all the people.*

Mother bustled back in, her slippers scuffing the floor. "Look! Aren't they adorable? You were devastated when she disappeared, weren't you darling?" She passed the photo of Melanie and me in the back garden to Callum who held it close, scrutinizing it. He looked up at me then back at the photo. "What's the name of the girl again?"

"Melanie, Melanie Shoreham. That's right, isn't it, Marcus?"

I nodded, meeting Callum's eye and he smiled back, giving nothing away.

I didn't ring ahead but the warden buzzed me in anyway. Rita was right: she was no ray of sunshine, her lips pressed in a line as flat as a corpse's ECG. "He's in number twenty, through that corridor and up the stairs on the right." She nodded her head in the general direction and went back into her office, releasing a cloud of cigarette smoke and air freshener before banging the door shut behind her.

I walked down the corridor, my feet gathering static on the red nylon carpet tiles. I passed the entrance to what looked like the communal sitting room, set up for bingo with chairs arranged around small card tables, all facing a larger table with the cage full of colored balls and a pile of cards stacked neatly beside a microphone. A lone elderly woman dozed in one of the plastic-upholstered winged armchairs that lined the room.

The walls were painted a bland institutional beige, and the glass in the doors and windows had lines of wire embedded in it, segmenting the view into tiny squares like a page in a child's maths book. It didn't feel very homely. I passed a couple of doors to the flats; it was just after lunch and the smell of hot fat and stewed tea leached into the corridor. It was quiet, although the blare of a TV show and canned laughter indicated the presence of life somewhere. I don't ever want to end up here, I thought, and was reminded of a conversation, not that long before – but in a different world it seemed, another life: over dinner, with wine and good scotch, when there was talk of a stylish retirement with Eames chairs and luxurious linens, with beautiful young gardeners stripped to the waist tending the flowers, decent food and art on the walls. A villa somewhere in France or Italy perhaps: an old folk's home for discerning old queens and their pals. Then I thought of Callum and the photo of Melanie, and the way he squeezed my arm as he kissed me goodnight, the rub of my stubble on his chin. My mother's look of approval. The idea of a coupled life, with its inevitable disappointments and failures.

I took the stairs two at a time and was panting when I knocked at Charlie's door. He took a while to answer, shuffling and muttering before he opened the door. He was stooped, his shoulders curving in towards his chest, and thin – much thinner than I had expected – but he was still a man to be reckoned with, impressive even. His hair was still thick, with only patches of gray around his ears; not so much changed from when I last saw him, when Melanie had left.

"Yeah?" He said, looking me hard in the eyes, evaluating, weighing me up.

"Charlie, I'm Marcus, Melanie's friend. We were in school together, before she—" I looked over my shoulder, back out at the corridor. "Before she left." I turned back to him.

"Oh yeah, I remember you. What do you want?"

"To talk. I've just come down to visit my mum and I thought I'd drop by and see how you are."

He looked me over again, nodded and stepped back. "Come in then."

His flat was small, but neat and tidy. It was open plan, with the kitchen in one corner of the main room, a large window across the wall above the sink. Newspaper twisted into bird shapes hung limp on cotton threads instead of a curtain. It was touching, the tatty scraps dangling there, a reminder of his old life.

There was a puffy black leather armchair angled in front of a large flat screen TV, a side table supporting the paper and an ashtray, and a small pine dining table with two matching chairs. He invited me to sit, and as I pulled out one of the chairs at the table I glimpsed his bed and a chest of drawers through the half-pulled curtains that sectioned off his living and sleeping areas. He turned the volume down on the TV, leaving the racing on the screen. Red alarm cords dangled from the ceiling – one above the small fridge by the sink, one trailing down over his TV and another by the entrance to the bedroom. I imagined accidentally pulling on one and having to face the wrath of the squint-mouthed warden.

"Tea? Or something stronger? You look like a man who likes a drink."

I shrugged and he fetched a couple of cans of cheap lager from his fridge, handing me one and sinking down into his armchair. Both cans opened with a sharp fizz and we drank. He sipped his and placed it on his side table, while I gulped mine, opening my throat with that particular thirst that comes with nervousness. I swallowed. "Sorry. I'm thirsty." I squashed my lips in the cup of my hand and wrung out the moisture, my face cat-tongue rough.

"You always were polite." He took out his tobacco tin from his shirt pocket and began rolling a cigarette. "Want one?" He offered the tin.

"No, thanks." I waited as he finished rolling and lit up. He coughed as he exhaled and took another sip of his beer to settle his chest.

"You've changed, I wouldn't have recognized you. Not a skinny, shy kid any more, uh? I suppose we all have, look at me, an old man now. It comes to us all, don't it?"

"If we're lucky." I agreed and drank.

"Need another?" He tipped his can towards me.

"No, thanks."

"You just look like you need one." He drew on his cigarette, and had to relight it. "How did you find me here?"

"I went round to your old allotment and a woman called Rita, who says hello by the way, told me you were here."

"Rita? Big girl? Nice eyes?"

I shrugged and half-nodded.

"Yeah, she was always a nosy cow. Nice enough girl though," he paused, looked wistful for a moment, then, "How was my patch? Bet it's all planted up now."

"Yes, afraid so. You must miss your pigeons."

"I do, you know. Beautiful birds. I had some champions in my time. Never mind. So what brings you here? I ain't seen you in what? Twenty years at least."

"Melanie," I said.

"What about her?"

"I want to know what happened to her, after she left, why she left. I don't want to cause trouble, I just have questions."

"Yeah. Questions. But why now?" He looked at me, one bushy eyebrow raised.

"To be honest I feel guilty. I wonder if I could've done more to help her."

"Is that right?"

"Yeah, I do, and I don't know if you heard, but Steve Burrell's body has been found. He was murdered."

"Who's that then? Friend of yours?"

"No, he was with Chrissie, her partner."

"Oh right, that Steve. Yeah, so he was."

"I can speak to Chrissie if you don't want to talk, just give me her number."

His eyes folded shut then opened again, like a reptile. "You'll have a job, boy. She's gone."

"Gone?" He's enjoying this, I thought, or maybe he didn't trust me either, or he was just lonely and talking felt good.

"She passed away. About fifteen years now, she's been gone."

"Christ. I'm sorry. What happened?"

"Lung cancer. Quick too, thank God. Riddled with it she was, when they opened her up, they just stitched her together and sent her to a hospice. I think it was losing Mel that killed her, the heartbreak. It can you know. You can die of a broken heart."

"I'm sorry to hear that. What happened to the little boy?"

"He lived with the grandparents for a while, then he was fostered out when they passed on. His dad had done a bunk, just gone off. Wouldn't be the first bloke to dump his own little one. Poor kid, I always liked him. He's still around here, works in that tyre place in town; think he might even own it, actually. I don't speak to him. He was born after I left so I never got to know him really. Not like Mel, she was like my own. Lovely girl."

"His dad was Steve, right?"

163

"What's that?"

"Jamie, Chrissie's little boy, his dad was Steve Burrell, wasn't he?"

"Probably."

"I thought he was."

"You'll be right then."

"The police say Steve was murdered, and buried up in the old orchards."

"Was he? That explains a lot."

"Have you not seen the paper? It's been in the local news."

"No boy, I don't bother with all that. Murdered was he? I'm not surprised."

"No? Why's that?"

"Because he was a wrong 'un. Bent pig, nasty bastard, you know? Must've made some enemies. I heard he was on the take from some druggies. You know, "pay up and I'll look the other way" type of scam."

"Really?"

"Oh yeah. I never understood Chrissie taking up with him." He turned to the TV for a moment and watched the horses silently race across the turf.

"I know Mel was frightened of him."

"Yeah, well, he was a bit handy, if you know what I mean, with women and kids an' all. Good thing he left 'em."

"He'd come back. I saw him."

"Well, it's a long time ago now, nothing we can do about it. Get us another one, will you?" He nodded at the tin by his elbow. I obliged and placed them on our respective tables.

Charlie leaned forward, elbows on knees, his hands loose, dangling. "I'll tell you what I know about my Melly-Moo and then you'll leave it alone, yeah? Let her rest in peace." He sat back, and drank from the fresh can.

He met Chrissie in the George, she was a barmaid and he was on the darts team. They won a trophy one night and she gave him a congratulations kiss on the cheek, just him. He sat at the bar the rest of the night, until last orders, chatting with her in between her serving the other customers. She was the best-looking girl in there, funny too, had this spark about her. He knew she had a little girl, some blokes thought that was a problem, baggage, but not him. Little angel she was, dad was a Greek fella, done a bunk before the little 'un was born, but Chrissie didn't like to talk about it. He takes them out, mother and daughter. To the beach, the fairground, picnics. He spends more and more evenings there, in her house. His place not much to speak of, a bloke's place, you know? Then he's moved in and they've got married. Chrissie in a peach dress and matching jacket, little hat like Princess Di with a net covering her eyes, him in a suit. Room in the pub with a lovely spread and dancing after the register office, Melanie in a frilly white dress and a bouquet of flowers, like a little bride herself.

"Were you happy?"

"Oh yeah. Of course, in the beginning. We were a family, we were talking about having one of our own, a little brother or sister for Mel."

"So what went wrong?"

"Who knows? Chrissie was hard, like glass. Easily broken. You know? She would fly off the handle for no reason."

He spoke and I listened, both of us drinking. The sun hot on my back, intensified by the safety glass, creeping up my spine before it tilted over the roof and the heat spread elsewhere.

Chrissie did get pregnant, after four years of trying. But it was some other fella's, that Steve's, and just like that she told him. Home from work, his stuff on the doorstep, packed all neat though. She washed and ironed all his clothes before folding them into his bags. Not his kid. Sorry. Don't be angry. Sorry. Melanie sitting at the top of the stairs, almost a teenager, big eyes all sad, sending messages with those teary, long-lashed eyes – *don't shout, don't shout* – so he didn't and what was the point, what difference would it make?

"Just like that?"

"What else would I do? Beat her up? Beat him up? Nah, I'm not that sort. There's plenty that would, but not me. Anyway, I wanted to be able to see Melanie so I needed to stay on Chrissie's good side."

"And then?"

"I left. She had the baby, moved him in. I saw Mel a lot in the beginning, I think they both wanted rid of her; she got in the way of their little family. Then hardly at all. Melanie changed, grew up. Then he left. End of story."

"Did he hit Mel?"

Charlie lifted his head and looked at me down the barrel of his nose. "Mel never said so."

I let it go, waiting. We drank, finishing our cans and starting another. Drinking more slowly.

"She went through a lot, as a kid."

"What kind of thing?"

"Just trouble. Chrissie did her best, but she couldn't protect her from everything, no parent can."

She'd always wanted to travel. She hated school, even though she was a bright little thing. Taught herself to read before she was five by all accounts. She used to make up stories about her adventures, how she'd travel to Mongolia and ride horses all day and sleep under the stars. She felt hemmed in. She liked to just go off, disappear for a bit. He always encouraged her dreams, bought her an atlas, and had a savings account for her to buy her ticket when she was old enough. He even paid for her passport, went up town with her and waited all day so she had it ready, for as soon as school was done.

It could make sense, it could be true. I listened and listened.

"Look Charlie, I suppose what I want to know is if anyone knows that I helped you that night?"

"What're you talking about?"

"The night before she left."

"She was always good at that. Vanishing. Leaving."

"Except she always came back."

"Well, it wasn't her fault was it? God only knows what happened to her. Bless her heart. Couldn't even have a funeral."

"But that night, when I helped you, when I helped Mel, who knew about that?"

"What you talking about?"

"C'mon Charlie, I think you know."

"Listen," he sat back in his chair, looking tired, ancient. "I don't know what your game is, but that never happened. You never helped me do nothing, I don't even know you."

"C'mon Charlie, give me a break. The night Melanie left, what happened?" I needed to find purchase, to hold on to what I knew because the old man was pulling me under with him. "Did it have anything to do with Steve? That's all I want to know, Charlie."

"That's it, get out. Look at me, I'm an old man, you come around here tormenting me. What the fuck is wrong with you? Now out, or I'll call the Old Bill myself."

"Charlie, I don't want any trouble. But the man was killed and—"

"OUT." He stood and reached for the red alarm cord hanging over the TV.

"Charlie, be reasonable. Please."

He shook his head. "For all I know you did it, you killed him. Coming here, accusing me. What's wrong with you, boy? Now get out."

167

1989

There are two types of liars – the ones that are fucking with others and the ones that are fucking with themselves. Melanie's mum was the second type. Who knows what kind Marcus was? Perhaps both. Perhaps everyone is. Chrissie had this habit of speaking with her eyes closed, as if she needed to protect her eyes from the words she spoke. It was like she was blanking out the world, or maybe not wanting to see the world's reaction to her. But she was a liar; she lied about everything: her health, her day at work, the neighbors, Melanie. Perhaps even she didn't know the truth about her own life.

Once, Melanie and Marcus were sitting on the low wall that edged the short parade of shops that served the estate. Waiting for the Chinese take-away to open for the lunch session; talking about music probably, and which books they were reading, or what it would be like to sleep with Kurt Cobain, and most likely debating whether to order egg fried rice and spring rolls or vegetable chow mein, watching people go in and out of the Co-Op, the Post Office and the launderette. Anyway, as they sat there an older woman stood watching them for a moment before coming over.

"You're Chrissie's girl, ain't you?" She had copper hair, the color of a two pence piece. She was tall and broad, almost as tall as Marcus, and wore a red Co-Op overall over her skirt and blouse. She had surprisingly slender ankles. Her brown eyes were ringed with blue eye shadow right up to her penciled-in eyebrows. Her nametag said *Maureen – here to help.*

"Yeah, I'm Melanie." She looked up, her hair dropping back over her shoulders.

"This your fella?" The woman winked and cocked her head in his direction.

"This is Marcus."

"How do you do?" He stood and offered his hand. She shook it, twisting her chin over to her lifted left shoulder.

"Oh, hark at him, he's a gentleman, ain't he?" She laughed to herself for a second.

"You don't remember me do you, babe? I'm Auntie Mo. I used to look after you when you was little and your mum worked up Marcani's with your Nan. I used to live above you in the flats. Remember?" She stared at Mel, hopefully, watching for recognition.

"Oh yeah! I think I remember." Mel nodded, "Auntie Mo. Yeah."

"I knew you'd remember. Lovely little thing you was, always smiling, no trouble. Look at you now! All grown up, spit of your mother an' all." She sighed and stood there, and they waited for her to speak again. "How is your mum?" she asked finally. Behind her, the owner of the take-away was turning the door sign over to OPEN and sliding back the locks on the door.

"Mum's fine, thanks."

"Is she? Oh, am I glad to hear that! When I heard she had the cancer, all I could think about was you kiddies. How you all coped I don't know."

"Sorry?" Mel stood, as if she had to get closer to hear better.

"She got the all clear now, has she? Had chemo?"

"Erm." Mel stood there, looking down at her shoes, her mouth open as if waiting for words to come from thin air.

"Have I put my foot in it?" Maureen stepped back, looking from Mel to Marcus and back again. "I'm sorry, darling. Your mum told me and Denise a while back and I just thought, well, I..."

"No, it's totally fine. It's just a bit of shock still, really. But Mum's fine. All clear. I'll tell her you asked. Thanks."

Relieved, Maureen's face dropped into a smile, "That's beautiful news. I'm so pleased. A brain tumor is nasty, bloody nasty. Oh I'm so pleased. Right then, I'll let you get on. I've to get back meself. Bye my darling. You look after yourself. Give your mum my love."

"Bye," Marcus said and watched as she strode back into the shop; when she reached the door she turned and looked back, but Melanie had slumped back down onto the wall.

"I didn't know your mum had been ill." He moved closer to her, but she was folded in on herself, unreachable.

"She's not," she said.

"But then why did that woman...?"

She turned and looked at him, the tip of her nose bright red like she'd been rubbing at it. She gulped and shook her head before speaking. "I'm gonna head back, OK? I'll see you." She stood and turned to go.

"What about our food?"

"Later, yeah?" She half smiled, nodded at him and began walking away, past the shops.

"Do you want me to come with you?"

"You're alright," she called back without turning her head. Lifting her hand in a half-wave she crossed the road, heading in the direction of her home.

She never mentioned her mother's illness ever again, and by then Marcus had learned it was best not to ask questions. Winter gathered itself around them, and she appeared in class so regularly that the teachers stopped registering surprise at her presence and instead enjoyed her snappy intelligence. She drew everyone in: like cold beasts drawn to the warm glow of a fire, they huddled round her, kids and adults. In the dining hall, during lessons, when she was quiet they were, when she talked they listened, but she didn't seem to notice or care. One or two of the girls didn't like her, obviously, but everyone else flocked to her like gulls around a dropped bag of chips.

The Darrens had pretty much left school: a couple of them to join their dads in the building trade; the tough, spotty one – Darren MacNamara – had been sent to Borstal after he put his own dad in hospital, though rumor was his dad had it coming, and Shine kept his head down. Vulnerable without his gang, he was no longer the top dog. He started seeing a girl from the year below, Jennifer, a small blonde with a row of gold hooped earrings punched into the curved rim of her ears, and they were inseparable, walking the school corridors hand in hand between lessons. Marcus had settled in, was almost comfortable.

It wasn't long before a new gang of wannabe tough guys in the year below started throwing their weight around, stealing lunch money from the first years, tripping people on the stairs, shoving their victim's head down the toilet and flushing, or punching them in the arm until the chosen one could take it no more. None of this really bothered Marcus and Melanie: as fifth years they were pretty much impervious to those stunts and most of them, even Darren Shine, were working hard for their GCSEs. Until one Wednesday, just before the Christmas holiday.

Marcus and Mel had gone over to the cloakroom, to have a last fag before lunch finished. By then he was a committed, dedicated smoker. It was a rotten place that stank of stale fags, sweaty trainers and the fug of teenage hormones. The rough wooden floorboards were littered with fag butts, sweet wrappers and torn Rizla packets. It was one of those prefab huts, flimsy and asbestos-riddled, brought in on the back of a lorry as the school outgrew the original building and propped up on a few stacks of bricks. But as it was self-contained and set away from the main school and the teachers, it was fairly lawless and was known as a good place to hang out and smoke, or fuck, or beat the shit out of someone.

They walked in and made their way to their usual corner, pushing past the racks of coats and PE kits towards the back, where they were concealed from any surprise visits from the staff. A small group of kids were huddled in the opposite corner, jostling and nudging each other. Laughing. Ignoring them, he and Melanie sat down and sparked up.

"Go on, cut it off. Do it," urged a voice from the corner, followed by a wail and more laughter.

"Please don't!"

He looked over at Mel, waiting for direction, or to see her reaction at least. She did nothing, just watched the smoke unraveling from the tip of her cigarette. The laughing and wailing and jeering rose in volume.

"Could you be a bit more quiet, please?" Marcus said, surprised at himself and a little pleased by his own bravery. He looked over again at Mel but she hadn't moved. He was disappointed that she hadn't acknowledged his courage and ashamed that he'd needed her approval.

"What?" One of them had turned towards him, his head too big for his skinny body. It was the ringleader of the newly appointed tough kids.

"You heard," Mel said. "Keep it down or you'll have the teachers in here." She still hadn't looked up.

"Give us a fag then." He had thin lips, almost non-existent in his wide, flat face. He moved closer.

"I don't think so."

"Then get out. This is our place and we'll do what the fuck we want."

"Right."

"Yeah right. Go on, get out."

"I don't think so."

"I'm warning you, slag." He lifted his right arm an inch and inclined his head towards the blade he held in his fist. Marcus felt sick. Mel sighed and stood up, sauntering over towards him. Marcus hesitated and then moved behind her, knees shaking. The boy was holding a pair of scissors, not a knife, but the blades were long and sharp. He shifted his weight and behind him Marcus saw a little Asian kid, on his knees, a long plait uncoiling from the top of his head.

One of the others, a short, skinny boy, his breath rasping in and out of his chest, held a scrap of black fabric in his hand. There were three others: a girl who looked like she was wearing someone else's uniform, the wheezing kid and a boy he recognized from the bus who wore expensive trainers and never caused any trouble. They moved away from the kid on the floor.

"You alright?" she asked. The kid was crying and shook his head.

"What are you doing to him?" She turned back to the ringleader.

"None of your fucking business is it, Paki lover?"

"I think it is, Fascist."

"What? You gonna stop me, are you? You and him?" He laughed. "I'm gonna cut his fucking hair off and make him look like the boy he says he is. You can stay and watch."

"No, you're not doing that."

The kid blinked then took another step closer, cocky, his chin thrust out. "Ain't I? Maybe I should cut you instead?" He made a jabbing movement with the scissors, slicing just in front of her chest. She didn't even flinch, she laughed.

"If that's what you want. Do it."

"Come on, Mel. Let's go," Marcus said. "Let's call someone."

"No." She didn't take her eyes off the kid.

"Go on, do as your queer boy mate says." His little gang were watching him and Mel with absolute attention.

"I said no. I'm not going anywhere." She took another drag on her cigarette then flicked the butt towards the kid, bouncing it off his chest. "I ain't scared of you."

He jumped back, flapping at the front of his shirt. "You mental fucking bitch!" Melanie closed the gap between them, standing toe to toe with the skinny kid.

Jittery, his crew kept looking towards the door and then back at him, just as the bell for classes went.

"Come on," one of the boys said. "She ain't worth it." He threw the scrap of fabric on the floor.

"Nah, she ain't." The leader squared his shoulders and sauntered out with his mates. "See you tomorrow, Paki-boy, she won't fucking save you next time. And tell your dad I'll be down his shop later for me porno mag."

"My dad hasn't got a shop!" the Asian kid shouted back.

"Here you go," Mel handed him his hair covering and he wound his hair up into a knot on his head.

"Thanks."

"What's your name?"

"Adeep." He stood up and wiped his face, still in shock.

"That's nice. You alright now?" He nodded. "We'll see you around then. Look after yourself."

"That was amazing," Marcus said as they walked up to the science lab.

"Was it?"

"Yes! You're a hero. Weren't you scared?"

"Of course I was. Weren't you?"

"I was terrified! I thought he was going to stab you."

"So why would I be any different?"

To Remember Is to Lie

The purple scent of rosemary. The shrill call of birds in the trees above. Charlie saying, "Don't tell anyone she's been here." His car door pulling shut. Other voices, like shadows, at the edge of the dark; I was dreaming.

"There he is, officers. Can I get you anything?"

Mumbling and footsteps in the grass. I sat up, blinking. A sick taste in my mouth.

Ada Okonjo and a uniformed officer were walking over to me. I pulled the sun lounger upright.

"Afternoon Mr. Murray, I know you're not feeling well, but can we have a word with you?"

"Of course." I expected to feel panic, or anger or indignation when they came. But I didn't. I didn't feel much. I felt the heat of the sun, the damp cotton of my shirt, the acid weight of my stomach. But what was I feeling? I don't know any more. I've spent so long paying attention to other people I've become a stranger to myself. "I thought the Met would be dealing with this."

"The Met? Why would they?"

"Well because... I'm sorry, Detective, why are you here?"

"We're just following up, tying up loose ends. Speaking to people that knew the family of the victim." They stood, awkwardly, looking down at me.

"Victim?"

"Detective Constable Burrell."

"I don't understand. What's that got to do with me?"

"Just a couple of questions." She half shrugged; no big

deal her body said. She was wearing a wedding ring, I hadn't noticed that before.

"Where's Callum?"

"DI McMahon is busy. Can we sit?"

I nodded and indicated the table and chairs under the pergola, moving to sit down with them. My back was stiff as I stood and then sat again; everything was going to pot, running to seed. My body, my mind, my career – everything.

"OK, this won't take long. As I said, just a couple of questions to help us with our inquiries. OK?" Okonjo smiled – reassuring, patronizing.

"Lovely garden. Yours?" the uniform asked. He was in shirtsleeves, but he was sweating under the stab proof vest he'd kept on.

"My mother's. This is my mother's house."

"Right, of course," said Okonjo. "And you're staying here?"

"Just temporarily. I came to cover the story about the body, we thought, my boss thought, it was a bigger piece."

"You're a journalist?"

"Yes."

"But you're not covering the Steve Burrell piece now?"

"No."

"Why is that?" Okonjo asked the questions, the PC wrote it down, leaning one arm on the table to stop it rocking on the uneven ground.

"I've had a disagreement with my editor."

"That's right, so you have. Can you tell me about that?"

"Not really, it's confidential and what isn't I'm sure you know already." I shifted in my seat. Mother was at the kitchen window, watching.

"So it had nothing to do with your personal connection to the victim? No conflict of interest or anything?"

"Of course not, I told you I don't know the victim."

Okonjo lifted her head, tilting it to one side, frowning, "Hmm," as if confused. "But you knew his stepdaughter, Melanie Shoreham?"

"Melanie? Yes, we were at school together, but I didn't know her family, definitely not her stepfather."

"Right. But you were close to Miss Shoreham?"

"I didn't know her for long. She left a few months after I met her."

"And when was that?"

"I don't know. I was sixteen or so. Which would be, 1990?"

"Right, around about the same time DC Burrell went missing."

"I don't know anything about that."

"Yes, early April 1990 was the last time anyone had contact with the victim and that was also when Miss Shoreham was reported missing by her family."

"OK."

She glanced at her colleague and watched him write for a second before lifting her gaze back to me. "Why did she run away?"

"I don't know. She never told me. She just left."

"Just like that? A sixteen-year-old girl leaves all on her own without telling anyone?"

"Well, she never said anything about it to me." I shifted in my seat, trying to stop the pinching in my spine.

"What was the nature of your relationship to Melanie?"

"We were friends, school mates."

"That's it? No romance or anything?"

"No."

"Did she have a boyfriend?"

"No."

"As far as you know? Or are you sure about that?"

"I'm sure."

"A girlfriend then?"

"Melanie never showed any interest in having a boyfriend or a girlfriend. She never talked about it."

"And you didn't think that strange?"

"Not really, she was different, bookish, an introvert I suppose."

She paused, twisting the gold band around her finger before smiling at me. She had a beautiful smile. "It must've been hard on you, at the time, losing your friend like that."

"Yes, it was. I missed her."

"In the file it says you were very upset during your interview with DCI Sutton, or DC Sutton as he would've been then."

"Sorry?"

"Don't you remember? He came to your school, spoke with several of your classmates and the staff there."

"Oh God, maybe. Yes. It was such a long time ago." They'd questioned us one by one in the head's office. I remember the detective popping his knuckles one by one as I tried not to cry, the fluorescent light cutting shadows in the corners of the room. I remember none of the other kids gave a shit, about Melanie or being questioned by the police.

She watched me. "Did Melanie ever mention DC Burrell?"

"I don't think so. To be honest, I can't remember."

"She never said anything about him and her mother fighting? Or that she was scared of him?"

"No."

"Did you ever hear from Melanie after she left?"

"No, how could I? She was killed."

"The report says missing, presumed dead; her body was never found."

"Yes, I know what it says."

"How?"

"Her stepdad, Charlie wrote to me, he sent a letter to my mother's house."

Okonjo smiled, "Yes, Charlie Smart, he's a character isn't he? Got a sheet as long as my arm. How do you know him?"

"I met him once or twice, when I was with Melanie."

She looked over at the other officer and waited for him to catch up with his notes. "So you had met her family?"

"Well, Charlie and her mum, but that's it. It was years ago."

"True, hard to remember which stepdad was which I

imagine." She smirked and raised her eyebrows. "They were a bit dysfunctional weren't they?"

"Not really."

"Is it possible she's alive?"

"Who?" There was a buzzing in my ear, high-pitched like a mosquito. I flapped my hand to ward it off. Both of the police officers squinted at me, as if I was mad. The buzzing stopped.

"Melanie."

"Possible, yes. Likely, no. Is this an interrogation?"

"No, just a few questions. You're being very helpful."

"I've not heard from her since she went. I didn't know why she left or that she was planning to." The sun was right above us, laser hot. Okonjo fanned herself with her hand.

"What was her relationship like with Charlie?"

"They were really close, she adored him."

Okonjo frowned and tapped her fingers on the table. A black bird shrieked in alarm as it flew across the garden.

"So other than being bookish and – what did you say? An introvert – what was Melanie like?"

"She was a teenage girl. Normal. I only knew her for a few months and then she was gone. I honestly don't know what I can tell you."

"So nothing out of the ordinary?"

"Except that she disappeared? I don't think so."

"Did she have many friends? Anyone else we can speak to?"

"No, not really. Though there was a girl called Georgina that she sometimes saw, but they weren't very close, I mean as far as I know."

"Do you have a surname for this Georgina?"

"I'm sorry, I don't. I met her once maybe, she was in care though, I remember that much, fostered by a woman who lived opposite Melanie."

"OK," she said, we both watched the constable write it all down.

"And her mother? Chrissie Shoreham, did you ever hear from her?"

"No, I don't think so."

"What about any other friends, kids from school, anyone you and Melanie hung out with?"

"No, I didn't stay in touch with anyone after I left."

Okonjo nodded at her partner and stood up. "You've been very helpful, thanks. Can you stick around for a few days, just in case we need to talk to you again?"

I shook my head, "I was hoping to go back to London tomorrow, actually."

"Well, if you could stay another day or so, we'd be very grateful."

"I don't know if that's possible, I may have to go."

"Then we'll come to you, if that's the case. Just give us your address in London."

"No, it's fine. I'm sure I can wait another day."

"Good. Just one last thing. Why did you go and see Charlie Smart yesterday?"

"What?" Sweat rolled down my face. "How do you know that? Am I being followed?" I'd thought I was safe, I thought I was exempt; I thought I'd always done the right thing. It's easy to believe you're innocent when you haven't done anything wrong.

"No!" She laughed, like I was absurd, paranoid, and I almost believed her, I was almost comforted, embarrassed. "We saw your name in the visitors' book when we signed in yesterday."

"You've seen Charlie?"

"We're seeing everyone that might be able to help. So, why did you visit him?"

"I don't think that's any of your business."

"Maybe not. Thanks for your time. We'll see ourselves out." She shook my hand and as I watched them walk across the grass it occurred to me that I didn't sign any visitors' book at the home.

1989

Over the next few days they were followed by Adeep. At lunch, in the corridors, at the school gate – he'd be there, smiling, waiting. Marcus liked him: he was sweet and didn't say much, just stayed close, sheltering in Melanie's shadow. They ran into the little crew of thugs too, but they'd moved on to new victims and pretty much avoided Melanie, only giving her dirty looks and muttering to each other. She didn't seem to notice any of it.

The next Tuesday Melanie was even quieter than usual, she didn't even argue with Laugham about his interpretation of Hamlet. She fell asleep in Geography, her head on the desk.

At lunch Marcus asked her if she was all right. They were sitting at a table, picking at the mashed potato and beans that were the only vegetarian option. Adeep was next to her, eating a sandwich.

She looked past them, towards the door, screwed up her mouth, looked straight at Marcus, then at Adeep and said, "To tell you the truth, you are all doing my head in. Stop tagging along after me like a pack of bloody dogs. Leave me alone." Then she stood up and left.

"Wow. Should we follow her? Have I done something wrong?" Adeep looked as if he might cry.

"No, I think it's best if we leave her alone." Marcus said, trying not to look as shocked as he felt; he'd never heard her say anything cruel before. "She'll come back." But he had no idea if she would.

"I just wanted to thank her." He reached up to his hair as if making sure it was still there.

They finished their lunch in silence, both watching the door. Mel wasn't in class for the rest of the day. Nor the next, and then school broke up for the Christmas holidays. Marcus resigned himself to the friendship being over – he'd expected it, after all. Why would someone like her want to hang out with someone like him?

He moped and sulked while his mother and Joyce put the decorations up and hoisted a tree in the corner of the sitting room. He put Melanie's present under the tree, just in case, but it just depressed him so he put it away again.

"Why don't you simply phone Melanie? All this draping yourself over the furniture in sorrow isn't helping anyone," his mother said after he spent most of Christmas Eve in bed, ignoring his Granny, the vicar and the neighbor, Mr. Simmons, who were all gathered downstairs drinking port.

"I can't. She hates me."

"Well you're not helping yourself lying around up here. Besides, it's snowing out, look." She pulled back the curtain. "Switch off the lamp so you can see better."

He sighed and tutted because she still didn't seem to know that he wasn't a child and it was all just pathetic, but he switched the lamp off anyway and stood up to join her. They watched as thick clots of snow spiraled and caught in the wind before drifting to the ground.

"Isn't it beautiful?" she whispered. She looked young, her eyes soft and smiling, enchanted by the snow.

"Yes," he said. "Do you think it will lay?"

"Oh I think so. Look, it's already covered most of the garden." She squeezed his hand. "Merry Christmas, my darling."

"Merry Christmas, Mum."

The opening bars of "White Christmas" plonked up from downstairs, followed by the vicar's smooth baritone. "Ah, Granny is at the piano. I'd better go back down. Do join us, you can even have a glass of wine."

He nodded. When she'd shut the door, he opened the window and lit a cigarette, listening to the adults slur and belt out a medley of Christmas tunes. It was quiet outside: the snow does that of course, deadening all sound. And though there were other houses along the lane, the yew hedges and stands of trees gave the impression that he was completely isolated. The snow glittered in the moonlight and he fancied he heard an owl hooting above the music. His mother was right, he decided, he needed to stop being so wet. He stubbed out the cigarette and hid the butt in a metal tin that used to have his Dinky cars in, closed the window and went downstairs. He would phone Melanie in the morning.

But she beat him to it. He'd just finished opening his gifts and they were about to head off for church. His mother, his granny and him, all muffled and trussed in wool and tweeds and fur.

"Listen, I'm sorry I was a bit of a twat the other day. Do you want to come over to Georgie's? She's on her own and everything. I'll come round and get you if you like?" He could hear the TV and her little brother yelling in the background, then her mother and the deeper vibration of a male voice.

"I don't know if I'll be allowed out today and we're just about to go to church."

"Church?" she said. "C'mon, I've got to get out of here."

"Hold on, let me ask." He put the phone on the table and padded in to see his mother. She was pulling on her hat. He'd never been out or away from the family on Christmas day, and it felt like a blasphemy to even ask, to even consider it, but she said yes, just like that.

"OK, but not until after lunch, which will probably be finished around three o'clock, so Granny can watch the Queen."

"Nice. I'll see you then." And she hung up.

"Do you want to come in?" He stepped back and opened the door wide, but Melanie shook her head.

"No, it's alright. We best head off, it's a bit of a trek." She was wearing an old green parka, zipped up tight to her chin with the hood up, the gray nylon fur framing her face. Her hands were rammed deep in her pockets and a plastic carrier bag dangled from her wrist.

"Hang on a minute then." He pulled on his coat, hat and snow boots.

"Blimey, you look like you're ready for an Arctic expedition!" She laughed and lifted her own wellington boot. "I look like a farmer! And I'm freezing."

"Do you want to borrow some socks? Granny gave me some beauties as a present."

"I'll pass, thanks. Let's get going."

Marcus shouldered his bag and called goodbye to the women snoozing in front of the TV, still wearing their paper crowns.

They walked side by side through the still-fresh snow, the only people out and about. Colored lights flashed in the windows of the houses, and one or two had gone overboard and had flashing reindeer and snowmen on their front lawns.

They reached the main road that cut through town and led out to London shortly before dusk; their breath and voices hung in wisps of vapor before cooling and binding with the air. The chalk cliff, created when they cut through the old hill to build the new High Street and flyover, merged with the snow; the white, soft bones of sea creatures, not yet stone, still damp from being buried under fathoms of the heaving abundant sea and the pale temporary solid water that lay on it now.

They got to Georgie's not long after four o'clock. The lift was out of order – which Mel said was a blessing as it stank of piss and the lights didn't always work – so by the time they got to the seventh floor and knocked on her door they were sweaty and red-faced, despite the cold.

"You're here! Come in, come in." Georgie grabbed them both, pulling them close for a hug. "I'm so glad to see you!

I've got presents and a tree and everything!" They followed her down the hall after taking off their coats and boots, past the bathroom into her living room, where a small, green, plastic tree, wound with red and gold tinsel and flashing white lights, took pride of place by the TV. A single bed was pushed up under the large window that looked out over the town, with the river behind running khaki and dangerous like an enemy combatant lying low. A row of patchwork cushions lined the bed, converting it to a sort-of sofa. A breakfast bar separated the living area from the small kitchen area. The whole place was spotless and smelled of fresh paint and air freshener.

"Jesus, this place looks amazing," Mel said, pulling out a couple of presents and tucking them under the tree and then handing the bag to Georgie. "There's some chocolates and a bottle of Bacardi from me mum in there for you."

"Oh bless her, say thanks for me. D'you really like it? I'm saving up to get carpet, so I've just got this for now," Georgie wrinkled a round yellow rug with her pointed foot. "But I painted all the walls meself, and got the bed linen and everything, and..." She turned and walked into the kitchen area. "See, I've got a fridge and a cooker and a washing machine! The social sorted that out and me bed. All brand new an' all." She put the bag on the counter and started opening the kitchen cupboards as if she were a glamour girl displaying prizes on a Saturday night TV show. "A fitted kitchen too."

"It's brilliant," Mel said and Marcus nodded, unsure what to say.

"I've even got some stools so we can sit and eat proper too."

"Perfect."

Georgie poured beer into glasses – there was no way they were drinking from the can in her gaff – and brought through little bowls filled with peanuts and wrapped sweets.

"Wow, this is really nice, Georgie. Thank you."

"Really?" She said, watching Mel's face like a hungry dog.

"Totally. You're a proper hostess."

"Thank you, I wanted to make it all special, me first Christmas in me own place and everything." She sat down on the floor with them and they toasted her flat, and each other.

"Bloody hell, I forgot to put the music on." She jumped up and pressed the switch on her CD player, adjusting the volume until Frank Sinatra crooned the opening lines to White Christmas. "I got the Rat Pack Christmas album, like me mum used to have."

"Nice touch." Mel sipped her beer while Marcus gulped his.

"I love the Rat Pack," he said and belched. The girls laughed.

"Let's have our presents!" Georgie said as she sat back down. Marcus pressed himself back and leaned against the edge of the bed, watching as Georgie unwrapped her present from Melanie.

"Oh my God," she sighed over the tiny figurine of a blue bird with jeweled eyes and outstretched wings, balancing on a twisted wire branch. "It's beautiful." She hugged Mel and turned to place it carefully on the window ledge by her bed. Then she opened the hastily wrapped lavender soap that Marcus had nabbed from his mother's collection of unwanted gifts from his father's faithful old parishioners. "Thanks, Marcus. Nice one."

They watched him open his gifts, Melanie cross-legged and straight-backed, Georgie leaning against Mel, her curls twisting up away from her head. There was a box of liqueur chocolates from Georgie; from Mel, a tiny framed portrait of Kurt Cobain hanging on a silver chain.

"Put it on," Georgie said, kneeling up to help fix the clasp around his neck. He pressed his palm flat against the frame, pressing it against his chest.

"It's great. Thank you." Melanie smiled and winked.

"Your turn," Georgie said and as she moved back to her seat beside Mel she grabbed one of the presents from under the tree and tossed it to Mel.

"Hmmm." She held it up towards the flashing lights and squinted. "What have we here?" She sniffed at it and then shook it gently, her head cocked as if to detect the smallest noise.

"Just open it!" Georgie bounced up and down. "Come on!"

"OK." Mel laughed, but she unwrapped the paper carefully, slowly easing back the tape as if it were of great importance to preserve the wrapping at all cost.

"You're doing me head in, you are such a wind-up!"

Finally, Mel had peeled back all the paper and dropped it to the floor; Georgie grabbed at it and scrunched it up into a tight ball and threw it out towards the kitchen.

"Do you like it?"

Mel turned the small black leather pouch over in her hand. "What it is?"

"It's a manicure kit, silly, look." Georgie took the pouch and undid the fastening on the other side. "See, you've got a nail file, a cuticle thingy, a buffer, some nail oil. Everything you need."

"I don't know how to use it." Mel gazed at the tools Georgie was waving about.

"I'll teach you. Seriously, one thing I've learned now I'm a professional is that you have to be well groomed at all times. It's essential. Look at me hands." She gave Mel the manicure kit back and turned her hands over to show off her perfect grooming. "I even do me toes." She thrust her legs out and wiggled her painted toes, flashing the dolphin tattoo that leaped from the arch of her foot towards her ankle.

"Excellent. We can do Marcus too." She widened her eyes at him. "Professional and well groomed. That's us. Thank you, G. You're a star."

"Now my present for you." He handed her a flat square parcel. "It's pretty obvious what it is so you don't need to sniff it or anything."

"Is it a teddy bear?" Georgie shouted and poured more beer into her glass. "Who needs another drink?"

"Me please." He waggled his empty glass.

"Come on Mel. Drink up."

"I will," she said, gazing down at the present she balanced on the palm of her hands.

"What are you waiting for? Open it!"

He laughed, "Go on. You'll like it."

She looked up at them both. "I know I will, I just want to enjoy this moment, before I know what it is. Just for a second." She closed her eyes for a just a fraction longer than a blink and then ripped the paper back.

"You got it," she whispered. "You remembered." He nodded as she finished pulling off the paper and turning the record over started reading the sleeve. It was the best gift he would ever give anyone.

"What is it?" Georgie twisted forward to read the cover. "Oh, one of your noisy Grunge bands. Nice one, Marcus."

"Bleach. I've wanted this for ages." She smiled at him, her eyes locked on his with such happiness that he could've believed it to be a permanent state of being, a fixed bond between them. Did he believe that that was enough? One present? That one thoughtful action would be enough to sustain a friendship? "I love it."

Not even Georgie's lack of a record player could dim her joy. She kept it on her lap even when the Chinese take-away arrived with the chow mein and Georgie's pork dumplings. She didn't move it when she gave them both a chopsticks lesson and she clutched it to her chest when they played the "Who?" game as the three of them lay in front of the soothing light of the TV, chewing on chocolates handed over from the large tin of Quality Street that Georgie had in her lap.

"Who would you most like to be? It can be anytime, anywhere, but it has to be a real person. One who's been alive. Right?"

"OK. You first then," he said, reclining on Georgie's bed, lolling against the cushions, half-drunk on the weak lager Georgie kept pouring into his glass.

"I would be Princess Di."

"Really? Why?"

"Because she's beautiful, and kind, she's like an angel. She hugs them AIDS patients and that. She even went to Liverpool to visit them football fans in hospital. I love her. And I'd have blonde straight hair – I would love to have blonde straight hair."

"Fair enough," he said. "What about you, Mel?"

"Easy. Kim Gordon. Cool, genius, strong, brilliant. End of story."

"Good choice."

"Who's that then?" Georgie said, getting up and tidying away the foil trays and the scraps of wrapping paper.

"Only the most amazing guitar player and singer on the planet."

"Don't forget songwriter," Melanie chipped in.

"Good point, well made." He raised his glass.

"Oh right, fair enough. Your turn, Marcus, who would you be?"

"I want to be Melanie," he said. Straight out, no hesitation, no umming or ahhing, no false modesty or weighing up the consequences of what he might say. It was the most honest moment of his life, maybe.

"Don't be daft," Georgie said, her round cheeks glowing on/off, on/off with the tree lights. "Someone famous or rich and a man, obviously."

"No," he slurred. "I want to be Mel."

"He can be me if he wants," Mel said and finally finished her glass of beer. "But he can't take back my present."

"Alright then. Weirdoes. Where do you see yourself in five years?"

"Where do I see myself?" Mel stretched her arms over her head, pressing her shoulders up against her ears, and yawned.

"Yeah, your ambitions, you know. Me social worker always asks me this. She says it's crucial to aim high and to have a plan." She undid the cap on the bottle of Bacardi that Mel's mum had sent over.

"What're yours then?"

189

"I've got loads, but the main ones are lose weight, get promoted, get married and have a honeymoon and a white dress, get a house and a garden, and then eventually, after we've had some holidays and saved up some money, I'd have a couple of kids and be a brilliant mum."

"You'll be a brilliant mum, Georgie."

"I will, won't I? I'd never let 'em down, I'd hug 'em and give 'em sweets and dress them beautiful in little Levi's and dresses and Kicker boots. I'd marry a good bloke, with a car and a job. We could live here while we were saving up and I'd never see a social worker ever again."

"Sounds lovely. What about you Marcus?"

Shrugging, he said, "I'm going to be a journalist and expose all the wrongdoing in the world. Move to town, have a flat in Chelsea and a sports car. Something like that."

"No wife or kids?" Georgie asked handing him a tumbler of Bacardi and Coke. A look flashed between him and Mel, almost invisible.

"Yeah, eventually, of course." He slurped the drink and coughed, head swimming.

"I'm going to travel the world, I'm going to dip my toe in every ocean and sea there is," Mel said, standing up and walking over to the window. "And I might not come back." She was still holding the record.

"What about your mum? You can't just leave your family and that. This is where you're from. You'd have to come back eventually, you belong here."

"No I don't. This is just a place, that's all."

"But it's dangerous. What if you get kidnapped by some foreigner? Or catch something from the water? And flying! I tell you what, there's no way I'd bloody get on a plane, what if some nut job blows it up like that Loccurbie bomber? Boom! Just like that – you're scattered in tiny pieces over the ground like bits of rubbish."

"How will you go on honeymoon if you won't fly, then?" he asked.

"We'll go somewhere nice here. Or get the ferry to France. There's no way you'd get me on a plane. I'd scream me head off."

"Well, I'm going as soon as I can," Mel said, leaning her forehead against the glass. "I'd rather be dead than stuck here."

Blue Peter

W hen Mother woke me the next morning I was still flat out on the sofa.

"Have you heard from Callum?" She stood at the end of the couch, looking at me. She seemed a long way away.

"No."

"Well, have you called him?"

"Yes. I've called him."

"I can't understand why he didn't let you know they were coming, he seemed so nice."

"It's his job."

"But why did they come to see you?"

"I told you yesterday. Asking questions about Melanie."

"But why?"

"I don't know, Mother, maybe because you made such a song and dance about our friendship to Detective Inspector McMahon."

"But I don't understand why they need to ask about her now?"

"The body they found, the policeman? He was her stepfather."

"Oh God, that's terrible! Could that have something to do with her going missing?"

"Maybe. The police seem to think so."

"What did you say to them?"

"What could I say? I don't know anything."

"No, of course you don't."

"How could I? It's ridiculous."

"So there's nothing we need to talk about?"

"What do you mean?" I pulled myself up to sit and groaned. My head was pounding.

"Nothing... Just I care very much that you're OK, and—"

"I'm fine. I'm fine. I've got no job, I'm hiding at my mother's, my reputation is in tatters and I might face criminal charges, but I'm fine."

I got up stiff and crooked, my breath thick with stale wine. The room swung and rocked around me, its clutter adding to my nausea. Objects tilted in and out of view: the wilting plant in a pot with dry soil; the small bell, shaped like a lady wearing a crinoline; an oval gilt frame holding a sprig of purple vetch pressed and dried by my mother's sister when she was a little girl, not long before she died of meningitis; a photo of my father in tennis whites, one hand on his hip and the other holding the racquet almost as if it were a cane and he was about to launch into a song and dance routine. He was grinning at the camera, his eyes screwed up against the sun. There was stuff everywhere – clean, recently dusted – but just stuff, dragging us down. Ghosts. I staggered out of the room to be sick, leaving my mother to call after me.

I remember the day my father died. Or I think I do. Blue Peter was on TV and I was sitting on the floor watching. It was summer, and I was wearing black plimsolls with an elastic tongue because I couldn't manage laces. I'd been playing in the garden and had grubby knees. Granny was there and what seemed like a huge crowd of other adults, strangers, were gathering in the study. Someone brought me a glass of squash to drink, but it was too strong and I couldn't swallow it. I wanted my mother. I knew that Daddy was ill and in the hospital, Granny had told me to pray for him when she'd put me to bed the night before. It felt almost like Christmas, or a party: lots of adults standing around talking; the change of routine. I was just a little boy, but some things remain sharp in my memory.

At some point, the bishop – my father's boss – came in and sat on the chair beside me. Simon Groom was reading out a viewer's letter, and a golden retriever sat with him on the Blue Peter sofa.

"Hello Marcus, what's this you're watching?"

"Blue Peter." My throat felt sore and itchy. The room was hot and all the windows were closed.

"So it is. May I turn it off?" He stood and leaned over to turn the switch. The picture disappeared with a buzz. "I need to talk with you."

He squatted down in front of me, a slender man with thick gray hair and a neatly trimmed beard. He was wearing his purple shirt and white collar and black trousers. "Can I sit here?"

I nodded and he lowered himself down to sit almost cross-legged with me, like another little boy. He told me that my father had died, had gone home to Jesus, though I don't really remember the exact words, just his sitting on the floor. But I do remember clearly that he said, "You have to look after your mother now and be brave." Then he patted me on the head before pulling himself up to stand and leaving the room.

When I switched the TV back on, Blue Peter had finished. That upset me more than the news about my father because, I reasoned, surely he wouldn't be long at Jesus's house? Wouldn't he be back soon? I told my mother as much when she came in later to say good night, and she pressed her lips tight together and briefly closed her eyes, before running from the room. Of course, I never mentioned my father coming home again, though I continued to hope for a long time that one day he'd be back, playing the piano, or reading in his study, or in the back garden, waiting to bowl for me, and I wouldn't have to look after Mother any more.

1990

He watched her lift her hand and brush her hair from her forehead, mentally rehearsing the gesture so he could better copy her. He followed her out of the brightly lit library into the dark. He was taller with longer legs, but somehow always a few steps behind, unable to quite catch up, as if the universe went easy on her and made shortcuts through space just for her.

Her smile was warm in his guts, keeping out the chill. He'd said, "You're my best friend," because she'd asked him why he was always so good to her, so kind.

"No matter what?" she'd said.

"Yes, of course."

"Unconditionally, no limits?"

"Absolutely. No doubt."

"Honestly? I'm hard to love you know."

"No you're not! Who told you that?"

"My mother says so."

"She doesn't know what she's talking about."

"What if I killed someone? Would I still be your best friend then?"

He laughed. "You won't kill someone, but yep, even then."

He didn't notice the shadow of a bruise under her skin or the blank look on her face.

All These Questions

I drove back to see Charlie, checking that no one was following me. They weren't as far as I could tell, but it was hard to know. It was possible they were switching cars or changing who was watching me. It was possible that no one was watching, I understand that and I understood it then, maybe, though it's hard to remember precisely. I'd had no response from Neil Mason or anyone else. Nobody wanted to touch the story: it and I were dead, finished. Even David was ignoring my calls and my source had vanished without a trace.

I parked and sprinted up the concrete slope to the door. The warden was standing there, as if she was waiting for me, as if she knew I was coming. She opened the door and I stepped inside.

"Back for Charlie?" I nodded. "Best come with me."

She had thin legs, spindly really, and had that awkward gait of a wading bird, knock kneed and flat footed, raising the knee and placing the foot down as if climbing an invisible stair. I followed her into her office.

"Take a seat."

I sat. Her desk was neat, an ashtray half-full of butts (against the rules, though she had the appearance of someone who upheld all rules), a phone and a desk diary sat alongside a photo of her and what I presumed was her family of husband and two teenage kids. A row of numbered hooks organized the spare keys to the residents' flats. There was no visitors' book visible. She unclipped a small black device from her waistband and put it on the desk. She noticed me looking. "The receiver for the residents' alarms."

"Oh, yes." I nodded.

"So, Charlie. I have some bad news, I'm afraid."

"Is he alright?"

"He had another stroke. A serious one this time, I'm afraid. He's in the hospital but they don't think he'll recover. I'm so sorry."

"When?"

"Sorry?"

"When did this happen?"

"Right, yesterday afternoon, not long after the police had been to see him. He was obviously upset, poor old dear. Why they bothered an old man I can't imagine. Dreadful."

"What did they want?"

"How should I know? They wouldn't speak to me. Just barged in."

"How long did they stay?"

"At least an hour or so, I'd say, around lunchtime. Disturbed all the residents, of course."

"And they didn't speak to you?"

"No. You're as bad as they are. All these questions."

"But you said they didn't ask you any."

"They didn't, you know what I mean."

"Did you speak to Charlie after they'd gone? Did he say anything?"

She squinted at me, assessing my criminal potential. "I didn't see Charlie again until I responded to his alarm call. Then I found him, on the floor, when he was beyond chatting, let me tell you. It was awful."

"Of course it was. I'm sorry."

"It's funny, he's had nobody visit him for years, then all of a sudden you all turn up. You, the police and that other fella; no wonder he had a turn. Probably too much for him."

"What other fella?"

"Another old friend came, after the police had gone. You're all creeping out the woodwork now, it seems."

"Did he give you his name or anything?"

"No, he didn't. And I'm not sure I'd tell you if he did."

"So he didn't sign the visitors' book?"

"What visitors' book?" She shifted in her chair, turning to face me full on. "What's going on here? This seems a bit fishy to me."

"I'm sorry, you're right. I'm in shock that's all. He was fine when I saw him and I'm just trying to get my head around it."

She nodded, she understood: I was shocked, upset. It's natural. "Right then, I don't suppose you know of any of Charlie's friends or family? We don't have anyone listed in his file, you see, and we need a next of kin."

"I don't, I'm sorry."

"Well, at least he isn't suffering. It happened so fast, he wouldn't have felt a thing."

"How can you tell? Sorry, stupid question."

It struck me that Charlie would've wanted to know, to face up to what was coming. I can't imagine anything more demeaning for a man like Charlie, to be blindsided by a stroke like that. A coward's way out, ignorant and mute. I rolled my lips into in a sad unsmile.

She softened. Patted my hand.

"What happens now?"

"Well, if no family are found, then there are procedures the social services and the hospital follow and in the event of his death, the council will step in. Do you want to leave your name and contact details so we can let you know?"

"No, it's OK. I'm leaving soon anyway. I just wanted to see him while I was here."

"I understand," she said, hardening again, used to this: the feckless, criminal friends of the lonely elderly. "At least you got to say goodbye."

"True. I'd best go."

"Right you are, take care."

I left and she didn't follow me, nor was she watching when I got in the car. That was it then, if Charlie couldn't speak, or didn't recover. It was over. There were no other witnesses, no one else to tell tales. But what had Charlie told the police?

I started the engine, put the car in gear and then slid it back to neutral. Killed the engine. What if I was sent there to cover this story because someone knew what happened? What if it wasn't coincidence but part of setting me up, destroying me, finishing the job? I dropped my head on the steering wheel. Think, think, think. Who? Edward? But how could he know about Melanie? About Charlie? I opened up the glove box to check on the locket. It was still there. It had to be a warning. What the fuck was happening to me?

I tried to slow my breathing and calm down. Told myself I was stressed, anxious. Things just happen sometimes, fate, luck, life. I swallowed hard. I looked around: there was the care home, solid red bricks, net curtains, fire escapes. There were cars, metal, heavy and durable. There were birds in the trees; a pigeon tapped at the pavement. I was the only thing that wasn't solid; I was the thing that was warping the world. Slow down, I told myself. Slow down. What could Charlie have said to them?

I phoned my solicitor.

"It's good you called," she said, cool, calm, expansive. "I've not been able to get hold of you."

"Yeah, I've been keeping my head down."

"Just as well."

"Any more news from the Sentinel?" Sweat was pouring from me, so I turned the ignition and flicked the air-con on high.

"No, no change there."

"There's another thing."

"Which is?"

"The story I should be covering, down here."

"The dead policeman in the orchard, I've heard about that. What about it?"

"Did you? How? Who told you about it?"

"Yes, it's on the news, Marcus." Deadpan. She sounded honest. Of course she did, I paid her to sound honest.

"Is it? Right. Well I might be involved, or I think they're going to make it look like I was."

"What?" She sounded less calm and cool. "Are you involved?"

"No, I don't think so."

"You don't think so?"

"It was a long time ago."

"So how are you involved?"

"I knew his step-daughter."

"And? I don't follow."

"Neither do I, just really odd things are happening. I think I'm being set up."

She sighed. "Have you spoken to Edward or another journalist and intimated that you are going to pursue the St. Clair article?"

"No, I haven't spoken to anyone. I emailed a couple of people, but they didn't reply."

"I made it very clear you weren't to talk to anyone." Her voice rose in pitch as if it was being squeezed through the line.

So did mine, as if I was trying to harmonize with her. "I want to clear my name. This is my life. My life. Anyway, why is that relevant now?"

"I didn't say it was. I just want you to do as I tell you and sit tight and speak to no one. I'll call you later, when I can. Alright?"

"Fine." I hung up.

Princess Diana's death made my career. Put me on the map. I was in Paris, covering a nothing story about an aging actor and his latest project as a restaurateur and professional gourmand. It's fair to say that up to that point I'd not quite lived up to my promise: in the words of my editor I lacked the guts to chase down a story, and I was hanging on by the skin of my teeth writing fluff pieces, desperate to keep the job for as long as possible. Edward meanwhile was rising to the top and it was Edward who called me at two in the morning, his voice gruff and salty.

"Where are you?" he said.

"In bed. What's up?" I was in the cheap hotel the paper had booked for me, foggy from the really cheap bottle of red I'd had at dinner.

"Still in Paris?"

"Yes, I'm back tomorrow."

"Princess Diana has been in an accident, a serious one. Get to the Salpêtrière hospital now."

"Are you sure?" I sat up, my head spinning, the air conditioning hissing in the background.

"Yes, I'm fucking sure! A contact in the French police just called me. Now do you want the fucking story or not?"

"Of course I do, I just—"

"Marcus, just get there." The line went dead.

I was in the right place at the right time, I knew the right people. I know, weary old tropes. But there I was, a serious journalist at last, waiting in a hospital corridor as police, doctors, diplomats and officials hurried back and forth, gleaning the details I needed to file a respectful but detailed piece about the tragic circumstances of Princess Diana's death before anyone in the UK had woken up. Quickly followed by an exclusive interview with a source close to the Al Fayeds, and then I wrote my piece, Pride and Protocol, about the public's fury at the Palace's lack of evident mourning and I was in. Reputation established, feet firmly under the table.

Even Edward congratulated me for my "knack for knowing just what the punters want, for reading the crowd." But I can't really claim that investigative accolade. Visiting my mother when I got back from Paris, I talked to Joyce. Royalist to the core and seething with anger at the Queen, she rocked back and forth on her feet: "You should tell 'em. Write it down in the papers. You tell 'em it ain't good enough to hide away in them palaces of theirs. They should honor that poor girl. She's worth more than the lot of 'em put together." So I did. I put it in the paper. Dumb luck, opportunity, connections, whatever you call it: how was I ever going to top that?

Memory, if we're honest, is a servile, biased little beast, delivering up half-remembered scenes that cast, at the very least, a flattering light over even the worst moments. In my experience, one is either the hero or the victim in the reconstituted fragments we assemble as our memories, making significance out of coincidence, tying up loose ends, connecting the dots. Memory creates a story out of random events, a plot with a beginning, middle and end, scenes and a climax, dramas and tragedy. We hunt like toothy little animals for patterns, for meaning, scurrying about gathering our special tales to line our nests and keep us warm at night. Mel taught me that, but I paid no attention. It's what I'd spent my life doing.

April 1990

"She was fucking her mother's boyfriend."

"No way!"

"Yeah. Her mum came in from work, and there she was, giving him a blow job on the sofa."

"How do you know?"

"Her mum told my Auntie Jan. She kicked her out then and there – naked in the street."

"Yeah, that's what I heard. Naked in the street, screaming her head off. Covered in blood. My brother saw her running towards the old people's home."

"I heard her real dad was an Indian bloke, with a turban and everything."

"No way!"

"Seriously."

"That would explain a lot."

"It's not the first time, neither."

"What ain't?"

"She fucked her mother's husband before. He's got a BMW, he gave her lifts to school. Bold as brass."

"Didn't she lose her virginity to Darren Shine's older brother when she twelve?"

"Wouldn't surprise me. Paki slag!"

"I ain't seen him around neither."

"Who?"

"Darren."

"Nah, working with his brother now. Lucky cunt."

"She right reckoned herself, didn't she though? I went to Infants and Juniors with her and she was the same then. Weird. Too clever for her own good."

"I heard the police were coming in to interview us all."

"No way! Here? In class?"

"Yep."

They were laughing, four of them, hunched over their fags and cans of Lilt and bottles of Tippex thinner in the pale spring light on the grass behind the science block. Three girls and a boy gathered ten feet away to his right. Marcus sat with his back to a tree, a book in his lap, unnoticed by them as they continued their nasty little story.

"Whatever happened, she was asking for it."

"Yeah. She's a whore."

"Do you think she'll come back?"

"Fuck no! She wouldn't dare. Everyone knows what she's done."

"To her own mum an' all."

He got up and walked away. There was sniggering and a burst of laughter behind him but he didn't look back, just kept going until he was climbing up the three flights of stairs to the school library. Library was a pretty grandiose title for the place. It was barely bigger than a classroom and the few shelves held little more than set textbooks and one or two Catherine Cookson novels. After nodding at the librarian, he sat at a desk near the back and pulled out his books. There was no one else in the room. He crossed his arms on the desk and laid his head on them, careful not to catch his cheek on his watch. The swelling had gone down but it was still sore, and the bruises on his ribs and stomach were only just fading to a sick yellowy-green. Those kids were right about one thing: Melanie wouldn't be back. Not after what he'd done.

River View

T he phone rang and rang and rang, an old fashioned trill that I hadn't changed. I ignored it, waiting for my solicitor to call back. I'd driven out of town, out past the industrial estate and into a newly created park with cycle routes and a kid's play area and long walks marked out with signage and arrows and accessible pathways. I parked by the river, watching the water drag at the mud banks. I wondered how long I could stay afloat out there. It had finally clouded over, raw-edged stacks billowing up and out into the atmosphere, blocking the sun. My phone rang again and I turned it over to look at the screen, but didn't recognize the number. The ringing was replaced by the chime of an incoming text message: MARCUS, ANNA HERE. I CAN HELP YOU, I KNOW WHAT THEY'RE DOING TO YOU. CALL ME.

She answered immediately. "Where are you?"

"River View Park."

"Sounds gloomy."

"It is. So what do you know?"

"Let's meet, I'll come over to you. Wait by your car."

"OK. Anna, how did you get my number?" But she'd already disconnected.

She pulled up twenty minutes later in a sleek Prius, just as the rain started, the fat warm drops slick on the hard ground. I got in her car, making room for my feet in the pile of food cartons and drinks cans on the floor. She was wearing the same clothes she'd worn at the press conference, her hair in a knot on her head. She looked healthy and young, despite her diet of fast food and fizzy drinks. I was like her once, impervious and fearless. I think I was anyway.

"Thanks for coming," I said.

"Sure. You alright? You look terrible."

"Tired, that's all. There's a lot going on."

"Yes, I've heard. Can I get you anything? There's a café out near the play park."

"No, it's all right." I waited for her to speak. She cleared her throat. I watched as another car pulled up alongside us, but it was just a mother with a couple of small kids.

"So, you've been fired?"

"Yes."

"It's not true though, is it, about the article? You didn't invent or exaggerate the evidence?"

"Of course I fucking didn't. What do you think I am?"

"I know, I had to ask. I'd really like to tell your side of it all, right some wrongs for you. I'd like to help." The car doors slammed shut next to us and the woman walked her mewling kids towards the play area, in spite of the rain. Desperation. "Pardon?" Anna said.

"Nothing. I didn't say anything."

"I thought I heard you say... Never mind. Let me help you."

"I can't talk about it. I'm not allowed." The rain had stopped.

"Just give me your source, I'll do the rest."

I almost laughed in her face.

"Listen, this isn't easy. I respect you. You know that, right? And I want to help you, God knows you need it and I really do want to help. But, there's more to all this, isn't there?"

"Of course there is, they're setting me up. They know I'm right."

"Maybe, but I don't think anyone will listen to you, not now, not unless you tell them where you got your information. The government has just announced massive new investment and jobs up North, it's a triumph apparently. I'm surprised you haven't heard."

"I've been avoiding the news. Anyway, what does that have to do with me?"

"It's all funded by the St. Clair group: hundreds of new jobs, urban renewal, reinvigoration. "Britain Reclaims Manufacturing Glory," I think that was the Sentinel's headline. Lord Sunbury is a hero. You can forget about proving your corruption theory now, I doubt even The Whistler will run it along with all the other nut job stories."

"Are you taking the piss? Is this true?"

"Absolutely. But you have other things to worry about, don't you?"

"Like?"

"Like Detective Burrell and your involvement in his murder."

"What?" My head felt like it was being crushed in a fist. I couldn't breathe: suffocating in her cramped car; the crap everywhere, her perfume too strong for such a small space, the rasp of her breathing. "Who said that?"

"I heard it from the police, actually."

"The police?"

"Yes."

"What the fuck is going on? Is this a conspiracy?"

"I thought you said there wasn't any conspiracy? 'Conspiracy theories are for the ignorant,' didn't you write that? I'm sure you did."

"Don't play games."

"I want to help you."

"Like fuck, why are you doing this? I can't believe it."

"This is my job. You know that, this is the world we live in. You help me and I help you. Quid pro quo. A story for a story. I'm following a lead."

What was it Melanie said? Something about my needing romance and glamour and rags. She said I romanticized everything, that it wasn't enough for me that life was mostly ordinary. Yes, she said that. Telling stories as if that will contain the mess of life. Stories.

"Marcus?" Anna clicked her fingers in front of my face.

"What?" I could see her, sitting cross-legged in my room, her face in shadow, hidden. Her voice remained. She'd warned me.

"Did you kill Burrell?"

I shook my head.

"Did you kill him?"

"Fuck you." I reached for the door.

"So, no then?" she said as I pulled myself out of the car. Dizzy, unbalanced, the ground shifting under me. I staggered, out of synch with gravity, back to my car. Behind me, Anna rolled down her window, "I'm sorry Marcus. Really. And I'm sorry to hear about your old friend Charlie. Let's hope he makes it." She reversed out and pulled away.

I got in the car, positive that I was being watched. I locked the door and used the mirrors to check around me. I didn't want them to know that I knew. I had to get out of there carefully, without arousing suspicion. I checked the glove compartment for the locket. It was still there; they hadn't moved it again. I could feel them watching, perhaps they were in the trees. Perhaps they had bugged the car and were listening. A helicopter chipped at the air above me, then angled out in the direction of the North Sea and shrank from view.

It was that easy to break me, that easy to disorient me like a blindfolded child at a party game. I wasn't the person I'd always believed I was. We are a tale we tell ourselves: editing, adding, mythologizing, and of course we do it to each other too. It's hard now to imagine why I believed so completely in my ability to be objective, to see the truth and only the truth; it took me all that time to realize that I only saw what I wanted to, what served me. Perhaps that is an admission of guilt. But at that point I was the subject in another author's narrative and I was afraid, and lost.

So I called Callum. I called him at the station, getting put through from the switchboard, so he'd have to take my call. I called him because if the police had told Anna that they suspected me, or if Charlie had told them what had happened, and they knew that Anna was meeting me, which I believed they did, or would, then if I didn't call it would be obvious that I knew. I might've been losing my mind, but I knew how this works. I'd upset the wrong people and they were out to get me. There would be no escape.

"What have you said to the Press?"

"Marcus? Is that you?"

"What have you said?"

"What are you talking about?"

"Don't play games, Callum. I've just seen Annabelle Walker from the Messenger. She told me that I'm your suspect. She asked me if I'm a murderer."

"Marcus, whoa! Slow down. What are you talking about? I don't know anyone called Annabelle."

"She's a journalist from the Messenger and she was at the press conference with me when we met."

"With you? I don't remember her."

"Well it doesn't fucking matter, what matters is she said the police had told her I was a suspect."

"She said what? When?"

"Just now. She was very clear she had information from you."

"Wait, wait let me talk to someone about this. I'll get to the bottom of it and call you back, alright? What was her name again?" I told him and he disconnected the phone. He sounded genuinely disconcerted, but I couldn't be sure. What had Charlie told them? There couldn't be anything to tie me to Steve. How could there be? I turned the ignition, and pumped the gas pedal, the car revving, a big, normal sound. I drove.

Trying to put the details of that night in order. Evidence. Actions. Consequences. Was there any evidence? Had we covered our tracks? I couldn't think. I couldn't remember. It was all so long ago, and I was innocent. I'd done nothing wrong.

Callum called back just as I arrived back at my mother's, sounding worried, calm. Genuine.

"Are you OK?"

"Not really. I want to know what's going on."

"I called the Messenger and they say there's no Annabelle working there, they've never heard of her and they've sent no one to speak to you. No one has said anything to the press, Marcus. Alright?"

"I spoke to her just forty minutes ago. Face to face."

"If you say so."

"I do say so. I was just sitting in her car. I'm sure your surveillance team can corroborate that."

"My what team? Marcus, you're not making any sense. Are you sure you are OK?"

"I'm fine. I just need someone to be straight with me, because nothing adds up. How did she get my number for a start?"

"Right. Listen to me. You're under a lot of stress, right now. Come into the station tomorrow and we can sort all this out? Come in around two p.m. Yes?" I could hear the din of an office behind him: voices, clatter, keyboards tick-tacking.

"Why tomorrow? Why not now? What do you need to do before then?"

"Marcus, get some rest. Come tomorrow, we'll talk then."

"I can't tell you anything else though. I don't know anything about Steve Burrell."

"Tomorrow, OK? Then it will all be over."

"Yeah," I said. Everyone was lying. Everyone.

"Go home and rest. Take care."

He'd gone. Everyone was lying. But those were the facts, as I thought I knew them.

February 1990

"I've bought us tickets to the Valentine's Day disco."

"That's so funny. Do you have any idea how tacky they are? A disco ball and flashing lights set up in the school hall with a dodgy DJ and the teachers watching our every move."

"It will be fun!" He took the maths textbook from her lap and flicked back a few pages, read the pencil notes she'd jotted in the margin and handed it back to her. "Take our minds off all this revision."

"You're not wrong there." She sat up straight and flexed her spine, pressing her belly and chest out like a sail caught in the wind. Stretching her arms up overhead. "I'm hungry."

"What do you want? I'll get us something."

"I don't mind, anything. Surprise me."

When he walked back into the study, the tray of cheese on toast and bourbon biscuits balancing on one arm, she was standing by the window staring out at the garden.

"The most important thing we need to decide now, of course," she said, turning around, "is what to wear to this night of debauchery."

Mel wore two white lacy slips, one over the other, that she'd bought from the charity shop for fifty pence each, with black tights, pink stiletto heels and a tweed jacket. He wore loose jeans, a t-shirt with Elvis on that Mel had customized by sewing a bow tie under Elvis's chin, and gray suede Vans that Mel had chosen for him, his Kurt Cobain necklace around his throat. They both had black eyeliner smudged around their eyes and sticky coats of mascara clumped on their lashes. They were standing outside the off-license in the cold, waiting for a willing adult to take their ten-pound note and buy four cans of Tennent's Super and a packet of fags. They'd already asked a couple of blokes, one old enough to be their dad, his belly hanging below his jumper, and one in his twenties with long hair in a ponytail. They both said no, though the old bloke had at least given them a fag each and asked Mel if she had a boyfriend.

They were about to give up when Darren Shine pulled up in his brother's car, Happy Mondays blaring from the stereo. He wound down the window and turned the volume down.

"What're you two doing?"

As always Marcus looked to Mel for direction and she shook her head at him, no.

"Waiting for someone to get us some beer," Marcus said. Mel tutted and blew smoke from her nostrils in two long thin streams.

"What?" Darren said as he squinted through the orange haze of the street lamp.

"We want beer, and don't have ID." Mel snapped. She was starting to shiver.

"You got cash?" Darren got out the car, leaving the engine running and walking over.

"Of course."

"What do you want then?"

"What does it matter? You're not old enough to get it, you're not old enough to drive that car." Mel chucked her cigarette on the ground and crossed her arms tight over her chest.

"You're freezing. Wait in the car and I'll get you your drink."

"Are you sure?" Fed-up and freezing Marcus was willing to risk trusting Shine, even if Mel wasn't.

"Yep."

He looked at Mel but she just shrugged her shoulders and turned away.

"OK. Four cans of Super T and a packet of B&H please." He gave him the cash.

"Right. Get in the car then, I won't be a minute."

They climbed into the souped-up VW Golf, Mel in the back, Marcus in front. An exhaust pipe fit for a Ferrari throbbed and shook under them, warping the go-faster stripes stuck on the paintwork. A pink plastic rosary dangled from the rear-view mirror.

"This is not a good idea."

"It's fine. He's being nice. Anyway, we weren't getting anywhere waiting outside were we?"

"No, I suppose you're right." Clutching her hands around her knees, she looked like a little girl. A little girl dressed in her mother's petticoats playing at being a woman. But then she pushed her hair back over her shoulders and turned towards him, the streetlight catching the curve of her cheek and lip. She seemed so much older to him then, as if none of this was new to her, or that's how he felt, while he was excited, nervous, buying booze, going out and dressing up. Sitting in the car, the heater blowing hot dusty air in his face, waiting for Darren.

"Alright?" He yanked the door open and passed over a carrier bag with the beer. "Your change is in there." He slid into the driver's seat and revved the engine. "So where now?" He turned to Mel in the back and reached his arm across the back of the front seats. A large gold sovereign ring almost covered the knuckle of his little finger.

"We're going to the Valentine's thing at school. You?" Marcus could smell his Kouros aftershave mixed with the scent of washing powder on his clothes. The gristly machine of his heart pumped hard in his chest, like a piston in a cartoon blowing steam.

"Supposed to be meeting Jenny there, ain't I? Let's drive up the back of the barracks, drink this lot and then go up the school. Yeah?"

"What about the gavvers?"

"What about them?"

"If we get pulled you'll be in trouble."

"Nah, we won't get pulled. They'll think it's me brother, and everyone loves him."

It was true. Darren's brother was local celebrity, an amateur boxing champ about to turn pro. He was always in the papers, posing with his belts or his blonde girlfriend or with a massive cheque that he was donating to the kid's home or the police benevolent fund. Darren was right: they were safe in the reflected glow of his brother, Mikey. As long as they didn't piss Mikey off, that is.

The old army barracks was up on top of the hill overlooking the town and the wide turn of the river as it opened up into the estuary. Built for the Napoleonic war and left vacant and boarded up in the 1970s, the crumbling brick walls were topped with rusty razor wire. It stood next to common land, mostly used by dog walkers and kids. At night it was used by older kids to fuck and drink and get stoned. It was a part of town that was new to Marcus, despite living there all his life, like pretty much everything since he'd started at Danner Comp.

The moon was high and full, but in the murky sky it was as gelid and sticky as egg white, casting almost no light. He opened the beer and Darren turned the music up.

"D'you like this band?"

"Yeah, it's alright." He began nodding his head in time with the beat.

"What about you, Melanie?" Darren had twisted in his seat to look at her, draping his arm across the seats again, his fingertips close to Marcus's neck.

"Primal Scream ain't bad. I like this one, it's catchy."

"You both like that American grunge shit, don't ya?" He pressed his shoulders back into the seat and raised his hips, pushing his right hand into the pocket of his jeans and pulling out a small plastic bag.

"Yeah," Marcus said, "But I like this too."

"Yeah, this lot are proper up for it, not ponces," he said, then leaned over to the glove box and took out a torn packet of Rizlas. He extracted two sheets and licked one, his thick tongue sliding down one edge, before sticking the sheets together at right angles. Marcus gawped as he rubbed his fingers together at the tip of a cigarette, leaving a line of tobacco on the middle of the rolling paper. Then he looked back at Mel to see if she was shocked too, but she was looking out the window, her head nodding to the beat, a can of beer in her hand.

Pinching his thumb and index finger together, Darren sprinkled the weed onto the tobacco just like Marcus's mother added herbs to her stew. He almost laughed at the domesticated little gesture, but held it in, pressing his lips together. Darren picked the papers up between both thumbs and fingers and began rolling the spliff back and forth, getting it tighter and cylindrical. Back and forth, back and forth he rolled, then he tried to tuck one edge under so he could roll it up, but it wouldn't work. Back and forth, back and forth, he tried again and again.

"Fuck! Hands are too fucking cold. You do it," he said, extending his warm hands in Marcus's direction.

"I don't know how to," he blushed.

"Pass it over," Mel said and took it in one hand. "And the Rizlas, these are worn out."

She laid the scrappy lump of papers and weed in her lap, extracted the Rizlas, licked and stuck them together in a second, put the fresh geometric papers in her lap, tipped the weed and tobacco into one hand, picked up the Rizlas, transferred the mixture back into the papers and had the whole thing rolled up and licked shut in a couple of seconds. She finished by tearing a piece of the Rizla packet off and rolling it into a filter and pushed it into the end.

"There you go." She handed it to Darren.

"Shit! Not bad. You get first go, you rolled it." He held it up and admired the perfect joint that she'd made, then handed it back with a lighter.

"Not for me." She shook her head, widened her eyes at Marcus and drank her beer.

"Suit yourself." Darren lit up and sucked on the spliff, its bright cherry swelling and contracting with his breath. He handed it to Marcus, his fingers soft at the tips. Darren was one of those kids with rich fathers – builders, plumbers, mechanics – who'd done well under Maggie, bought big houses, had nice cars, wives who didn't have to work, holidays in Florida and a timeshare in Spain. But they still went to the same pub every Friday and considered themselves down to earth, unpretentious. They'd moved off the estate – but only just. Their kids had everything – designer label clothes, box-fresh trainers, new cars and could even go to University – but woe betide them being queer or marrying anyone different or getting ideas above their station. Richer than Marcus and his family, they still thought that he and his kind were posh, not to be trusted. But sitting there, Marcus thought Darren was more than that: tough like his brothers and father, yes, but also funny and generous, warm. He was sexy.

He took a drag, a tiny one and held it in, like Darren had, as if he were holding a lungful of oxygen underwater; his lungs burned. As he exhaled, managing to keep it a small cough, his head filled with the most amazing and hilarious weight. He handed it back to Darren and watched him as he drew deeper on the joint and tipped his head back on the neck rest of his seat.

"Turn the light off. It's a buzz kill," Mel said from the back.

"Yes, ma'am," Darren said, his voice suddenly softer. He reached up and clicked off the interior light, then swapped the CD in the player for another one. "When I buy a car I'll get one with a Changer in the boot."

"Cool," Marcus said, not really knowing what he meant. He sipped his beer and looked at Darren in the soft glow of the dashboard lights. With the door sealed, in the dark, and the dope, it felt as if they were as remote and secluded from the rest of the world as a chick in an egg. Safe and entirely alone on the planet, alone under that sticky moon, he was in paradise.

In profile, Darren's face was noble, his full lips pressed together under his nose like a prince on the side of a coin. His right elbow was propped on the window edge of the car door, his right hand just hanging there in front of his face, the fingers scissored around the joint, ready to bring it to his lips. Then he turned to Marcus and he swigged his beer fast to cover the direction of his gaze.

"There you go, have a toke on that." Darren passed the joint to him again. This time the smoke was hotter and singed his mouth and throat as he gulped it down. He gagged and spluttered, almost puking. Darren banged and then patted his back while taking the joint from between his fingers. "Whoa there, keep it down, tiger."

Marcus sat back up, his skin raw from his touch. "You alright?" He nodded and sipped more beer, concentrating on breathing.

The bass line of the music kicked in and Darren turned the volume up. In the back Melanie said, "I love this tune – I need to dance, c'mon shift. Let me out please."

Darren opened his door, got out and moved his seat, letting her slide out. He thought she'd break the seal on this perfection and let the rest of the world in, but she didn't. Darren wound down the windows and turned on the headlights, and she danced in the pale granular beam in front of them, their world expanding but still hermetic, still safe from harm.

They watched her dancing, raising her hands above her head, twisting them as if she were gathering the air to her body. Her hips swayed and curled. She was beautiful, of course. Unselfconscious, dancing for herself, singing the words, not caring what anyone else thought. Dancing under the hard chemical light of the stars. She wasn't afraid, that was the difference; the difference between her and the rest of them. She faced everyone and everything openly, with a smile. That's not to say she was naive or innocent, not at all. He guessed it was love. She loved. It's fear that destroys, destroys everything. She was better than him. Better than everyone. She deserved better. She deserved more.

"You like her a lot, don't you?" Darren had put the joint in the ashtray, letting it go out and opened another can of beer.

"Yeah. I do. I think she's amazing."

"You sound a bit like her you know?"

"Do I?"

"Yeah, it's weird, like you're becoming her or something. You even move like her." He raised his hand and flicked it as he tossed his head, imitating perfectly the gesture they made to dismiss an idea or thought or conversation. He was spot on.

"Do I really?"

"Yep. It's normal I suppose. We all do it; we all copy each other, don't we? I guess it's how we learn to talk and that. Are you really seeing each other?"

"Of course." He finished his beer and opened another, Darren drained his second and popped open his third.

"OK. If you say so."

Melanie disappeared into the dark and reappeared at the door singing, "I wanna be adored."

Darren laughed and ruffled her hair, "You're adored. Like the Stone Roses, do you?"

"I do actually. What's the time?"

"Don't know, why?"

"I think we've missed the disco, you guys," she grinned.

"Fuck the disco."

"But what about Jennifer?" She leaned forward resting her arms on the window edge, her face so close to Darren's he could kiss her and for a moment it looked like he would; they stared at each other for a second and Marcus's stomach contracted with jealousy. But for whom? For both. He wanted them both for himself.

"Fuck Jenny."

"Let me in then," she said and climbed in over Darren, sliding between the seats, singing to herself.

"What shall we do now?" Marcus said, wanting to stay right here, but not like that, not the three of them. For the first time since he'd met her, he wanted Mel to leave. She was in the way.

"Let's stay, drink more, smoke more."

"No, I'm going to go home I think," she said.

"Really? Don't go."

"Yeah. I should."

"Then we'll drop you home."

"Really? You'd do that?"

"Yeah. Can't have you wandering the streets at night." Darren turned the ignition of the car and it roared into life.

"OK. Thanks Darren."

They drove her home in under ten minutes. She made Darren pull up at the end of her road so her mother wouldn't see her get out of a car; she kissed them both on the mouth as if it was the most natural thing in the world.

"Bye, chaps." She saluted, turned away, fading out of view, then reappearing under a street light and shutting herself inside the house.

"Was she drunk?"

"I don't think so, she only had one can of beer."

"She's a wild one."

"Maybe."

"Where now then?" Darren said.

"I don't care." He laughed, drunk, stoned and flirting with the most dangerous boy in his school or maybe even the town, but who measures these things?

So it began. In an empty car park, they finished the joint, drank the rest of the beer and then somehow there was Darren's tongue and hot mouth, his hand on the back of his neck. His body, stronger than Marcus, bigger, but soft and fragile too. The curve of his spine as it arced towards his bottom, the hair curling over his ears, his hands grabbing him, holding him, pushing him. Soft whispers and laughter, their secret, their precious beautiful secret.

Then it carried on: parked up on farmland at the edge of town; in deserted garages; the school playing field; his dad's office surrounded by tea mugs, filing cabinets and pictures of page three girls. Driving up to London in a borrowed car, taking E, going to Heaven and dancing, bodies pressing, sweating, shirts off, surrounded by other men kissing, holding each other, belonging.

His face, almost crying when he came. It probably lasted a month, maybe a little more, but it was the most intense, exquisite time of his life. For that short time, Marcus was completely himself. No pretense, no lies, no stories. Just himself.

Marks and Spencer

M other was in the kitchen when I walked in, the phone in her hand. She watched me, a suspicious look on her face. "Marcus, are you OK?"

"No, I'm not."

"What's going on? I've just had a call..."

"Did you know about Sunbury and the jobs?" Her face was a pale round blank.

"I don't know what you're talking about, calm down."

"Fuck! Just be straight with me. Did you know about St. Clair and Sunbury creating all these new jobs, creating a new economic dawn or some bullshit?"

She stood in the doorway, watching me.

"You knew, didn't you?" She nodded.

"Why didn't you fucking tell me? I don't stand a chance now, not a chance, and the fucking police want to question me for murder." I bumped my fist against my head to stop the buzzing in my brain.

"Marcus! Stop, you'll hurt yourself!" She was crying.

"Mum, be quiet. I just need to think."

"But you're not yourself. Please just stop for a minute."

"You don't seem to understand. I'm losing everything, Mother. Everything. So stop the hysterics and leave me alone."

"Please don't shout, Marcus." She looked afraid; I don't think I'd ever frightened her before and at that moment I didn't care.

"I'm not shouting." I felt faint and leaned against the wall, head spinning.

"Darling, please. Let me help you. Why don't you go take a shower, have a shave, maybe take a nap and we'll talk when you feel more like yourself."

"Are you part of all this?"

"What, darling? Part of what?"

I shook my head. I thought: I can retell this, move the narrative in a different direction. I just need to take control again. It's my story, not theirs. I need to rearrange the order, the facts. I believed I could.

"Nothing, I'm fine; I'm just upset and stressed. Over-reacting."

"I understand. That's OK."

As I moved past her, she reached out for my hand and held on for a second, but I kept moving, pulling my hand from her grasp. She didn't follow.

Mother was in the study, reading the paper as if nothing had happened.

"What does it say about St. Clair and Sunbury?"

"Only what you already know." She'd been hiding the paper every time the Sentinel and St. Clair was mentioned, for my own good I suppose. I hadn't told her not to, either.

"I'm sorry I didn't tell you, I just didn't want to upset you more."

"I'm the one who should be sorry, Mum. I came to stay for a day or so and I've brought nothing but trouble with me. It's a bloody mess."

She folded the paper and pushed her glasses up on to the top of her head, scraping her hair back into short gray spikes like a silver crown. "I'm so worried, darling. Why won't you let me in? Please, talk to me." She patted the sofa beside her. "Come on, sit with me."

She's hiding something, I thought. But she's my mother. That was all there had ever really been, her and me; all I remembered of my father was a sickly man, stooped over his desk, a ghost. My memories of him are false, informed by photos and stories I've been told. I walked over to the window, where it was cooler, clearer.

"Are you sure you can't find a way to sort this out?"

"I don't think so."

"Can't you tell them who told you about it all?"

"It won't help, and it doesn't matter any more."

"Why not? If you've got nothing to hide, then tell them."

"What do you mean, 'if' I've got nothing to hide?"

"Nothing, it's just a figure of speech. Callum phoned, he's worried about you too."

"Is he really?"

"Yes. He said to make sure you go to the station tomorrow, he sounded genuinely concerned."

"What did you say to him?"

"Nothing."

"Are you sure? Did he ask you anything?"

"No, just if you were OK, that's all. He cares."

"Mum, don't be naïve. This is about his murder case: he's been using me for information. Getting close to me, using me, using you."

"What information?"

"It doesn't matter."

"Why won't you talk to me? Let me help. Whatever it is you've done, I'm here for you."

"What makes you think I've done anything?"

"We all make mistakes, darling. All of us, we're only human. Let me help."

"So you're assuming I'm guilty too? So what? You think I'm a liar and a cheat or worse?"

"No, Marcus. Please, that's not what I'm saying at all."

I turned to the window, away from her, and the black Audi was there, bold as brass, parked outside our drive.

"Fucking hell. Look, who is that?"

"What?"

"Come here and look, that car. It's following me. I'm being watched."

She walked over, pulling her glasses back onto her face.

"I don't know, darling." The car pulled away, turning left at the end of the road. "It could be anyone, a neighbor or a visitor. You're under a lot of stress, darling, I know that, but no one is out to get you, least of all me."

She stroked my arm, her hand warm. "Come on, sit with me. Talk to me. We always used to be so close, remember?"

I sat with her. It was easier that way.

She sat, my mother, all her other selves folded in, striations, layers: the little girl sent to boarding school, the daughter, the sister, the wife, the mother, the Honors graduate, the widow. Mostly unknown to me. She must've wondered what life would be like if she'd made a different choice: married someone else, had more children, other children, ones who'd give her grandchildren and noisy Christmases and family events, or if she'd not married at all and faced different disappointments. Sitting here, I was only capable of seeing her as my mother, the fleshy conduit into this life, my life. All ego and self-centered, rendered down to the bare fact of me. Freud must say something about that, the tyranny of a child or something. I don't know. I'd forgotten what I didn't know and I didn't know what I'd forgotten.

Was she in on it? My mother.

Once I took her to the Ritz for tea, making up for not visiting, missing her birthday, Christmas or something. Then I took her shopping, offering scarves in cashmere and silk, a handbag, purse, shoes. Bond Street, Selfridges, Harrods; she turned her nose up at everything. Finally she marched us into Marks and Spencer and let me buy her a blouse. She continued to wear it, years later. That seemed to sum her up. Loyal, steadfast. She wouldn't have turned on me. She wouldn't.

"You are so like your father."

"Am I?"

"Oh yes. You have his hands, and his mannerisms. The way you stand, lightly, like you're about to spring away, that's just like him."

"I don't remember much about him."

"No, I don't suppose you do." She looked away, as if in the distance she could see the past. "He was a serious young man, thoughtful. Driven. Maybe not the marrying kind."

"What do you mean?"

"Only that his work was important to him. I think he would've liked to have continued his missionary work, but I wanted to come home."

"I thought you were happy."

"We were, he wasn't the resentful type. He did what was right. Happiness comes from different sources; you know that as well as I do. He was a reserved man, distant sometimes, always loving and polite, kind; but hard to know, hard to reach. Like you can be."

"I'm an open book."

She reached for her glasses and slid them down her nose to peer at me. "If only that were true."

The clock ticked, the pendulum's arc determined by a sliding brass weight. A slight shift could slow or speed time. She reached into the sleeve of her cardigan and pulled out a handkerchief, blowing her nose then tucking it back again, smoothing it under her cuff.

"Would you like me to come with you tomorrow, to the police station?"

"No, thanks."

"Callum said it was just a formality, nothing to worry about."

I nodded, shrugging. There was nothing to say, she would only argue, or continue trying to reassure me. The point was, neither of us knew what was going to happen. We didn't know what Charlie had said, or what they'd found.

"Yes. I'll be heading home in a day or so, if that's OK?"

"Of course, stay as long as you like. It's been lovely having you here."

"Bar the police visits, my getting sacked..."

"Well, now you put it like that," she grinned and reached to ruffle my hair. I sat still and let her, before smoothing my hair back into place.

"Everything will work out, darling. Trust me," she said. Trust me.

March 1990

"Ah, so that's where you've been." Mel raised her eyebrow and smiled, tipping her head to the right. They were walking from the science block to English, side by side, through the paved picnic area. Daffodils in the sparse flowerbeds bobbed about in the breeze like corks on a stormy sea. Darren had walked past, his hands in his pockets.

"Alright?" he'd said.

"Alright," Marcus replied. That was it, nothing else.

"What do you mean?" He blushed, of course he did.

"You and Darren. It's obvious." Looking around, she checked there was no one listening.

"How?"

"The way he looked at you then. The fact that I hardly see you outside school any more, that you hum to yourself and daydream during class. You're in love," she teased, linking her arm through his.

"No I'm not!"

"I believe you." She cuffed his arm.

"D'you think we're disgusting?"

"Of course I don't. But I think you should be careful."

"Why? People already think I'm gay. What does it matter?"

"Yes, maybe, but you and Darren? Listen to me. Be careful."

"He's not stupid you know. He's not like the others, he's different."

"Perhaps, he is. But trust me, if this gets out he'll turn on you just like the others, and if he doesn't it's the family you'll have to watch for, his brothers."

"So we won't get caught."

"OK lover boy. I've missed you though," she said and pushed through the door into English, saluting Mr. Laugham as she dropped into her seat.

When he was four, Marcus trapped his finger in a door; so young he wouldn't remember, but this is the kind of experience that the body – and that lizard part of the brain – never forgets and is always vigilant for. Testing the world for the potential of pain. Watchful. He'd cried and screamed and to his little befuddled mind it took forever for his mother to arrive and save him. He thought she would never come. Does this explain anything? Who knows, these are just stories.

Old Blood

The room was small and drab, with pus-colored walls, plastic chairs, a rectangular table topped by a tape recorder with its red light flashing, a video camera in the corner. Etcetera. You've seen cop shows on TV, and they're strikingly authentic. And of course, the obvious question, which is real? The police station on TV or the one I was in? And neither of those questions was new either, only it was the first time I'd asked them.

Okonjo was sitting opposite me, her hands clasped and resting on the table, her posture saying, "I'm listening, I'm non-threatening." Etc. A new habit, I was done with collecting and reporting all the details. I was tired. The strip light above fizzed and clicked. The vending machine coffee Okonjo had brought for me was cold under the greasy film that had formed like a scab on the surface. Etc. Just things. Words.

"So tell us about your friendship with Melanie."

I told her. I told her about school, I told her about our friendship, I told her she was clever, brilliant. I told her very little. Okonjo was laying bait for me, which I avoided. I knew how to interview. Perhaps she didn't know that? I thought I was being clever. Self-possessed. She got up and left the room; when she returned, Callum was with her. He sat in the corner, barely looked at me, though he was listening, his head to one side like a parrot.

Okonjo pressed Record again on the tape machine.

"Let's start again. We just want to clear some details up with you, OK?"

I nodded, lifting the tips of my fingers up to my mouth.

"You're a journalist, that's correct isn't it?"

"Yes, I am an investigative journalist. I write, excuse me, wrote for the Sentinel."

"Politics? Big business?"

"Mostly." Callum was looking to one side, his mouth pressed tight.

"But you're not working for the Sentinel now?"

"No."

"Why's that?"

"There has been a misunderstanding."

"A misunderstanding?"

"Yes."

"OK, let's go back a bit. Why did you choose to come and cover a murder case? Bit out of your usual remit, isn't it?"

"Not really, the location the body was found in could have been an embarrassment for the government. Potentially political, you see?"

"So it was your decision to come here?"

"My decision? I wouldn't say that, my editor felt strongly that I should work on this. He's the boss." I sat back in the chair, keeping my eyes on Okonjo. She smiled, her cheeks pressing up into her temples.

"Your boss," she checked her notes for a moment, "Edward Campbell, said you insisted you take this story. He said you were aggressive."

"He said what? When did he? Why have you spoken to him?"

"All part of my job, Mr. Murray; checking facts, establishing the truth. You know about that as part of your work, don't you or maybe not?" She smirked. "Did you insist on covering this story?"

"No, I didn't insist on coming here, not at all. Quite the opposite."

"So you wanted to avoid coming here? Any reason why you'd want to avoid your home town? Your mother lives here, doesn't she?"

"Now you're twisting my words. Come on, you can do better than that." A shrill ringing had started in my ears, like a digital whine just in my range of hearing.

"So you weren't avoiding covering this story?"

"No."

"But you knew the victim? Detective Constable Burrell?"

"No, I didn't know him."

"So you never met him?"

"No."

"But you were friends with his stepdaughter, Melanie Shoreham."

"Yes." Callum looked away, his face tight.

"You were very fond of her. Charlie, Mr. Charles Smart, was Melanie's former stepfather, is that right?"

"Is what right? I'm confused by your question."

"Sorry, that Charlie was her mother's ex-partner?"

"Yes he was, or so I was told."

"Good. Well, he said that you idolized Melanie. 'Worshipped her' is how he described it. Would you say that was true?" She was picking up pace, getting into her stride. Had she suspected me from the start, is that why she didn't like me? How long had they suspected me?

"When did he say that? When you interviewed a very sick man and nearly killed him? Is that when?" My throat was dry; I reached for the cold coffee then set it down. My hands shook.

"Did you 'worship' Melanie?"

"No. We were friends, that's all." I cleared my throat, the sound of a guilty man. I tried not to swallow or blink. I kept my hands folded on the desk.

"So, you wouldn't have done anything to protect her?"

"What do you mean?"

"I mean if she was in danger, you might have tried to help, no matter what."

"Whatever it is you're implying, why don't you just spell it out?"

She leaned back, leaving her hands flat on the table. Her fingernails were short, but filed into perfect, shiny ovals. No ragged cuticles, no hangnails. She sat forward again, reestablishing our connection. "Did you know that Melanie's neighbors had called the police on numerous occasions because of domestic disturbances?"

"No, I didn't."

"Yes, it would appear that DC Burrell and Melanie's mother, Christine, had a turbulent relationship. Is it possible that he was violent towards Melanie?"

"I don't know." I blinked, swallowed, blinked. As if I was lying. Was I lying? I wasn't sure. I blinked again.

"Perhaps he was violent to Melanie and you had to defend her? It's understandable, you were close and she was in trouble maybe..."

"Seriously, you are grasping at straws. I've no idea what you're talking about." My skin had begun to itch, as if I were crawling with lice, the light from the fluorescent bulb vibrating in my eyeballs.

"Social services were involved with the family, did you know that?"

I shook my head.

"Did you know that Melanie had been hospitalized after being attacked when she was fourteen?"

"No, I didn't."

"Well, she was but she refused to tell the police who assaulted her. So you see why it would be understandable if you'd wanted to protect her?"

"I didn't know she'd been hurt." The image of Melanie that I'd carried for so long dissolved and reassembled. Unrecognizable.

"Just to come back to your editor, Edward. Why did he say you insisted on covering this story, when you say you didn't?"

"I don't know. He has a big problem with me, obviously. Look, I'm sorry, I don't think I can help you." I got up to leave. They both watched me, unmoving. I sat back down. Finally, Callum spoke. "What do you think happened to DC Burrell?"

"I don't know. From what I've heard from you, maybe he was killed by the gang he was undercover with, but who knows?"

"Forensics say he was killed by a blow to the skull by what looks like an iron. Bit domestic for a criminal gang, isn't it?" Okonjo raised her eyebrows.

"How would I know?" All three of us turned towards muted voices outside the door, the handle half dropped then flipped up again. Whoever it was had changed their mind about entering. They turned back to me. Okonjo reached inside a blue folder and slid out a sheet of paper. It was a photo of Chrissie's wall hanging.

"Do you recognize this?"

I looked closely at it; Elvis's face marked by the shadows of old blood, or dirt. "No," I said. "No." Shaking my head. I felt my lungs squeeze shut; my head spun and black spots appeared in my peripheral vision.

"The body was wrapped in it before being buried. Are you sure you've never seen it?"

I shook my head. Tried to breathe.

"Did you ever visit Melanie at her mother's home?"

"Once maybe, twice, I can't remember."

"So you don't remember seeing this at Chrissie's house?"

"No, no I don't remember."

"Because Charlie said it was hers."

Charlie. Good old Charlie. Fucking Charlie. "He would know better than I would."

Okonjo shook her head and exhaled hard. "We know you're hiding something and I don't want to be rude, but you don't exactly have the reputation of being an honest and upstanding citizen right now. So why don't you just tell us what happened?"

"I don't know what happened."

"And yet you were the last person to see her alive and well in this country."

"No I wasn't."

"We have witnesses who say that you were."

"That's impossible." My neck and shoulders cramped sending a spasm of pain through my jaw. I rolled my head from side to side, the joints popping and cracking. Okonjo watched me, almost sneering. I settled back in my chair, the ache spreading down my back and up around my skull. The floor felt a long way down.

"And yet, we have two people who claim they saw you with Melanie, covered in blood on the night she left."

"That's a lie."

"Really? And we're supposed to believe you?" She raised her eyebrows, incredulity reshaping her face. "Did you kill Steve Burrell?"

"No."

She softened, morphing from interrogator to confidante with a subtle shift of her shoulders and face. "Not even to protect your best friend?"

"Am I under arrest?"

She pulled back. "Not yet."

Callum touched her arm to interrupt and leaned forward to speak. "How tall are you, Marcus? Six foot one or so?"

"That's right."

"And how tall were you when you were sixteen?"

"I don't know! This is ridiculous."

"Is it? Because the forensic evidence shows that he was struck from behind, with enough force to kill. The size and shape of the injury gives us a pretty good idea of the height of Burrell's killer. So roughly, how tall were you?"

"Not much shorter than now, five eleven maybe."

"And Melanie? How tall was she?"

"I don't know. I'd guess five-five or something. Average height. I can't be precise. I mean I'm not her parent, I didn't keep a record of these things."

"No, but we tend to know these sorts of things about our close friends. Don't we?"

"Yes, I suppose so."

"So she was average height and with a slim build, would you say?"

I nodded. "Can I speak to my solicitor now?"

March 1990

He stood on her front step, blood stinging his eye. His hands were scraped raw, the knucklebones exposed and slick under the streetlights. He was covered in blood, though it looked worse than it was. Head wounds bleed a lot, considering how thin the skin is, stretched over the skull, the particular bones of the face. He tapped on the door, afraid of disturbing the neighbors, or her mother. There was no answer so he thought about leaving, finding his way back. He thought about the mess he'd run from and whether he was dead. Then she came and opened the door. The light behind her picked out her shape.

Like a Breakfast Egg

"All done?" Okonjo and Callum stood at the door. I nodded, sliding my phone into my pocket. They sat down in tandem, as if they'd rehearsed the movements and the timing over and over. Their twinned faces searched mine for a reaction. I looked straight back at them.

"If you admit that you were wrong about St. Clair, then this will all go away. It's that simple."

That's what my solicitor said, or that's what was implied, or that's what I remember, or that's what I heard. And I agreed. I gave in, weak as I always was, even if I pretended for a little while that I wasn't. And I write all this down as if I remember every detail, every word spoken, every gesture, every facial tic and expression as if I'm a recording medium, a technology able to reproduce the scenes perfectly, like my father's God. But I'm not, and now I wonder how much I've got wrong.

"As I said, the victim was struck from behind, with a fair bit of force. Now he was a big man and the blow came down," Callum stood raising his arm and brought it down in an arc. "Like this. So it's likely he was on his knees or crouched down close to the floor, facing away from his attacker. He was hit just the once, which suggests it was, well it suggests this wasn't a frenzied beating." He sat back down, watching me.

"Perhaps someone was just trying to make him stop, perhaps it all got out of hand." Okonjo drummed her fingers on the table then asked, "What do you think?"

"I don't know."

She sighed, "So, let's say you didn't kill him, Marcus. Let's say it was someone else and we just need to fill in some of the gaps. You could help with that, couldn't you?" She waited for me to agree. I nodded. Disgust at the dark reach of St. Clair was replaced by relief and fear that flushed through me like cold water. It was over. Of course they knew it wasn't me. They knew all along. They knew it was Charlie. All it took was to stop telling the truth. I would let lies replace an exhausted reality. It was that easy.

"Talk me through it then. What happened that night after your friend Melanie killed DC Burrell?"

"Melanie didn't kill him, she couldn't."

I looked down at my hands, trembling in my lap. My head felt loose on my neck, unattached. Separated into distinct parts. New details, new facts sliding into place. Melanie? I imagined the possibility of blood, the skull cracking like a breakfast egg. The parabola of the iron, swung and dropped like a drowsy morning spoon. Melanie. Her face, her hands. Small.

"If it wasn't Melanie, then who?"

"Not Melanie, she wouldn't hurt anyone," I shook my head.

"But you say you weren't there, so you don't actually know?"

"No, I wasn't there."

"So you don't know."

"No."

"What do you know about that night?"

"I've told you, nothing. I don't know anything. I was a kid."

"It's just, with an injury like that there would be a lot of blood, a lot of mess to clear up and then there's the body to dispose of. It's a long way from the Shoreham house to the orchard where we found the victim, and he was a well-built man. I can't believe that Melanie could've moved him, even with her mother's help, let alone dug the grave. Chrissie Shoreham couldn't drive, so I wonder who helped them?"

I said nothing, a series of images flickering through my mind.

"Why did you go and visit Charlie Smart? Was it to threaten him? To warn him to stay quiet? To get your story straight? Did you and Charlie... "

"No."

"No, what?"

"I didn't visit Charlie to threaten him. I just wanted to see him."

"You just wanted to see an old man you barely know, after what? Twenty years? Doesn't that strike you as strange?"

"No, it doesn't. Are you going to arrest me or can I go?"

Okonjo pursed her lips and looked over at Callum. "When was the last time you saw Melanie?" She reached into her jacket and handed me a tissue. I was sweating. I mopped my face. Maybe there were tears.

"At school, I think. Not long after Valentine's Day. There was disco at school."

"Did she mention anything? Seem worried or afraid?"

"Yes, maybe."

"Did she? What about? Because before you said she hadn't been any different from usual."

"Did I? When?"

"When we spoke at your house, Marcus. Remember?"

"I'm very upset. I'm under a lot of pressure right now."

"I have your statement here from 1990, do you remember now, being interviewed by our boss, DCI Sutton?"

"Not really. Vaguely, I'd forgotten until you reminded me."

She passed a sheet of paper to me. "Is that your signature?"

"Yes."

She pulled it back across the table so she could read from it. "Here you've stated that you and she were good friends. That she often talked about leaving home and running away but that you had no reason to believe she was unhappy. Do you still believe that?"

"I don't know."

"Why run away if she wasn't unhappy?"

"She just wanted to get away from here, she wanted to travel."

"She didn't leave because of DC Burrell?"

"I don't know. I really don't know."

"Did you help Melanie move the body?"

"No. I did not."

"Did you help her leave? Because that would be aiding and abetting, you'd have helped her get away with murder. You understand?"

I pictured her face, her dark eyes, the smell of coconut shampoo. "No, I didn't help her."

"Do you know who did?"

"No. She just left."

Callum leaned forward. "And you never heard from her after that?"

"No. I never did." Time spread out in all directions. I felt as if I were overflowing, spreading out like water, that I was everywhere I'd ever been or was going to. I felt it as distinctly as I feel the seat under me now. As if I'd dissolved in the air like salt in water, mineral atoms diversified, soluble, inseparable yet distinct from my element. I gathered, pulsed and flowed. Melanie disappeared from me again.

"Will you be OK? You look terrible." Callum walked me out of the station, down to reception. I was free to go. Free as long as I kept lying.

"No, I won't be OK, Christ."

"Marcus, I was doing my job. You understand that, but I did have feelings for you, real feelings."

"Real feelings? What are they? I know who you are and I know that you're a part of all this to silence me and you've all won. You tell whoever it is that's pulling your strings that they've won. I'm done." I pushed past his extended hand and out through the automatic doors. I walked down towards the old Library building, my keys and some change jangling in my pocket. There was a breeze, cool off the river, cutting through the summer sun. The Union Jack outside the library lifted and rippled, clanging against the pole.

I imagined the possibility of blood, the skull cracking like a breakfast egg. The parabola of the iron, swung and dropped like a drowsy morning spoon. Her face, her hands. Small. Her dark hair, her skin; a bruise wrapped like a cuff around her wrist. Her neck. Burnt flesh. Vanishing. Burrell's hands on her, twisting her like dough. Melanie.

Was it possible? Making him stop. Making it stop. The wrapping up and disposing of the body, cleaning up the mess, the fear, the hysteria. Who did that? Charlie? Mel? It was my fault. And Chrissie? Where was she? I imagined the digging, listening out for sounds of discovery, the body – a dead weight, limbs flung loose and slack before rigor set in. The head lolling and rolling, the gold tooth just a lump of metal, useless, the hinge of the jaw, the bone and flesh and matter. A ring of red marks and the purple dots of a fresh bruise.

How did I not see the trouble she was in? What kind of person was I to not see her clearly? And worse, what kind of a man was I to give in so easily, to fold and let a murderous cartel get away with profiting from terrorism? And for what? To save myself from trouble? The answer to all these questions is the same. I'm a self-absorbed coward. Actually worse than that, a narcissistic coward.

I used to think that if I had to live around there for the rest of my life I'd throw myself in the river, but there I was. Could I stay? What could I go back to? I turned right and headed down the High Street along with the mothers in their velour track suits and their shalwar kameez and their skin tight jeans, all pushing their chubby babies in their buggies; past the pound shop and the pawn shop and the charity shops; past the withered old ladies tugging shopping trolleys and the gangs of teenage boys with their legs lassoed by their low-hanging trousers. I wondered if Georgina was still here, married with kids just like she wanted, or if she was another written-off victim of the care system. I was half tempted to look for her, but what for? What would that achieve?

People are more interesting than you give them credit for you know, I could almost hear Melanie's voice. *Give it a rest, always judging.* The voice of my conscience, she had taken root in my head, shaping me, changing me in just those few months. I half expected to see her, as she was back then, hanging out round the back of the town hall where the skater boys did ollies and flips, or sitting by the river looking out down the estuary across the warehouses and docks, the dull metal sheets rusting and warping over steel frames. What did you do Melanie? What did we do to you?

I kept walking, past a group of Danner Comp kids gathered around the bus stop, their uniforms practically unchanged from when we went there. Turning away from the river and the center of town, I walked up the hill, through the narrow roads of terraced houses, their front doors opening directly onto the street; as I walked I could hear their TVs, their dogs barking, telephones ringing, their children crying. It's no wonder that it seethes with barely suppressed violence there, all those people in such close proximity, never any privacy or respite from one another. I didn't care if they were watching me: I was done, broken.

I think now of my father's book, and the image of violence as an unstoppable flood that requires diverting elsewhere, rage that can only be spent by destroying someone, even if they're innocent. It sickens me.

I turned right by the George and Dragon pub, its beautiful Victorian arched windows boarded up, the double doors padlocked, and into the estate towards Melanie's old house. I'd been walking for at least an hour and I was hot and thirsty. I got myself a bottle of water in the corner shop at the end of the street; standing outside to drink, I realized that I was opposite Melanie's grandparent's house.

July 1990

Only her grandmother was home when they knocked. She let them in and they followed her into the small sitting room. A green leather three-piece suite took up most of the space; a television hunkered next to the fireplace. A large studio photo of Melanie and her brother sitting on a sheepskin rug in front of a summer-blue backdrop was in pride of place on the mantelpiece.

Georgina had made him go, turning up at his door, red-faced and sweaty. Her fingernails were painted a metallic blue.

"Hello, what's up?" He pulled the front door closed behind him, blinking as his eyes adjusted to the sunlight.

"Have you heard from her?"

"No, no I haven't. Have you?"

"No, and it ain't right. Something ain't right."

"How'd you find me?"

"Why? What's it matter? Melanie's gone, ain't you worried?"

"Of course I am."

"Act like it then. Come on, I'm going to her nan's to see if she knows what's going on, 'cause this stinks, and you're coming with me."

"I don't think we should, I think we should leave it to the police."

"Are you having a laugh? I don't trust the filth and I don't trust her mum, not after what she let him do to Mel and get away with it."

"Who?"

"Him, that Steve, you know what he did, don't you?" She watched his face, her eyes narrowed. "You don't know, do you? I thought you were best friends, maybe not." She shook her head and paused. "Well, you're coming with me. And if you must know, Darren Shine told me where to find you."

"Would you like a glass of squash?" Melanie's grandmother had a tiny mouth and spoke as if she were up against a deadline, speaking fast and lisping a little.

"No thanks, we just wondered if you had heard from Melanie. I'm worried sick," Georgie said, wiping her face on the hem of her t-shirt, exposing her soft, freckled belly.

"Well, I'm not sure really."

They stood there, the three of them in the middle of the room, listening to the rumble of the bin men and their lorry outside, the squeal of garden gates as they picked up and returned the bins, and the whine and crush of the compacter.

"Can you tell us where she is? We just want to see if she's all right. We're her friends."

"We know who you are. Georgina and Marcus, right?" Her grandfather, tall and thin with a head of thick gray hair, walked in.

"They just wants to know where she is," the old woman said, looking from him to Marcus to Georgie and back again.

"Do they?" he said quietly as he moved past his wife, gently moving her from his path by pressing on her shoulder. "Have you spoken to her mother?" He sat down in the armchair opposite the TV. On the dresser behind him there was a gold carriage clock with the legend "Presented to Victor Shoreham, Celebrating 40 years service as Union Rep"; next to a postcard from Paris, a set of false teeth bathed in a glass of water.

"I tried, but she won't talk to me."

"And you?" The older man turned to Marcus.

"No, I haven't spoken to anyone."

"Right," he looked over to his wife, "Shirley, babe, what's the doctor said about keeping your teeth in?"

"I forgot, duck." She sat down on the sofa and pressed her tiny lips together.

"No one knows where Melanie is. You got it? No one, not the police, not her mother and not us. Now leave it and don't come back upsetting my wife again." He strode towards the front door, opening it and flicking his head towards the street. "Out."

"Why didn't you say anything?" Georgie huffed, trying to keep up with Marcus as he hurried across the street.

"Like what?" he snapped. Charlie would go mad if he found out they'd been there.

"Oh forget it, Marcus, you stuck-up dickhead. It's like you don't give a shit about her, like none of you do. She could be dead out there and you don't give a shit."

She turned and left him standing there, watching her go, wondering what he could've said to not make things worse, if he would feel less lonely if he told her what he knew.

Sweet As

I drained the water from the bottle and threw it in a bin. I was just walking, with nowhere in mind. And perhaps I was, but it seemed that nothing was random. Or just that in that small town, everywhere I went I would come back to her and still she will be gone. It was as if she was controlling me, watching. Exhausted, I crossed over and cut through the park towards home. *Someone* was controlling me, watching.

The black Audi was back, parked across from Mother's. Enraged, I headed over: police, hack, whoever he was, I was done, I'd had enough. I'd say anything, I was guilty, I'm a liar, I always have been, just stop. Just stop. He got out of the car and pushed the door shut, his arms loose at his sides. He was big, his shirt gaping over his belly, and he'd shaved his remaining hair to a stiff bristle.

"What do you want?" I panted, the heat was too much, I waited for him to step forward and hit me or shove me into the car. I wanted him to. I wanted someone to make it easier for me.

"Easy, mate. You don't remember me, do you Marcus?" We stood in the road, sweat stinging my eyes. He shrugged, turning his palms up. "It's me Darren, Darren Shine. Been a long time."

Darren. I rubbed my face with my hand, pushing out the light, the present, cutting myself off, scraping my chin. I looked up. Darren. "Fucking hell."

"You alright? You don't look too clever." He reached out but didn't touch me. He wore a wedding ring, solid gold wrapped around his finger.

"No, I'm not. I'm fucked." A tree reached up and out behind him, a house rose up behind that, a ginger cat arched its back on a wall. I had no idea where I was, but everything was familiar. I looked up and down the road, then behind me. We were alone.

"D'you want to sit down?"

"What?" I heard him, but I couldn't think of an answer. "Why have you been following me? What're you doing?"

"It's not me following you."

"Who is then?"

"You what?"

"Why are you here?"

"I live around here with me wife and kids." He smiled, shrugged embarrassment, but the gesture was tiny, gone and I could only half process.

"You live here?"

"Around here, yeah."

"Yes." He lived there; he wasn't following me. It was a coincidence, a normal everyday occurrence. "You look so different, I didn't recognize you."

"It's been a long time."

"Yeah."

"Right then, sweet as a nut, mate." He shook my hand and got back into his car. I stood there. As the engine flared he put his window down. "I'm sorry to hear about Charlie, he's a good 'un. A heart of gold, but you know that, don't you?"

"What's that?" I leaned in towards the open window; the scent of pine and new car was carried on the cold conditioned air. "How do you know about Charlie?"

"Small town, mate. Everyone knows everyone, and everything. Charlie, he told me to give you this." He flipped the sun visor down and pulled a narrow envelope out from the clip and handed it to me. "You take care now. It was good to see you." And he drove off.

March 1990

"Jesus Christ, what the fuck happened to you?" Mel stepped back, opening the door, her face white with shock. "Where's your shirt? Quick, come in."

He followed her through to the kitchen; a lamp was on in the sitting room and a book lay open and face down on the sofa. She was alone.

"Sit down and let me see."

He lowered himself slowly onto the chair.

"Let me guess, Darren?" She held his chin in her hand and turned his face to the light. "You're bleeding. Fucking hell." She turned and grabbed a tea towel from a drawer and ran it under the tap.

"I'll clean this up and then get you some frozen peas to put on your eye. Do you want me to call the police?"

"No," he croaked.

"What about an ambulance?" She dabbed at his face, wiping the blood and grit from his cheek.

"No."

She shook her head, and moved away to rinse out the cloth. "Should I call your mum?"

He started to cry and she put her arms around him, her hair soft against his neck.

They had been parked round the back of the football fields, behind the changing rooms and the clubhouse. No one ever went there at night, it was always safe. They were in the back seat, Marcus lying against Darren, his head against his chest.

They were smoking a joint and Darren held it to his lips so he could take a puff. It was cool out, the windows had steamed up.

"You need a drink." She got up and rummaged around in the kitchen cupboard before pulling out a bottle of brandy and pouring a couple of inches into a tumbler. "Here, it'll help the shock. I've seen it on TV so it must be true." She laughed softly and nudged him. "Come on, you'll be OK."

"He said he was going to kill me." He took the drink and sipped. It stung his lips and tongue but he drank it anyway.

"It'll be OK, I promise. These things blow over eventually, they always do."

They were laughing at something. It was hard to remember what, but they were laughing hard, clutching at each other. Then Darren stopped and turned his head to listen, saying, "What's that?" and out of nowhere there was a roar of banging on the roof of the car and fists pumping on the windows.

"Oi, Oi! Open up you dirty boy! C'mon let's see your bird. Oi, you little stud."

Darren sat up and pushed Marcus away from him. "Oh fuck, it's my brother."

Then the door opened and several faces, shiny in the automatic light pressed, into the space. "Come on you little lovebirds, let's have— What the fuck? Oh my god, you filthy queers!"

They'd forgotten to lock the door. Marcus had forgotten to lock the door.

They moved from the kitchen to the sitting room, Mel bringing the bottle of brandy through and refilling his glass. He still had a bag of frozen peas pressed against his throbbing face – even the teeth hurt at the back of his mouth.

"They'll tell everyone. Everyone at school will be laughing about me; I'm such an idiot. You even warned me. What am I going to do?"

"No they won't, they won't tell anyone. D'you honestly think Darren's brother will want people knowing about this? Or his dad? It'll ruin the tough guy Shine image. Trust me, they'll keep it quiet. You just have to keep your head down and stay away from him. At least for now."

When he was finally able to run, Darren was still curled up on the ground, his brother booting him in the stomach. Marcus hesitated, but there were four of them, and they were bigger, tougher. "You sick cunts, you fucking homos. In my bloody car an all." Over and over, the words and the kicks, the fists. Only the first couple of punches hurt, the rest he didn't feel, only knew that he was falling down. And once he was down he knew it would be over soon, and that it wouldn't be so bad. Gravel and broken glass in the flesh of his cheek and side, then his palms as he pushed to stand. Then he ran, over the football pitches, past the George and Dragon pub, straight to Melanie.

"Are you cold? I'll lend you a jumper if you like?"
"No."
"Let's have a look at your face then." She took the bag of peas from him and touched his face with her fingertips; she was so close he could see the flecks of gold in her brown eyes.
"I just left him there. I ran like a coward."
"You did the right thing," she said kissing his forehead.
A key in the lock and the scuff of shoes being kicked clean signalled the arrival of her mother.
"What's this?" Chrissie stood in the doorway, her cheeks flushed; behind her, watching over her shoulder was the man they'd seen at Leysdown. The one who watched them on the beach. The one who'd frightened Melanie so much she couldn't speak. He looked even bigger than before, his shoulders hunched in wads of muscle and sinew around his neck, his head too small.
"Marcus has had a bit of trouble, Mum."

"Oh right. So that's why he's half-naked on my sofa and you're drinking my booze? D'you think I was born yesterday? I told you, no more of this. Didn't I? I warned you. I bloody warned you." She moved over to them, dropping her bag on the armchair and gathered up the glasses and bottle of brandy.

"Mum, it's not like that. He's my friend, I'm just helping him."

"Yeah, helping him half-naked, drunk on my sofa, while your little brother is upstairs. You just don't learn do you? What's up with you?"

Steve shook his head and sneered, "Nothing's changed around here then, Melanie? I told you, Chrissie, didn't I?"

"Mum, what's he doing here? You promised me he'd gone for good." Melanie stood up and moved closer to her mother, her hands turned up to plead with her, or show her she was clean, innocent. Marcus's heart was racing, the brandy and the punches to his head were clouding his brain, he couldn't think.

"I decide who's allowed in my house, not you. You're a dirty little slut, Melanie and you know what's worse, you're a liar too."

Melanie stood rooted to the spot.

"I can't be doing with all this. I warned you Chrissie, I'm not coming back here if she is going to be causing trouble between us." Steve moved towards the door, his dark hair gleaming in the light.

"Don't go, Steve, we'll sort this. Please, babe," Chrissie said, pleading, then turned to Mel and hissed: "See what you've done? You ruin everything. Everything. God knows I wish you'd never been born."

Steve stopped, still turned to the door ready to go, waiting.

"Marcus, please tell her what happened, please," Melanie looked at him, her eyes wide, beseeching. But he couldn't speak, couldn't say the words. Shame and cowardice silenced him like a fist in his mouth. Melanie was begging him and he said nothing. Did nothing.

"See, your boyfriend won't even lie for you. Get out. Get out now."

"Mum, I'm begging you, please listen to me. Nothing has happened, Marcus was beaten up and I was just helping him."

"Right. Who beat him then? Why?"

"Marcus?" Melanie waited for him to speak up. She wouldn't betray him, she wouldn't tell them. It was up to him. But he couldn't.

She turned back to her mother. "It doesn't matter why. I wasn't doing anything wrong, I promise. Marcus is my friend, you know he is."

"Can't think of a lie quick enough can you? I told you'd be out if anything like this happened again. Didn't I? Didn't I? Now get out boy, before I fucking throw you out. NOW."

"Marcus, please. Just tell her what happened. For fucks sake! Please!"

He stood and walked out the door, shaking, about to be sick, her mother's shouting hammering at his skull. He pushed past Steve, his cheap aftershave and sweat, into the street, where he collapsed down on the curb, to wait for Mel, wait for her mother to calm down. He left her in there, alone with them.

Behind him, the screaming continued, and the neighbors came out, shaking their heads and folding their arms. One of them called over to him, "You'd best get out of it son, the pigs will be here in a minute." So he left. He left her there and kept walking until he got home.

The Envelope

There was a knock on my door. I was packing to leave. Charlie's envelope was in my back pocket, unopened. I needed to get away from there, at a safe distance to open it.

"Come in."

Mum walked in the room, her eyes small behind her glasses. "You could stay a little longer you know." She leaned against the desk, her arms crossed over her chest.

"I know."

"I can't see why you're rushing back. You've been through a lot these last weeks. Why don't you stay?"

"I can't, Mum. I have to sort myself out, I can't live with my mother forever, can I?"

I needed to get away from there, from that parallel universe of twisted happenings, from the ever-present past, but I couldn't tell her that. I let her think there was a job, a future.

"What will you do?"

"I don't know. Something will come up. Maybe I'll sell the flat, start again somewhere. Write a book. I just need to let it all go."

"And will you move on? Will you let it all go?"

"What do you think?"

"I think you'll pursue this story and try and clear your name."

"Maybe. Maybe there's nothing to prove."

"Just be careful, please."

"Don't worry, I'll be back soon."

"Will you? You always say that and then I don't see you for months."

I kissed her forehead and squeezed her shoulders. "I promise."

"Did you see the news about Edward Campbell?"

"I did, he's done all right hasn't he?"

"I should say so! Director General of the BBC and after what he did to you... It's criminal."

"Yeah." I made a move towards the door, needing to get out.

"It was her mother, wasn't it? Who did it?"

"So the police said."

"Yes. Well, they would know."

"I'd best be going."

"Yes, of course. Drive safely." She followed me out onto the drive. I leaned down and kissed her again and she gripped my hand. "You've got nothing to be ashamed of you know." I straightened and nodded. "I mean it, you can only do what seems right at the time."

"Yeah, thanks."

I got in the car and drove slowly out, watching her in the rear-view mirror as she waved from the door. The black Audi wasn't on the street or parked on any of the drives. But it didn't matter any more.

Just before the motorway I turned off into the old industrial estate, and drove up past the cement works and the paper factory. The concrete road ran out, finished by a scrubby patch of grass and low wall. It was deserted, the factories closed. I climbed out of the car and up the over the wall. The river opened wide, merging and heaving against the sea. Currents coiled and bucked at the surface, and across the water I could just make out the mud banks of Essex. A seagull tilting on the wind above. I pulled Charlie's envelope out of my pocket and tore it open.

March 1990

S he phoned first, her voice flat and thin as if stretched to the point of snapping. It was late and his mum was in bed. He was watching TV, still nursing his bruised face and back. He hadn't left the house, too scared of seeing Darren and his brother. He was half-expecting them to turn up on the doorstep at any moment, ready to kill him. They hadn't, but he half wished they would.

"Of course you can come, I've been so worried," he said.

Ten minutes later she tapped on the door. "You sure this is OK?"

He nodded.

"Where's your mum?"

"Upstairs, asleep."

She paused and seemed to reach an agreement with herself and looked up at him; her face was swollen – from lack of sleep or crying it was hard to tell. "Charlie is in the car outside, he wants you to go and speak to him."

"OK." He looked down the drive and saw the car parked by the hedge, its engine and lights off. "You wait inside, in the sitting room."

He trod lightly and then jumped to the lawn edging around the gravel drive and skirted towards the car that way, as quietly as he could. Charlie leaned over and opened the car door from the inside. He got in and as he reached to pull it shut Charlie gripped his arm. "Quiet." The heavy door slipped into the mechanism, only partway closed. "You alright?"

"Yeah."

"Nervous?"

Marcus nodded, though he didn't know why he should be nervous.

"Don't be, you're a good friend, a good boy. We'll look after her, alright? Keep her here tonight, and don't tell anyone. You hear me? No one. Not your mum, not the police, not a soul. Promise?"

"I promise. What's going on?"

"Nothing, Marcus. Nothing is going on. Mel's just had some grief with her family, that's all. You understand that don't you?"

"Yes, I understand."

"I'll be back for her tomorrow night, same time. Can you keep her hidden that long?" His big hands rested on the steering wheel. A tree-shaped tag hung from the rear view mirror, scenting the air with pine.

Marcus thought about his mother and Joyce and their unvarying routine. The next day was kitchen day, cleaning and restocking the cupboards, scrubbing the slate floor. "Yeah, that won't be a problem."

"Good, you're a good lad." Marcus pushed the door and started out. "Marcus." He stopped and turned back, one leg still on the pavement. "You're a part of this now, you understand? You have to keep your mouth shut or we're all up shit creek, especially Mel. It's important you understand what I'm saying to you. I'm trusting you now."

"I understand, and I won't let you down. I promise."

"Good lad. You'll have no trouble from the Shines from now on, either. Just keep your mouth shut, alright? You ain't seen Melanie and you don't know where she is." Charlie smiled, his teeth yellow in the streetlights.

Melanie was sitting on the corner of the settee, her knees pressed together. She sighed and shrugged off her jacket, letting it fall behind her into the gap between her body and the cushion. He noticed that her hair was damp, freshly washed;

the scent of coconut shampoo lifted off her in warm waves. She looked like a little girl, her eyes huge like a seal pup, reflecting the flickering apparitions from the TV. He reached to turn it off. "Leave it on," she whispered. He sat in front of her on the floor. She was wearing white trainers with black laces, thin ones, like formal shoe laces; she had a thin bandage around her hand.

"What happened to you?"

Surprised, she looked at her hand as if she'd not realized it was there. "Nothing, I burnt it on the iron. I was ironing. A silly accident."

"Ouch. Does it hurt?"

"It's fine." She tucked her hands under her legs, her elbows winging out in triangles from her body. She looked thinner than usual.

"You need a drink? Food?"

"No thanks."

"What happened with your mum?"

She blinked, her slow focus settling on his face. Nothing.

"I tried to call you but there was no answer." He reached for her arm and she moved back, sitting up straight.

"No, she unplugged it."

"What's going on?"

"This is a lovely house." She turned her head and stared at the photos on the mantelpiece. She stood up and walked over to the fireplace. "Do you light this?"

"What?"

"The fire. I'd love a real fireplace, I bet it's lovely."

"Sometimes, Mum likes it. Listen, tell me what's going on."

"I told you, nothing. I just need to leave." She picked up a photo of his father; in tennis whites, he looked like Fred Astaire, grinning at the camera. She put it down carefully and adjusted it so it was in the exact same position as before.

"But Mel, that doesn't make sense. Is it my fault? Because I'm sorry, I didn't know what to say to your mum. I was scared;

I know I should've said something, explained. I was just so scared."

"It's not your fault."

"But you're leaving home, this is terrible..."

"Marcus, it's not one of your dramas, it's not telly, it's nothing. Ordinary, boring life. No big deal."

"It is a big deal; I don't understand why you're going. It doesn't make sense."

"Because it doesn't, OK? We aren't all like you, with history and logic and photos to prove who you are. Sometimes it doesn't all add up. My life isn't a science project or a fucking novel that ties itself neatly in a bow. Maybe it's all too roughed up to show, but there it is. It's what I've got. Besides, it's pointless. D'you know what my fucking mother said to me? She said, 'This is all down to you. All I do for you, after all I've gone through.'"

As Mel spoke, she pulled her lips back over her teeth, imitating her mother, the hard bones of her face reassembling, becoming her mother. She began pacing back and forth reciting the words, "'We're not hunks of meat – a beating doesn't soften us up, no, no it doesn't. These scars make you hard, you hear me. You have no idea what you're talking about. You've got a lot to answer for my girl, and let me tell you something. You don't know you're born, you spoiled little bitch, whatever happened to you, you asked for it. Slut, slut, slut. I wish you'd never been born, I wish it was you who was dead.'"

She stopped speaking as suddenly as she'd started and stood at the window looking at herself, at the room, Marcus behind her reflected in the night-blackened glass. Her body was rigid, accommodating only the heave and contract of her ribcage. "Now leave it. Be my friend and help me. Please."

"But Melanie, I don't understand."

"I said leave it."

He took her upstairs. She slept on the floor, though he offered her his bed, and he woke early, listening for his mother.

He made a space in the wardrobe for her to hide, just in case someone tried to come in. He sneaked her some juice and toast and told his mother when he passed her on the stairs that he hadn't managed to sleep all night, so he would rest that day. She agreed, stroking his forehead and lightly brushing his black eye and cheek with her fingers. "Back to school next week though, alright? Or I will call the doctor."

They read and dozed all day, not risking talking, though neither had much to say anyway. She lay back against the bed at one point, and he saw the purple curve and red dots of a new bruise around her neck, but knew better than to say anything and looked away before she realized he'd noticed it. That was how they spent their last day together. Lying in his room, side by side, but she'd already gone. Charlie came for her at eleven thirty, in a different car, a white Ford Fiesta with a nodding dog perched on the parcel shelf.

She hugged him, tight, the smell of coconut shampoo pressed deep against him. Then they were gone.

Elena Santi

I was sitting in a lecture hall, jetlag working like grit behind my eyes, swallowing my Starbucks coffee with her locket around my neck, the chain tarnished and gray, not silver any more. I'd put it on after I opened Charlie's envelope and not taken it off since.

I turned to watch as students filtered into the room, so definitively American with their sportswear and well-fed bodies and perfected teeth. They climbed the stairs to find a place among the raked seats, pulling out notebooks and pens, flicking through their phones, chattering and flirting and laughing. The room was filling up. The title of the lecture was projected onto the screen above the rostrum: Ethics and the Nature of Language. In a smaller font the name of the Professor: Elena Santi — the name scrawled by Charlie on a scrap of paper, a scrap of paper folded into the crude shape of a bird; the name that Charlie had tucked into an envelope and asked Darren to give me; the name on a bird-shaped piece of paper that I have pressed between the pages of my passport.

She wasn't hard to find. Her faculty page was impressive in an institutional, establishment way. The Director of the Center for Ethical Studies, she's on the advisory board for Sedenco, the energy giant, and an advisor to the current administration. According to her bio she holds a BA, MA and PhD from Harvard, where she was the recipient of the W.G. Michaels Fellowship and the Kennedy School Prize.

She'd written a lot, mostly academic papers, research and analysis, articles responding to government proposals, a monograph on Justice and Morality, the kind of thing that flies beneath the radar unless you are in the same field: important, but not mass media worthy. The only photo of her online is a formal headshot, where she is smiling against a beige backdrop and looks like a thousand other women in their forties. I could find nothing about her private life, she had no public social media page and her Twitter was strictly professional and pretty sporadic.

So why was I there? Why did I fly all the way to Boston and book into an expensive hotel without emailing her first? But what would I have said? *Hi, I was given your name by an ailing old man. Do you happen to know anything about a girl called Melanie? Did you kill Steve Burrell? Who are you?* So I booked a flight, because what else could I do?

A woman entered the hall and stepped up behind the rostrum. She moved the microphone, and turned briefly to check the screen. She had no notes or prompts that I could see. She cleared her throat, swallowed and raised her head. She smiled, and looked around the room, taking everyone in. The students fell silent. Sitting there in the front, I caught her eye, and for a moment the woman looked back at me with Melanie's slow, calm gaze and time fell in on itself, collapsing around me like the pixelated world in a computer game, leaving only us two balanced in the void. She made no move to show she'd recognized me.

She began, her accent Bostonian with a hint of something else. It would be hard to place if you didn't know, but I could hear the glottal stops and flat vowels of Estuary English. There she was, almost unrecognizable, well groomed, grown-up, professional and still entirely familiar. Talking as if the universe was an open book and she knew all the words by heart. I watched her: the slow way of blinking, the slight turn of her head, the way she looked as if she was just outside of time, just beyond the world around her and was only there to observe; and it was like she'd never disappeared, she never left.

"Language is so constructed as to require... It's necessary always to make distinctions... not I, not us... this or that... you or me. Black or white. You see, our survival as a species has depended on these binaries in order to distinguish what was safe from what was potentially dangerous and yet now, it destroys us. This false taxonomy of being... this fascist impulse at the heart of our language... This is what Nietzsche asks of us... and Derrida, the deconstructive impulse is..."

As she spoke, her whole body lending itself to her words, she was spellbinding, and behind me I could feel the whole room was caught up too.

"We construct our reality, a concoction spun from words and our feeble human perception and then we fight and kill and destroy to defend it. Language, it is sometimes said, is what separates us from, elevates us even, above other animal species. I wonder if that is wrong. Perhaps, in our acquisition of speech and the multitude of signifiers we use to distinguish ourselves from the world around us, we have diminished ourselves in demanding meaning and certainty where there is none." She paused. "Any questions?"

And a young man stood and garbled something about the impossibility of communication without words. We watched him redden and puff his chest, the rising inflection of his voice pitched to defend. She nodded, listening, considered his question and answered slowly, carefully, affording him a deep respect as if he'd made a major contribution to the world of human knowledge. Then she smiled as if she and he were in on a private and deeply serious joke, and said, "Of course, and there is our problem."

And by the way he beamed at her and agreed, we knew she'd won him over. It was that slow, gentle way she had of watching and letting nothing get to her that she'd always had. You couldn't touch her. No one could touch her. As approachable as she looked, glossy and fine-boned and smiling, she was impervious, unknowable. And yet it was a kindness, a generosity, because if you couldn't hurt her, you couldn't hurt yourself. He sat down, still smiling, unable to help himself, and recovered in the cocoon of her attention.

I left with the others, hidden in the push for the door and the last of the summer sunlight. I wondered if she'd call my name: she didn't. I knew she wouldn't. It was enough that she was alive. Melanie is alive and Charlie had protected her all along.

I went back to my room and packed up my things. There was no need for anything else. No need for questions, or the answers. No need to tell her that finally, I understood why she vanished, I understood why she couldn't tell me what happened. I wouldn't destroy the life she'd built. Maybe she was Melanie, but she was Elena too. I know which one I'd choose to be.

So you see, she was a figment of my imagination. Flesh and blood – but a story, a myth, a series of actions and consequences folded into my own history. That was my fault. Isn't that love? Making someone into a story of wonder, no matter what, and turning yourself into the perfect character to fit alongside them? To be them? It would be foolish to imagine one's life as separate from all others, as singular and clearly defined, stupid not to see how connected we are, our lives bouncing and colliding, merging and dissolving into one another. I am her and she is me. So I left, I boarded the plane. I left Elena where she belonged and took Melanie home with me.

Acknowledgments

I would like to thank Ford Dagenham, Lindsay Parnell, Eadaoin Agnew, Rebekah Lattin-Rawstrone and Luke Seomore for reading endless drafts and offering patient, incisive and invaluable advice and sometimes puzzled questions about what I was doing!

Thanks to Julia May for invaluable insider journalism info and advice.

Thanks to Gary Powell for guidance on police procedure.

Special thanks of course to Hetha and Lin, you guys are the dream team.

And brilliant Kevin.

But most of all, thanks to Joe, Raif, Boo, Indi, Rose and Jay. I love you all.